ONCE UPON A MCLEOD

BY

KAY SISK

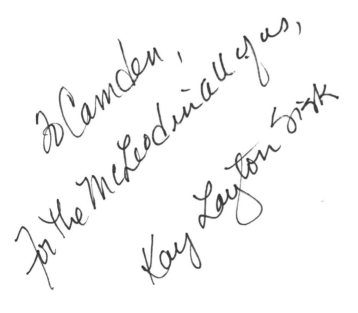

To Camden,
For the McLeod in all of us,

Kay Layton Sisk

Once Upon
a
McLeod

KAY LAYTON SISK

Cover by Lyndsey Lewellen

Chapter One

"**Y**ou ladies need help?" Bry Phillips adjusted his sunglasses to better avoid the glare of the late afternoon August sun. He watched the two women spin around on the concrete roadside picnic table at the sound of his voice. He'd not meant to startle them, but then there wasn't any way they'd heard him coming over the Webber music blaring from their open-door vehicle.

"Do we look like we need help?" It was the redhead who jumped to her feet. Her sandals skidded in the gravel of the tourist park that overlooked the West Texas town of Cummings. She cocked her hip as she caught and balanced herself with one hand on the table edge, like a cat who'd tumbled from her perch but wanted the world to think she'd done it on purpose.

"Well—" he hesitated and shifted his weight as the sweat began to trickle down the back of his neck from under the faded golf cap. Just as he'd cooled down in the car after walking eighteen holes, he'd stopped to offer assistance, and it looked like his getting all hot and sweaty again wasn't going to be worth it. They might not need any help but helping was built into his job description and his personality. So he'd pulled over. The hood of their new white SUV wasn't raised and he'd

1

noted the tires were healthy. "I don't guess you do."

"Well, of course, you were just being helpful." It was the other one, the blonde, who answered now. She smiled and swung her tanned legs around so she could face him while maintaining her perch. Their accents were unmistakably honeyed deep South.

Bry shut his mouth on a smile. The attitude, the accent, the out-of-state license plates, the age appropriateness of forty, give or take a few—well, that's all he needed for confirmation. It had been a worthwhile stop after all, certainly worth a trickle of sweat down his neck. He knew who these two were, and the fun—for himself and the town—was just beginning.

"Then you don't need a ride into town?" The devil made him do it. He couldn't even resist the grin that came with it as his whole attitude changed.

The redhead lowered her sunglasses to the tip of her nose and narrowed her green eyes at him. "Are you really trying to pick us up?"

"Only if you need it."

Her mouth dropped open as she blinked, searched for words. Her friend grabbed her arm and pulled her back onto the rough table. He decided against any more conversation and smiled at them.

"Good day, ladies." He touched the brim of his cap for good measure and strode back to the white truck he'd left running on the other side of their vehicle. He resisted the temptation to turn around and see their response. Circling out of the parking lot, he headed down the hill toward town, reaching for the CB radio as soon as he cleared the gravel.

"Sam, come in." Clicking the mouthpiece, he tried to maintain a certain solemnity, but he couldn't. He'd been the first to spot Joe Tom's bitch niece and entourage and the betting pool at Sally's Grille now belonged to him.

"Here, boss."

"Want to run some plates for me?" He paused for just an instant. "Georgia plates?"

The innuendo wasn't wasted on Sam. "Aw, what luck, Bry." The older man could see him swing an imaginary hat to the floor. "That's no fair. You been out roaming for them."

"No way. Just lucky. Call Sally, tell her I'll pick up my money in about five minutes."

"It's really Joe Tom's bitch niece?"

Bry made a mental note: Cummings would have to watch itself or someone would call her that to her face. She was just here for the funeral and the reading of the will. How hard could it be for them to be polite?

He clicked the mouthpiece. "The one and only peach pit herself. And she brought a friend."

"Criminey. You have all the fun."

***

"Bethann Fox, you're not going to live long enough to see Joe Tom buried!" Kiki Wright launched from the picnic table and dusted her denim-clad bottom. "You are absolutely the rudest person I have ever known!"

"What did I do?" Bethann stayed where she was and pulled the band from her red hair. She finger-combed the curly mass and reached to get it clear of her neck. Redoing the ponytail, she hopped off the table and stood beside her friend. Turning around to face the sun, she took a deep breath and tried to control her irritation. From the roadside park overlook, the last place she wanted to be was spread at her feet.

Cummings, Texas. Heart of cattle country and all attendant pleasures. Including one Joe Tom McLeod, her late husband Marsh's uncle and source of supreme vexation throughout her married life. Joe Tom: bachelor, rancher, raconteur, all-around-good-ol'-boy, whose main goal in life had seemed to be to get the better of Bethann. Now the old man was dead and she was here to see he remained so.

"What did you *do*?" Kiki repeated as she moved to stand nose-to-nose with Bethann. "Did you not see the truck he was driving?"

Bethann raised her eyebrows. "No, I did not see the truck he was driving." She mimicked the cadence. "I'd have thought that for all his gallantry he was on a white charger."

"It had words on the side."

"Like 'Need a ride? Call 1-800-IMA-STUD'? And a middle-aged one, at that!"

"Like maybe a ranch. Like he owns a ranch?"

"Ooh, I'm impressed. Never met one of those

before." She started toward their car. "Are you coming?"

"You know, Bethann," Kiki held onto the topic as they climbed in and she adjusted the music level down to bearable, "you are all alone and that tall, dark, and handsome stranger who might own a ranch and who is ever so gallant—"

"You read too much."

"—might just have made our stay here so much more interesting for you if you'd let him."

"Tell me he looked like anything other than a good ol' boy in a gimme cap." Bethann buckled her seatbelt and put the car in gear.

Kiki positioned the air conditioning vents for her comfort. "You have no imagination."

"You have too much."

"Bethann, you absolutely have to be here for three days. You might as well be nice and behave yourself."

"If—and I repeat if—Joe Tom's lawyer had not insisted I come because the will was going to be read and Ted is in it, I'd have sat out this performance in Atlanta." She glanced sideways at Kiki. "I shouldn't have to remind you that Joe Tom is the reason I'm a widow!"

Kiki twisted her mouth and took a deep breath. "And I shouldn't have to remind you that you can catch more flies with honey than with vinegar."

"Okay, okay." She slowed the car as they entered the city limits. "Truce. I'll try and be nice."

Kiki cocked her head. "You're going to have to do more than try, Bethann. You're going to have to have a change in attitude for the next three days. Get a new one, as my girls would say."

"Three days, is that all? Three days and then I can go back to being—what was it Ted let slip they called his mother out here?" She thought for just an instant although it wasn't necessary. Bethann had all her Texas nicknames memorized. "Oh, I remember. Joe Tom's bitch niece. Or was that Joe Tom's peach pit niece?" She chanced a glance at Kiki and grinned like a jack-o-lantern. "Now I ask you, do I look like a bitch or a peach pit?"

"I think it was your attitude, not your looks, that got you those names." She smiled hesitantly at Bethann. "But then, you probably earned them both."

"You're some friend, Kiki." She swung the SUV into the empty parking lot of the Wel-Come-On Inn. Good thing they had reservations.

"Just remember that 'cause I'm all you've got for the next three days."

***

The parking lot of The Cummings Brothers Funeral Home and Chapel of Rest (*Three generations of service to you*) was full when Bethann and Kiki pulled in at five till eight. "Maybe there's another visitation going on," her friend observed.

"How many people can a little place like this have die in a day?" Despite Kiki's counsel, Bethann found her attitude slipping back to its previous low level.

They circled the lot, maneuvering the sport-utility between dented pickups and dusty Suburbans before Kiki spotted the lone empty space marked for family. Although there were several family spots, they were already occupied. The white truck from the afternoon occupied the end one.

"Let's get the name of that ranch!" Kiki started off in the opposite direction from the funeral home doors.

Bethann met her in front of the SUV and wheeled her around. "I'd rather be ignorant. And can you imagine the gall of these people parking in the family spots!"

"Well, how many did we need?" Kiki huffed. "The fleet stayed in Atlanta."

They reached the double doors, only to have them open for them from the inside. "Mrs. Fox?" the tall, thin man asked as he looked directly at her. Bethann marked him as the director even as she felt herself scrutinized. He shifted his gaze to Kiki and froze his thin face in a smile of aid and regret as he looked back at Bethann.

She extended her hand. "Bethann Fox. This is my friend and business partner, Kiki Wright."

"Milton Cummings," he said as he took their hands in turn and pressed them gently. "So pleased to make your acquaintance, Mrs. Fox, although I do regret the circumstances. And may I say now how sorry we all were about your husband's untimely demise here two years ago." He furrowed his brow. "Your uncle is in the Cummings Family Room. Lawyer Smith did tell you all the arrangements had been made some time ago?"

"Yes—"

Milton continued. "And paid for. Joe Tom wanted no problems for you and Little Tom." The smile returned.

It was Kiki who broke through the sharp intake of Bethann's breath. "Little Tom?"

Mr. Cummings looked momentarily ruffled. "The boy? Your son?"

Bethann nodded knowingly and Milton Cummings led them through the lobby to the first visitation room.

"Score one for Joe Tom calling Ted Little Tom," she hissed out the side of her mouth. "He knew his name was Theodoe Thomas—for my father. How typical!"

"Bethann!" Kiki's whisper held a warning as she clamped down hard on her friend's upper arm.

"I'm sure you'll be pleased by all the folks who've come to pay their respects." The director moved aside to reveal a room filled with people.

They stood nervously in the double door entrance. Bethann tried not to stare back at those gathered. Sunday suits mixed with blue jeans. The crowd was varied in age, from a young woman with a child on her hip to a group that sat along the wall, their walkers in front of them. A path cleared slowly between them and the casket, as the conversation level dropped to zero.

Bethann and Kiki walked silently towards the casket, Bethann focusing on it, Kiki looking around as she gentled her grip on Bethann's arm from warning to support. "Spotted him," she whispered in Bethann's ear.

"Huh?" She couldn't take her eyes off Joe Tom's face as they stood by themselves beside the casket. The conversations in the room started back at a low level.

"The rancher. He's in the back corner. Cleans up pretty good."

"Hmm." Bethann pulled her arm away and clasped her elbows, rubbing them distractedly as she studied the ninety-three-year-old legend. His balding head was powdered, his nose larger, harsher than she remembered. When he was last in Atlanta five years ago, he'd been heavier. Now the like-new suit seemed to engulf him. His six-foot frame was shrunken. His cheeks were hollow, his hands thin, helpless in their repose. Whereas in life Joe Tom had been a formidable man, in death, he was frail and vulnerable.

"Personally, I'd have put him in his Levi's with a chaw of tobacco in his mouth, but old prim and proper Cummings wouldn't hear of it. You could insist though."

Bethann looked down at the source of the acerbic comment. Barely coming to her nose was a slender old woman of indeterminable vintage. Her purse was hooked over her arm and her dress was Sunday-quality. Her white hair was cropped close to her head and very curly. Pale blue eyes peered alternately through trifocals at Joe Tom and then Bethann.

"Well, it would have been more interesting." Bethann extended her hand. "Bethann Fox." She turned slightly and indicated Kiki. "My friend, Kiki Wright."

"Edna Earle Williams." The old woman extended her

hand to them in turn. Her grip was sure and firm. "Knew your Marsh and then your boy. I'm the one took to calling Marsh The Marsh Fox back when he was small. Never seen anyone could hunt like that. He had a nose for game. Never understood why he went and made a salesman."

"He was a very good salesman."

"I'm sure he was." Her eyes flicked back to Joe Tom. "Never liked him though, did ya'?"

The question caught Bethann off guard. "We had our differences."

"Didn't we all." Edna Earle started off toward the back of the room.

What a strange conversation, Bethann thought, but before she could make sense of it, someone else was by her side, hand out in sympathy. "Brother Bob Buchanan, Sister Fox. I'll be laying Brother McLeod to rest."

From his hair to his shiny suit, Bethann found Brother Bob the epitome of pastorly sleaze and the last sort of preacher she thought Joe Tom would have picked to deliver his service. "Joe Tom was a member of your congregation?" Surely her incredulity wasn't showing.

"Well, in all honesty, Brother McLeod didn't have a church home. He just asked Brother Milton to choose someone." He brushed at his lapels. "He did request just a graveside service with appropriate words from friends and relatives. Will you be wishing to deliver a eulogy?"

Bethann had to stop herself from laughing out loud. Now *there* was a tempting thought. "I don't believe so," she managed to say. Just imagining giving the eulogy would provide her the necessary satisfaction. Which would she mention first? The fact that Joe Tom had locked his new bathroom door and pretended he only had an outhouse during her first visit twenty years ago? How about his last visit to them in Atlanta when he had plugged up the sewers for three houses by dumping tobacco remains down the upstairs toilet and then beating a hasty retreat?

"Very well. The funeral home will send a car for you at ten. Brother McLeod's neighbors will be serving lunch at the home place after the service."

Bethann merely nodded as she watched him slide away.

Slowly, they were politely surrounded by Joe Tom's neighbors and friends: the banker, the man at the feed store, the boy who serviced Joe Tom's pickup when he became too feeble the past spring to do so, the young woman with the child, the waitress at the Wel-Come On Inn's coffee shop. The poker buddies came en masse and some of them showed up again with the domino players. It was obvious the old man had not lacked for social activities, even if church attendance was not among them. Gradually, the group in the room dwindled.

A rotund man with thinning hair and a well-worn summer suit glided in near the last and introduced himself as Bethann and Kiki stood alone. "Mrs. Fox, Delmar Cummings Smith, Joe Tom's lawyer. I spoke to you on the phone. I hope you had a smooth trip out. Your sister accompany you?" He looked expectantly at Kiki, waiting for his proper introduction.

"My friend and business partner, Kiki Wright. Surely Joe Tom mentioned to you that I was part owner of a catering business?"

"Yes, I'm sure he did." Lawyer Cummings answered distractedly. "I don't want to seem rude or to hurry you, but as I said on the phone, my wife and I have planned a little trip and we are scheduled to leave tomorrow evening for the airport. I will be bringing Joe Tom's will out tomorrow to the ranch and have us dispense with the reading then and there. It's a very simple thing, really. Just a formality."

"You wouldn't rather I came to your office tomorrow before the service?"

"It would, of course, suit me fine." The words tumbled out. "But Joe Tom was a friend and valued client and he requested that I share his last wishes with you at the ranch."

Bethann quirked a brow. "Sort of set the scene?"

"You might say that. But the neighbors are fixing lunch, so we'll just kill two birds with one stone."

"I smell a rat, Mr. Smith."

He hedged. "We both knew Joe Tom, Mrs. Fox. He was a man of many surprises. Such as your son's generous college trust fund. Anyway, I think you'll better understand everything tomorrow. I'll see you then?" The smile was frozen. He didn't wait for a confirmation, just turned and left, surprisingly agile for one of his bulk.

Bethann twisted to look at the casket. "Old man, did you just wink and grin?"

"Don't put it past him."

The women looked up at the speaker. Once again, the man from the afternoon managed to surprise them.

"Joe Tom was an amazing man," he said. Now that the golf cap was gone, Bethann could see the richness of his brown wavy hair, just beginning to lighten to gray at the temples. Blue eyes twinkled in a tanned face as if he knew something she didn't. But then, that attitude could very well describe everyone in the room, including the corpse.

"Not exactly my choice of words, Mister—"

"Phillips, Bry Phillips. I see you made it into town just fine."

"Yes, exactly. We just told the car to follow its nose." Bethann scooted sideways as Kiki dug into her ribs with her elbow. She paused. "However the trip did make me tired, so we had stopped to rest. You were a close friend of Joe Tom's?"

He glanced at the figure in the casket and drew a deep breath. "The last few years, he was," he hesitated, "he was a good friend." Something in his voice told Bethann he found that description inadequate, but that was all he was willing to reveal. "Whenever Marsh and Little—Ted—were in, we'd hunt together." He shifted his weight and let his next words rush out as if he'd wanted to say them for a long time. "I sometimes think if I had been there when Marsh—"

13

Bethann drew a deep breath. "Regrets do us no good, Mr. Phillips. I'm just glad Ted was with me at the time." Bethann found it impossible to get the steely edge out of her voice. They lapsed into an awkward silence.

Bry finally gave his head a quick nod. "I'll see you tomorrow then." He turned and walked to the doorway where he was joined by Edna Earle. The old woman glanced over her shoulder at Bethann as she and Kiki took one last look at Joe Tom.

"Old man, whatever do you have up your sleeve?" Bethann murmured.

Chapter Two

Bethann and Kiki rode in silence to the cemetery. Their driver, as decrepit as the old white Cadillac limousine that had been sent to fetch them, didn't speak either beyond the perfunctory comment about the weather. Once through the black wrought iron gates they could see an impressive line of vehicles crowding the narrow gravel cemetery roads.

Mr. Cummings materialized at the door of the limousine. "This way, Mrs. Fox, Mrs. Wright." He took Bethann's elbow, leaving Kiki to follow over the sparse, roughly cut grass. The warm wind offered little relief from the midmorning sun.

They were seated side-by-side under the tent which provided shade for Joe Tom's casket. Flower arrangements covered the ground around it, and an American flag, evidence of his stint with the Army, was already properly folded in a triangle and placed in a plastic cover.

Bethann leaned back, trying hard not to survey the knot of people that had closed in behind her and to the sides of the tent. Kiki nudged her with her elbow and deftly indicated the six pallbearers lifting Joe Tom's casket from the hearse. Each one, including Bry Phillips, was in a law enforcement uniform. Impressive for Joe Tom to have such as escort. Still, she felt a twinge of betrayal: the rancher in the golf cap was what—the sheriff?

Only three days, she repeated inwardly. *Now two. After tomorrow, I'm gone.*

Brother Bob Buchanan appeared from the group and raised a hand for silence and prayer. To his credit and no doubt the sun's, the service was mercifully brief. Bethann and Kiki joined the Cummings community in laying to rest one Joseph Thomas McLeod beside his mother, father, sister and brother-in-law—Marsh's parents—with solemnity and little fanfare. Marsh himself was buried in Atlanta. Bethann listened dry-eyed.

Fifteen minutes after they were seated, Bethann and Kiki stood for the final prayer. Brother Bob was first to shake their hands, then the pallbearers. Bry was the last of them, laying his carnation on the casket with seriousness, then turning to Bethann, offering his hand as the others had done.

"No tears, Mrs. Fox?" She withdrew her hand from his larger one as she studied his badge and nameplate.

"No, no tears, Sheriff." She accented the title, the look in her eyes emphasizing that she didn't appreciate his not telling her who he was the day before.

He appeared to ignore the censure, smiling slightly and inclining his head. "See you at lunch."

"Humph! Pallbearers must be invited," Kiki

commented as he moved off toward someone else in the group.

"Either that or the bequest list is long. After all, he did say that Joe Tom had been a good friend." She shifted her weight on the carpet of funeral home turf, let her temper edge through. "So Bry Phillips is the sheriff."

"Get real, Bethann, you could hardly expect him to tell you that on first meeting. You didn't exactly inspire a torrid welcome mat yesterday afternoon. Anyway, it's probably a game around here to see who can zing the niece first."

Before Bethann could reply, the rest of the congregation came with words of condolence. It was a repeat of the night before. Most of the faces were familiar, but now they were hot from the sun and eager to get back to air conditioning.

"That's interesting." The sympathy line had trickled through and Bethann's eyes roamed to the small hill at the entrance of the cemetery. Kiki looked, too. A Jeep sat at the gate, its two occupants just shadows as they observed the proceedings.

"Herself, that's who that is." Edna Earle's voice was derisive as she approached Bethann and extended her hand. "I knew she couldn't stay away. Though she's done a damn fine job of it for seventy years!"

"Seventy?" Bethann flicked her eyes from the Jeep to the speaker. "Grudge match?"

"Something like that." Edna Earle tugged on Bethann's hand to get her attention. "That's May June

Cummings, ninety-two if she's a day and still riding in a Jeep. I'd like to see her get in and out." Bethann couldn't help but smile at the old woman's chagrin. "I had to give up those high step-ins last year, count of my arthritis, but then I'm not waited on hand and foot." She squinted. "Always got some young man to see to her."

"That's Cummings as in Cummings County, Cummings Funeral Home..."

"Cummings Feed, Cummings First National Bank, et cetera. The matriarch Cummings. Had to come see him dead! Her nephew there," she jerked her head in the direction of the hearse, "wouldn't tell me if she came to view him. Too good to sign the book."

"Edna Earle wearing you out about something?" A sheriff's deputy, his nameplate declaring him to be one Sam Taylor, grinned as he walked up. His brown eyes were kind, as he leaned his broad, over-six-foot frame down and extended his arm to Edna Earle. "Bry says come on if'n you don't want to walk."

"Don't think I couldn't!" She turned back to Bethann and Kiki. "Hope you two aren't too good for fried chicken 'cause that's what I cooked for lunch. Marsh said you never did fry nothing. I figured you didn't know how. And you a Southern girl." She took Sam's arm over the rough ground as they walked to a standard sheriff's car. She sat in the front while Sam drove. Bry headed for the truck.

"She looks pretty well taken care of to me," Bethann commented.

"She must be eighty." They both continued to watch Edna Earle and her entourage depart the cemetery. "What do you think—mother, son, grandson, favorite aunt, nephews?"

"Hell, I don't know. You know how small towns are, everyone's always kin to everyone else." Bethann folded her arms and felt her anxiety level start to rise once again. The day wasn't half over, and while she'd survived obstacle number one, the funeral, obstacle number two, lunch and the will, loomed large.

"Ladies, is there anything you need to ask or see to?" Milton Cummings stood in front of them. Did the man not make noise when he moved? "Shall we deliver the pot plants to the ranch? Leave the sprays here?"

"There won't be anyone to take care of them at the house, Mr. Cummings. We're leaving tomorrow. Why not deliver them to the nursing home we saw on the way in or a doctor's office? Brother Bob's church?"

"Very well." He handed her the encased flag. "If there's nothing else, do you want the limo to take you back to the motel or on to Joe Tom's?"

"Motel. We'll make our own way out to Joe Tom's."

***

Bethann stopped the SUV at the open gate to the McLeod property. The mailbox swung by a point from its post. A once-proud split-rail fence was falling down every twenty feet. The only appearance of care was in the sign that boldly proclaimed "Ranch McLeod" over the entry to the road. It hung straight, its unpainted carving done by a craftsman who took his time and well-used his talent. Cattle grazed on one end of the sign while on the other, horses ran wild.

The gravel of the entry quickly gave way to dirt. Parts of the road were deeply rutted, evidence of the monsoon spring and almost-drought summer. A grove of pecan trees framed the drive. Bethann shifted into four-wheel drive.

One-half mile from the gate the road curved and the two-story white native stone house came into view. The wooden porch railings were in much better condition than the rest of the buildings surrounding the house. The barn was almost as dilapidated as the mailbox. There were two or three outbuildings, wooden, barely standing. The windmill drooped, with half its blades missing and one leg appearing much shorter than the other three. The deputy's car, sheriff's truck and a Cadillac were the only signs that anyone was about.

Bethann parked by the front porch. "Joe Tom really let this place go," she observed as they left the cool interior. She hadn't seen it in fifteen years, but the ranch house looked as if it hadn't been cared for in twice as many. She craned her neck toward the roof as she got out. "I don't see it."

"Bethann, don't upset yourself." Kiki tried to put her arm around her friend. "Like you said, the place is neglected."

Bethann deftly moved out of her way. "Marsh falls to his death trying to put up an antenna for the old man, then Joe Tom doesn't even have the decency to show up for his funeral, now there's no antenna, and I'm not supposed to be upset?"

Kiki crossed her arms. "I don't have any better answers now than I did two years ago. But you can't go in there all mad and embarrass yourself. Those people are just trying to be nice to us." Bethann glowered at her. "Walk it off!"

"I don't like you, Kiki."

"I'm a bitch, I know, I hear it all the time. It must be the company I keep. Now walk to the barn and back."

Bethann rolled her eyes at Kiki's solution to every problem—walking it off. She dropped her shoulder bag at her friend's feet, let the keys bounce on top of it and started off. Halfway there, she turned around and came back.

"That was quick. All better now?" Kiki asked.

"There's a satellite dish behind the barn."

"At least there's not cable."

***

Just inside the living room Delmar and Sam stood by the water cooler, their distance from the window unit, Bry noted, carefully calculated so they couldn't be seen from the outside. "What's she doing?" Delmar groused.

Bry heard the question as he came up behind them,

iced tea in hand. His practiced lawman's eye recognized the stance, the body attitude, the shake of the head from the afternoon before. He watched as Kiki stood in the bright sun, not seeking the shade of the porch, as her friend marched halfway to the barn and back. He knew full well the circumstances of Marsh's death: slick soles on an old metal roof, a trip over the antenna wire, a two-story plunge to the concrete top of the capped water well. Damn Joe Tom for having the reading here. He shook his head.

Bry was spared from framing even part of this into words by Edna Earle's appearance. Wiping her hands on her apron, she joined them at the window. "What in hell are you three gawking at? Girl lost her husband here. One thing to come back to Cummings, another to stand on Joe Tom's porch!" She opened the front door and leaned out with the screen. "I can't keep these men off this chicken much longer. Are you coming in or not?"

"Be right there, Edna Earle." Bethann picked up her keys and purse. Dusting them off as she took the porch steps two at a time, she and Kiki entered the house while Edna Earle still held the door open.

"Jeez, it's as bad as I remember." Bethann stood just inside the large room that ran the width of the house. Bry watched her shake her head as she reassessed her surroundings. What did she expect from an old man who hadn't felt like caring for his home since *her* husband had died? Cracked linoleum covered the floor while multi-colored rugs played chase across the expanse. Two huge stone fireplaces faced each other from north and south, each with its own sitting area. The southern one boasted the television, a relic even the secondhand store would refuse, while the northern held the infamous yellow and black McLeod couch.

"Tell me I lied." Bethann turned to Kiki, a woman who, Bry felt with certainty, didn't normally stand anywhere with her mouth open and her eyes unblinking. He gave the room a quick once over to discern what they found so uninviting. It was clean—except for the cobwebs gathered on the twin antler chandeliers. There were assorted ladderback chairs, two tables, a wall full of pictures, then one totally blank except for the prerequisite cowhide and longhorns, bookcases whose contents had not been inventoried in fifty years. Two water coolers ground away in opposite corners, trying their best to cool a house whose owner had resisted most modern conveniences, certainly air conditioning. A wood-burning stove could be glimpsed in the hall, a feeble attempt, Bry knew, to heat the whole house from one location. But the room was dominated by the twelve-foot long, yellow and black plaid custom-made-in-Scotland couch.

Kiki moved further into the room and nudged the large central rug with her toe. "Don't be too hasty, Bethann," she murmured as she put her hands on her hips and swept the room a long glance, "this is Navajo. Old Navajo."

She started toward the couch when Edna Earle took

charge. She shot Bry a sharp look before grabbing Bethann's arm and shaking Joe Tom's bitch niece out of her lethargy. "Come on, I set up at the kitchen table. We'll eat around it."

***

Whatever Bethann had expected lunch to be, silent wasn't it. But that would be the best one word description: silent. Lots of fried chicken and fluffy biscuits, lots of crumpled paper napkins, lots of iced tea. Lots of silence. Edna Earle commanded the dinner table as efficiently as any general. Grace was dispatched and they sat down.

"Maybe we do need lessons." Kiki muttered as she pulled the skin from her third piece of chicken. "Better than my grandmother's."

"I'm still amazed at the dishes." Bethann turned the saucer over in her hand. "Last time I was here it was Melmac."

"It is a unique concept." Their caterers' eyes had immediately been drawn to the lunch plates. No two place settings were alike, which spoke well of the imagination of various dinnerware manufacturers, yet all had a common western theme. Colors ranged through all the brown tones to the green of Frankoma's serving pieces. Western scenes and cattle brands were displayed in some fashion on all.

"I think you could say he got a hoot out of

assembling all these," Edna Earle said. "Never passed up a flea market."

"That much was obvious."

Sam muffled a laugh. Bethann caught it. "Deputy, do go on. Just because I gave up visiting Joe Tom a long time ago—and my reputation and opinions seem to have lived on in my absence—doesn't mean I wouldn't enjoy a Joe Tom story or two. I can even contribute."

He smiled in relief, touched his mouth with the paper napkin. "Well, I do know a few, just like everybody else." Edna Earle cleared her throat. He turned to her and his tone became belligerent. "This is the strangest family funeral meal I've ever been to. Where are the stories, huh?" He swiveled to Bethann and Kiki. "Mrs. Harkness, now she was president of the historical club some time back, and you know how they're always looking for something new to slap one of those historical markers on."

"Sam, were you even born when this took place?"

"Edna Earle, I heard my mama tell it a dozen times. Anyway, seems this is one old stone house and she figured Joe Tom'd be proud to be on the tour."

Bethann saw the smiles start. This story must be well-known and oft-told, and she didn't feel that Mrs. Harkness came out ahead.

"She kept bugging him about letting her and the old girls in the club come on out and see it. Joe Tom always kept that front gate locked, you know. The men, well, we still come through Edna Earle's pasture next place over, if the gate's done up. Anyhow, she'd catch him uptown at the courthouse or call him on Sunday mornings, since he liked to sleep late then. I don't know if she just wore him out or if the idea came to him and he went for it."

"I was told the boys at the barbershop had something to do with it," Delmar added before closing his mouth on another ear of corn.

"So he called her up."

"No, he went over to her house during a meeting." Delmar swallowed. "My wife was in attendance."

"Maybe you should tell the rest, Delmar. Wasn't your wife also in attendance out here when it happened?" Edna Earle cocked an eyebrow. "I was told she was. After all, I was out of town at the time and had nothing to do with it."

"Sheesh, I started this story, Edna Earle, I'm going to finish." Sam turned back to his audience. Bethann was meticulously picking a biscuit apart and eating it in tiny pieces. Kiki was licking crumbs from her fingers and eyeing another piece of chicken. Sam took a deep breath. "Some way or other, Joe Tom got in touch with Mrs. Harkness and invited her and her committee over to the house. Kind of a preview session. See if it fit the bill, et cetera, for one of them markers. They were to come to tea."

"Tea?" Bethann and Kiki mouthed the word simultaneously.

Delmar cut in. "Missy should've smelled a rat right then."

Sam huffed. "He called it tea and they came. Four of them." Sam paused and the rest with him, the names of the gullible being mentally tabulated. When there was no protest, he continued. "He'd been over to the big nursery in the next county and got flower pots for the outside, so I hear it looked respectable. He'd even swept the porch. There was a linen cloth on the big table by the couch, and he'd set up the tea things there." He paused for effect. "But he'd also borrowed every hunting dog in the county and they were inside."

"Had been all day," added Edna Earle.

"It was June. It's not like it was going to wear them out for hunting," commented Bry.

"Anyway when he went outside to see to Mrs. Harkness and the ladies, the dogs managed to get rowdy before he got back in." Sam paused for effect. "He never was much for emptying the spittoons."

Bethann burst into laughter. "How long did they stay?"

"Dogs went home that night."

The laughter was contagious.

Kiki glanced over at a finally smiling Bethann. "Bethann can beat that."

"Do tell." Bry stretched back from the table and crossed his arms over his chest. "It would be interesting to hear some of Joe Tom's niece stories from the other side." He scooted away from Edna Earle as she hit lightly at his arm.

Bethann sighed and began to fiddle with her iced tea

glass. "Well, Sheriff," and she let the word linger just a bit, "I don't know that Joe Tom would have shared this, because I don't think he ever knew it."

"Must be the tobacco and plumber story." Bry smirked. "Marsh told us. But you're right. I don't think he ever did tell Joe Tom he backed up the plumbing for three houses by disposing of his weekend's worth of— shall we politely say?—tobacco spittle down the upstairs toilet and then leaving town."

Bethann narrowed her gaze at him and pursed her lips.

"That was it, wasn't it?" he asked.

Edna Earle got up abruptly, her chair scraping loudly on the worn floor. "Enough of that."

"What?" Bry asked as she jostled his chair as she went past.

"We'll have dessert on the couch. You can read the will in there, Delmar, although I dare say, you've got that document memorized."

Chapter Three

As they shuffled into the living area, Bethann watched the lighter mood of minutes before disappear from each of them. The Last Will and Testament of Joseph Thomas McLeod was to be read and the solemnity of the occasion was not to be marred. Kiki took the coffee tray from Edna Earle and set it on the long low table before the plaid couch. She poured mugs for the women, ignored the men. Edna Earle set the tray of pecan pie pieces beside the coffee.

Bethann settled on one end of the McLeod sofa, the large pottery mug balanced between her fingertips, legs crossed, her right foot swinging slightly. Kiki sat beside her, a welcome buffer between her and the strangers for whom and from whom there seemed only derision. Sheriff Phillips slumped into the cushions at the far end. He removed one of Joe Tom's pipes from the old rack on the end table, turning the carved buffalo head bowl over and over. Sam spun a ladderback chair and crossed his arms on the back of it. Only Edna Earle, sitting between Bry and Kiki, was outwardly calm.

"Well," Delmar began as he adjusted the bifocals on

the end of his nose and scooted the old wing chair into a position in front of the fireplace. He sighed. "It's really a somewhat simple affair, and I told Joe Tom I only saw one complication, but we'll get to that towards the end." Bethann felt the hair rise on the back of her neck as Delmar looked out from under his heavy brows and studied the group assembled before him. He sweetened his coffee before continuing.

"To give you some background, Mrs. Fox, I don't believe you were ever aware of just how much Joe Tom grieved the loss of your husband. It was like taking a son from him. He just couldn't bring himself to go to Atlanta for the funeral. He felt guilty, I think blamed himself for Marsh's death, was even embarrassed. You see the fruition of that in Little—," he caught himself, "—in Ted's trust fund. He came to me to set that up and to rewrite his will on the day of Marsh's funeral. Up until that time, Marsh had been his sole heir."

He reached behind himself on the chair and pulled folded legal-sized papers from his coat pocket. Bethann felt his audience catch their collective breath as he shook them open. "We all know how these things begin. No doubt Joe Tom was of sound mind, even if it was a bit on the contrary side." He flipped a page and began reading. "'To Edna Earle Williams, the thousand acres adjacent to her property that I won in a poker game from her husband Vernon in 1978.'" He looked over at Edna Earle and waited for her comment.

"That all? Hell, he cheated Vernon out of two

thousand."

"I believe we're talking the thousand out here to the west," he pointed, "that I have the deed to in my safe. Cheating has never been mentioned, Edna Earle, and Vernon had several years before he died in which to do so. This was the poker game over here, not the one at Blackerby's barn. That particular tract was sold fifteen years ago in an oil deal. I recall Joe Tom did right handsome off it."

Edna Earle huffed and sank back into the tartan cushions. "It's the least he could do."

"Well, no one's arguing with you on that." Delmar readjusted his glasses.

If this wasn't one of Delmar's "complications," a disagreement over a thousand acres, Bethann thought, what was? It didn't bode well for Ted.

Delmar continued. "'To Sam Taylor, whatever vehicles I own at the time of my death, including the old one in the barn. Enjoy!'" Delmar glared at Sam, daring him to fuss.

"Sounds good to me." Sam couldn't help but grin. "I know what's in the barn. Won't Renita and me be spiffy!"

"Just what you two need now," Edna Earle muttered.

But Bethann smiled at his uncontrolled joy. So it was still here, Joe Tom's late in life vehicular folly. Ted would be furious over this.

"Well, one happy customer. 'To Bry Phillips, the remaining land and livestock, if there is any at the time of my death,'" Delmar fixed a steady gaze on the sheriff, "—livestock, that is, and I don't believe so—" Bry nodded as the lawyer continued, "'with the exception of the house, the first big bass pool, and the hundred acres accompanying them to the road to make a good piece of property.' I have the map attached to this and the deeds. I believe that leaves you with about four thousand acres." He paused as if waiting for Bry to object.

"Well, looks like you can quit sheriffing and do a little ranching like you always wanted to." Edna Earle clipped off the words.

Kiki lightly flicked at Bethann's knee. "Rancher," she mouthed with a smile.

"Wouldn't Meg've been proud!" encouraged Sam. Edna Earle fixed him with a sharp look.

Bry ignored them and sat silent. His breathing had slowed and he seemed to be just keeping himself under control. How curious, Bethann thought.

"Very well, Bry, let's not have a comment." Delmar turned a sheet of the legal-sized paper. "The rest deals with Theodore Thomas Fox." He cleared his throat. Bethann set her coffee down on the table, folded her hands in her lap, and began twisting her wedding ring. Delmar drew a breath to start and then stopped himself. "Why don't I just tell you this part?"

Her stomach made a roller-coaster drop as Delmar put the will into his lap and pulled off his glasses. After rubbing the bridge of his nose, he replaced them. "Mrs. Fox, it was Joe Tom's wish that the remainder of his estate go to your son. As he is not yet of age, and Joe Tom seemed to think twenty-five was an appropriate age after which a young man's oat-sowing was about over, you are the trustee. In light of your history with Joe Tom, I've always thought you to be an odd choice, but he felt that as Ted's mother, you would best represent his interests."

He paused for effect. A dropped pin would have been heard as equally as a gunshot. "The rest of the estate consists of the designated hundred acres, the contents of Joe Tom's safety deposit box, assets from banks and stock accounts, et cetera, the house and all contents with the exception of Sam's vehicles."

Bethann uncrossed her legs and waited for the other shoe to drop.

Delmar did not disappoint her. "Now up to this point, I do not question Joe Tom's choices or generosity. But I want you to know that *from* this point on I fought Joe Tom. It was an uphill battle and I lost. Obviously." He tapped the will. "It's here, in black and white, and as they say, it is legal." He picked the papers back up, thumbed a page over and began to read. Bethann willed herself to breathe as she listened to Delmar's version of a complication.

"'In order for Theodore Thomas Fox to inherit, Bethann Tyler Fox, widow of my nephew, Marsh McLeod Fox, is to live for one year at Ranch McLeod. During this time, all normal household expenses will be paid from my accounts. This is not to include extensive remodeling, i. e., no air conditioning. She may spend five nights away without penalty. At the end of this time, eighty percent of my remaindered estate goes to Theodore Thomas Fox, twenty percent to Bethann Tyler Fox. If she declines to live at Ranch McLeod for the subsequent year or breaks the five-night rule, the estate is to be sold and divided evenly between the two parties named in the sealed envelope in Delmar Smith's office safe."

A complication, indeed. Bethann felt all eyes on her. She did not take hers off Delmar, but drew a quiet breath and moistened her lips. "Well, the old bastard got in one last turn of the screw. Just exactly what are we talking, money-wise?"

The lawyer smiled and visibly relaxed. "Joe Tom was certainly a good judge of character. You do indeed have a head for business just like he said. Cut right to the chase. Last quarter, we were probably talking somewhere in the neighborhood of twenty."

Bethann let her jaw go slack. "Did he think I was stupid? Or just gullible?" Delmar's back stiffened. "I'm going to leave a very solid business, move here and allow myself to become a prisoner for twenty thousand? Hell, after Ted's education fund and the big land grab here, I'm surprised there's that much left!"

Delmar's eyes lit and a slow smile touched the corners of his mouth, making Bethann grow wary once again. "Million, Mrs. Fox. The remainder of Joe Tom's estate was worth twenty million."

"Million?" Her voice squeaked and Kiki gasped.

"Million. He just didn't live like it. Sort of a point of pride, you might say."

"How?" Bethann's voice cracked with the question. Was that muffled laughter from the far end of the couch?

Now Delmar grinned broadly. "Let's call it skillful land management and lots of timely investments in, oh, oil, gas. He knew when to get in, more importantly, when to get out. And he never did spend much on himself. No wife, no kids..."

"No conscience."

"Edna Earle, your attitude has taken a turn for the worst in all this." Bry spoke to her somewhat harshly. "Up until we sat down for lunch, you were always in Joe Tom's corner. Why the change?"

"He's trying to be immortal by dragging this thing out for another year. All the town's going to be dying to know who the two lucky souls are if Bethann screws up and doesn't come live here."

Bethann found her voice. "And this is a decision I'm to make when?"

"Well, it does need to be settled as soon as possible. Joe Tom provided a week's grace period from the time of the reading of the will. Missy and I will be returning on just exactly that day, so I will need your answer in one week. Surely, you're not considering turning down your son's inheritance?"

"Mr. Smith, at the moment, I'm beyond considering anything. I'm in a state of shock."

"I understand. Joe Tom often had that effect on people."

***

Kiki reached for the plate of leftovers on the kitchen table in front of Bethann. "Of course, we'll have our lawyers look at it."

"For all the good it'll do." Bethann slumped forward and went after another cold biscuit, tearing it in halves, then quarters. When Marsh died, her world had collapsed. She hadn't thought it could happen again so soon.

The others had left shortly after Delmar stacked the papers, leaving Bethann a copy of the will. Edna Earle insisted on doing the dishes, as there was no dishwasher, while Sam ecstatically pulled Bry to the barn to inspect the year-old pickup and the vintage Corvette. The latter was all the evidence Bethann had ever needed that while Joe Tom might not have spent money on his environment, he wasn't above a bit of folly. Bry still seemed to carry a chip on his shoulder, even when they came back to get Edna Earle. Left to their own devices, Kiki inspected the house, while Bethann sat at the table with the will in front of her.

"What would you like me to say, Bethann, other than the lawyers will look at it?"

"I want a way out. I want to not feel this resentment—hatred—I feel. I want to hold Ted. I want to go stomp on Joe Tom's grave!" She ground her teeth, gave voice to the bubbling resentment. "How dare he be so cavalier with my life? How. Dare. He."

Kiki sat beside her. "Let's look on the bright side."

Bethann rolled her eyes.

"The old wagon wheel that doubles as a window in the upstairs bath over the tub is fantastic. Joe Tom had a certain style." Bethann cut her eyes at her as she rushed on. "Of course, I'm no expert, but from all those antique pricing shows on TV, I'd say the rugs are Navajo, the dusty bronze is a Remington, and there's a trunk full of quilts predating 1910. Granted, the set of rodeo characters from rail spikes and horseshoes is a bit much, but there may be value there as well. And if there's one pair of worn-out, scuffed up cowboy boots with sterling silver spurs in the closet, there's two dozen!" Her voice softened. "You really didn't pay much attention to this place when you were last here, did you? Even this table is wonderful." She traced her fingers over the quarter-sawn oak.

"Kiki, I don't need you to play devil's advocate."

"It's just a year, Bethann."

"Two words, Kiki. Atlanta Divines."

"I can do it by myself." Bethann raised her eyebrows. "Okay, I'll hire Marilou to take your place." Bethann set her jaw. "Sorry, wrong choice of words—no one can take your place—Marilou can just help. She'd love to."

"Damn straight. Marilou wants in. Has always wanted in. She'll take over."

"I won't let her. You can come back three days at Christmas, two in June. The busiest times."

"And in the meantime, what am I doing out here— tending nonexistent livestock and parrying words with Sheriff Bry?"

"Well, the last wouldn't be too bad, would it?" Bethann laid her forehead on the table, knocked it against the oak. Kiki ignored her. "I've been thinking about this while I took inventory and you sat in here feeling sorry for yourself. The cookbook."

Bethann raised her head. "Oh, that'll be easy. We're over a thousand miles apart and we're going to write our definitive Atlanta Divines cookbook."

"Knock, knock, Bethann, internet, email. Any of this ring a bell? We've been meaning to do it for five years and what's done so far? Nothing!"

"Is that house improvement and therefore banned by Joe Tom?"

"I think a business expense. We've been wanting to upgrade. Sounds like Joe Tom just bought us matching computer systems."

"Was this the same line of thinking that had ol' Jon overextending the car dealership ten years ago?"

"No, this is the same line of thinking that made him realize his mistakes, step back, retrench, do the right thing, and triple the business."

"I haven't made any mistakes here."

"Not yet." Kiki drummed her fingers on the table. "We'll take inventory and get the proper kitchen equipment. Find out how to draw on the accounts. Have those items I think are valuable appraised…"

"Why don't you come and stay a year? Sounds like you'd enjoy it."

"Jon would go nuts without me. And my children are younger than yours."

Bethann sighed and started the campaign from another angle. "What about Ted for this year?"

"What about him? He's not going to be living at home. He'll love having you here. Maybe he can help you get in good with the sheriff."

"Oh, thrill. What about my parents?"

"Oh, yes, Thomas and Lanelle. And just when did you last see Thomas and Lanelle?"

"March." She sighed. "Or was it April? On their way from winter in the Keys to summer in Bar Harbor."

"Um-hum. Twice a year, T and L breeze through, drop some largesse on Ted, marital advice on you, and take off. Now, really, other than giving them a new spot to park the Pace Arrow for a month, how do you think your being here will affect them?"

Kiki was tearing down every roadblock as Bethann voiced it. "What about my house?"

"Lease it. Or we'll watch it. It's just next door."

"You are entirely too perky for me. It's like you want to get rid of me."

"Oh, Bethann, no. No. I want what's best for you and Ted. I can't see you letting all this slip through your fingers. Twenty million dollars." She measured her words. "You'll never have to cater again. Ted can do what he wants, not what he thinks he has to. Think of the freedom!"

Bethann settled her chin on upturned palms. "What if Ted's named in that envelope anyway?"

"Tops, it's only half. What if he's not named?"

"What if you convince Jon that this is where you all want to spend Thanksgiving?"

"What if I convince Jon that this is where I want to spend Thanksgiving and he can stay home?"

They both laughed, the sound an antidote to the day's tension. "I used to lead such a normal life, Kiki. What happened?"

She shrugged. "Let's find paper and pen and start an inventory. It's not really as bad as you think. There're two bathrooms."

"One for me, one for the cats. You think Pen and Tux can be happy as farm cats?"

"Ranch McLeod cats, Bethann. Get it straight."

"How am I ever going to explain this to Ted?"

"Wait till he gets home in a week. Then start with a checkbook."

Chapter Four

The rich smell of bacon and coffee drifted in to Bethann. She turned lazily in the double bed, and stretching, touched the high wooden headboard with both hands, allowing her fingers to trace the carvings. The McLeod family bed, where Joe Tom and Marsh's mother had been born. Where Marsh almost was. The stuff of family legends. A new mattress and box springs would arrive today and she'd transfer all the fancy linens to it. Joe Tom's room was about to take on a decidedly feminine air.

Bethann reached down and pulled Pen closer, snuggling with the black and white cat that always slept with her. She glimpsed Tux on top of the dresser, watching, still very upset with this break in his routine. "What smells so good, guys?" Bethann bolted upright. Nothing should smell good because no one else was in the house. At least, no one was supposed to be!

"Jeez, what is going on?" She scrambled for her robe, knocking Pen from his perch and causing Tux to meow. Flinging open the bedroom door, she tied the sash as she tore barefoot down the hall and stairs.

Edna Earle stood in the kitchen, apron tied around her middle, whistling as the bacon sizzled. Bethann's coffee pot/espresso machine had been elbowed out of the way for a percolator. Homemade bread was sliced and ready to toast in the oven broiler. A carton of eggs lay open beside the stove. An old jelly glass held late-summer wildflowers, and two places were perfectly set at the kitchen table.

"Edna Earle, what are you doing here?"

"It's six thirty, Bethann. I've let you sleep late enough." She slid the bread into the broiler.

"That's kind of ignoring the question. What are you *doing* here?"

"Girl, I work here. It's a good thing I brought my own supplies this morning. All you've got in the icebox is yogurt. Care for coffee?"

"Sure." Bethann reached up into the cabinet for a mug, returning three to the shelf before finding one that wasn't badly chipped. "I know you worked for Joe Tom but—"

"And now I work for you." The old woman smiled and deftly turned the perfect overeasy egg. It swam in bacon grease.

It smelled too good not to eat it. The yogurt she'd bought the night before would keep. Still, this sudden advent of a housekeeper was not in her game plan. But then lately, what had been? "I don't need you to work for me."

"Sure you don't. You can fix eggs like this?"

"I don't want to fix eggs like this."

"Marsh loved them."

"No doubt. That's because he never got them at home."

"Precisely. Your culinary skills have serious gaps. You need me for that cookbook."

"It's not that kind of cookbook—and how do you know about it anyway?"

"Small town. Everyone had to know what you'd be doing for a year."

"So Delmar told them." Bethann was exasperated. "Why am I wasting my breath arguing?"

"I have no idea. Ready to eat?" Edna Earle handed her a full plate.

Bethann sat down and cast a sideways glance at the cook. "Why don't you just sit down here and explain it all to me, Edna Earle."

The old woman placed the toast on the table and pried the lid from a jar of homemade pear preserves. Seating herself across from Bethann, she fluffed out her paper napkin, smoothed it across her apron, bowed her head. Bethann did similarly, but never took her eyes off her. "Want me to pray, or you like moments of silence?"

Bethann gritted her teeth. "Whatever you and Joe Tom did."

"For what we are about to receive, we are ever grateful. Amen."

"Now start talking, Edna Earle. Don't leave anything out."

The old woman ignored her. "See you have a cat pan in the corner of the kitchen. Do you really want that smell in here?"

Bethann sampled her breakfast. The eggs were wonderful, the bacon just salty enough. She would have trouble maintaining the right amount of pique. "Where would you suggest I put it?"

"Outside. Don't those city cats know what the dirt's for?"

"They are quite capable of going outside. I wanted them to get used to the house first. A pet door is coming with the movers."

"Movers? What else is coming? There's not much room left in this house, y'know. It was enough trouble to keep it clean as it was."

"I'll be doing the cleaning. And I have no intention of surrounding myself with Joe Tom's artifacts for a year. It is mine now."

"Conditionally." Edna Earle sipped at her coffee. "So what are the movers moving?"

"Personal items. A computer. DVD. A real TV. Ceiling fans for every room. Kitchen equipment. Decent pots and pans." She measured the words and watched for the reaction. None was forthcoming. "Your turn. Explain it all to me."

"I started working for Joe Tom over twenty years ago right after Vernon died. Did the shopping, cooking on weekdays, left him something for supper. Let him forage for himself on weekends. Took his laundry home.

Cleaned. Maybe a better word is cleared."

"So if you were working for him all that time, how come I never ran into you on those horrible visits we made?"

"Joe Tom gave me the time off. Figured you could take care of it all."

"He paid you to work for him."

"Well, I didn't do it for my health. He didn't pay near well enough."

"I'm sure there's truth to that. So you expect to keep on."

"It supplements my social security." She smiled cagily. "He always paid cash so don't go looking for any check stubs. Uncle Sam's business is his, mine is mine."

"Are you going to tell me, or do I have to guess what your services are worth?"

"I may need to negotiate a new contract."

Bethann rose to get more coffee. It could be a longer year than she'd expected. "I don't need you, Edna Earle. My culinary skills are legend and my washer and dryer arrive this afternoon. Maybe you should take early retirement."

"My other job doesn't cover my expenses."

"You have another job?" Bethann cut a slice of bread and put it in to toast. "Who else do you work for?"

"It's a different situation altogether. And no, thank you, I didn't want another slice."

Bethann sliced another one.

"What do your parents say about all this?"

"What do my parents have to do with *all this*?"

"Known Marsh since he was little. I *know* about Thomas and Lanelle." She used the tone of voice reserved for dirty little family secrets.

"T and L will try to work Cummings into their spring schedule. They've always wanted an excuse to do the Texas wildflower trails." Bethann retrieved the toast.

"What did Ted say to his inheritance?"

"Wanted to quit school before he began. So I told him the first indication of slipping grades, and I would be in Atlanta for good."

"Good for you. Money's wasted without an education."

At last, something they could agree on, but Bethann held off feeling relieved as she watched the old woman's eyes twinkle. She felt the trapdoor under her feet.

"It'll be mighty lonely for you this year if I don't work here."

"I've been 'mighty lonely' for two years."

***

Edna Earle nodded to herself. Just as she thought. A little companionship should go a long way here. Companionship of just the right male kind. With a quick mind, a special wit, and a temper to match that rambunctious red hair, no wonder Joe Tom had alternately admired and reviled Marsh's wife. It would take some work, but this plan of hers, still in its infancy, was definitely worth a shot.

"I can make myself indispensable," she countered.

Bethann sighed. "Will it do me any good to argue?"

"What do you think?"

"I think I'm beaten. But you're here just till I'm moved in and settled. If you're not indispensable by then, you're off the McLeod family payroll."

"Fair enough. Just remember, I don't work weekends, do upstairs windows, or clean up after your hoity-toity affairs. I have my standards." Edna Earle walked over to the wall phone.

"Who are you calling at this time of morning?"

"Plumber for your washer and dryer."

"It's seven in the morning. Don't go getting me in bad with the serviceman."

Edna Earle only smiled as she placed the receiver to her ear. "It's okay, his name is Williams, too."

"So you have a complete staff of Williamses at your beck and call?"

Edna Earle nodded.

"In that case, I foresee the needs of a locksmith, electrician, carpenter..."

"Easy."

"And junk dealer."

Edna Earle humphed. "No dice. That one's a Cummings."

***

"Where are you off to?"

One hour later Bethann stood in the door of the kitchen watching Edna Earle sweep the floor. She felt ridiculous. A woman old enough to be her grandmother was doing what she should be. And now she was going to be cross-examined.

"Post office. Thought I'd get a box this morning, sign the signature cards at the bank, check with Delmar to see if there's anything else needs doing. You're here if the movers come early."

"Adjusting to a housekeeper real well, aren't you?" She swept up cat litter. "Those two have got to learn some manners."

"You're making me feel guilty watching you."

"So don't watch. Get 'em to give you Joe Tom's old box. Number thirteen."

"Very funny. Do we need anything while I'm out?"

"Don't think so. You seem well supplied with yogurt. You can eat leftovers again tonight. Unless you feel like cooking. After all, your culinary skills are legend."

Bethann shook her head as she turned and walked through the living room to the front door. She gave a chuckle to see Pen and Tux on opposite ends of the couch. A little cat hair would do it some good.

The ride into town was pleasant. The morning air held the merest hint of freshness so Bethann went with windows down. The car needed airing anyway. Two days cross-country with unhappy cats had not exactly lent a new car smell to the vehicle.

She reflected on the events of the past two weeks. Indeed the will was legal. Even knowing it was too great a chance to pass up for Ted, she still struggled with the decision. Kiki was resolute, determined Bethann would go. The idea of someone living with her things for a year had been too much, so instead of leasing, Kiki would watch the house. Still there were things she absolutely, positively could not live without for a year. Her kitchen and bedroom had practically emptied. She might not have central air for a year on the ranch, but she would have creature comforts. Two new state of the art computer systems were ordered, two business expenses paid for by Joe Tom. He would not get the better of her, not even from beyond the grave. It would take a year, but Bethann was determined to have the last word.

She squelched Ted's off-the-cuff desire to quit school and follow in Joe Tom's entrepreneurial footsteps. At least he understood about the Corvette since he knew Sam. Saying good-bye was softened by seeing him be slyly pleased at his absolute good fortune while all the time trying not to look anxious for her to leave and start his road to financial independence. He had helped her pack and carried the cats to the car. Not to worry, he told her, he would spend Thanksgiving, Christmas, and spring break with her.

Anything so she would not violate the five night rule and cost them their inheritance.

***

The Cummings post office was little more than a room with some mailboxes attached to the feed store. The service window opened just as she arrived and stated her business. She read the postmaster's name: Evan Cummings.

"You'll be wanting Joe Tom's old box?" Evan was middle-aged, short, balding. His glasses slid to the end of his nose and he pushed them back into place.

"Be fine."

"You need to fill this out and I need two forms of ID."

Bethann looked from the official form back to him. "Really? You don't know who I am?"

"Oh, we all know who you are. Uncle Sam just needs confirmation." He smiled. "But in the meantime, I'll let you have Joe Tom's mail since it is taking up considerable room." He shuffled to the back of the small office and returned with a foot-high stack, loosely held with an assortment of wide rubberbands. The bundle appeared to consist mainly of magazines, but the undeniable look of bill envelopes was there, too. He plopped the pile down in front of her. "I'll need that form back before I can make it official."

Bethann shot him her best "dirty look" and gathered up the slippery stack. Balancing the mail and trying to get her purse onto her shoulder took all her attention as she abruptly turned away from the window. All she saw was scruffed cowboy boots as she bumped into the person behind her and caused them both to drop their armloads. Mail scattered.

"Oh, I am so sorry!" She scrambled to pick up the pieces that had escaped the stack and slid in all directions across the aged wooden floor.

"Well, I'd heard you were coming back." Bry tilted his Stetson upward at the brim and gave her a long look. Her red ponytail bobbed as she reached for the scattered mail and tried to reassemble it.

She stopped what she was doing and levelled a look at him. "Is this your way of saying welcome to Cummings, or are you disappointed because your name's in the mystery envelope and now it looks like you won't collect?"

"Now how'd you think of that?" He let a slow smile ease across his features and started retrieving his mail, mostly manila envelopes and a few small boxes.

"I guess I'm just always thinking." Bethann had her envelopes and magazines back under control. Standing, she shot the other people in line a hasty glance, then righted her purse over her arm and marched out.

Bry placed the mail in the window, let it slide toward Evan. "Quite a temper, eh, Sheriff? Are we sure she's not Joe Tom's relative? Swear Marsh never was like that."

Bry ignored him as he continued looking in the direction Bethann had gone. Her perfume lingered in the air longer than her quick-tempered words.

Evan finished stacking the envelopes. "Well, Sheriff? Any truth to what she says?"

Bry snapped his attention back to Evan. "About what?"

"You in that envelope if it doesn't go to Little Tom?"

"Now why would I be there?"

***

Why indeed? Bry slowly pulled the truck out of the parking space and absent-mindedly drove the four blocks to the sheriff's department. He'd sure like to think he was in that envelope. But then, since Marsh's death, Joe Tom had led him to believe he was a major inheritor along with Ted.

Although, in all honesty, both with himself then and now, there was no reason he should have inherited anything. Ted was Joe Tom's only blood relation. The surprise came with Joe Tom's inclusion of Bethann. Was the four million a consolation prize for her "surviving" Cummings for a year, his last shot at a woman he couldn't abide? What *had* the old rascal been thinking?

But it still stung, even though two weeks had passed and the realization had had plenty of time to set in. Four thousand acres was nothing to feel scorned about. It was the ranch Meg and he'd always hoped to have as their own. Now it was there, just sitting and waiting for its new owner. Him. He needed to saddle up, ride over it, review the stock tanks, the herd sheds, try to feel gratitude instead of resentment. But all he had done was stop by Delmar's office to do the paperwork. He'd not set foot on the property. Joe Tom had strung him along for two years with the innuendo of inheritance. Had he thought Bry would desert him if there wasn't a promise of something coming? Hell, he'd loved the old rascal for years. Why had Joe Tom felt the need to lie?

Entering his office, he put the mail receipts down for Corinne, the dispatcher, to note the cash and then turned to the stack of documents on the counter, taking some of them with him into his private office. He slammed the door harder than he meant to but wouldn't open and redo it as his grandmother would have made him. He just let it serve as fair warning that the sheriff had already been trifled with once this morning and would stand for it no more.

With an accomplished twist of the wrist, he sailed his hat onto the rack and then settled at his desk, but he couldn't concentrate. Even the half-whittled block of wood sitting on the blotter held no interest for him. He laced his fingers behind his head, put his feet up on the well-worn blotter, and stared off into space.

The last image he expected to see popped up. Bethann Fox, perfumed and sassy, smiled knowingly and winked, took a pile of money from him and disappeared.

Chapter Five

"**W**ell, did you get all those pressing chores done?" The screen door slammed in Bethann's wake, as Edna Earle stuck her head around the refrigerator door.

"Most. Delmar was out. In court or something." She put the mail down on the kitchen table and it slid across, skiding into the jar of flowers. "Oh, hell." She picked up a manila envelope and brandished it in Edna Earle's direction. "Don't believe it. Got part of his mail."

"What did you say?" Edna Earle leaned around the refrigerator door again. She'd occupied herself with piddling chores until Bethann showed up as she'd already heard about the mail mix-up from three sources. Each informant had given a more lurid story. Adding up the accounts, she could see about two hundred people as direct witnesses and the match ending with Bethann slapping Bry. She didn't believe any of it for a second. For starters, if it were true, she'd already have heard from Bry. He hadn't called.

"Sheriff Whatever and I collided at the post office and the mail bounced everywhere. It wouldn't have happened if he'd been back behind that rope they have in normal post offices."

"Bry."

"Huh? Oh, yes, Sheriff Bry. Probably sneaking up behind me to find out my business. If he'd have just waited, I'm sure old Evan would have told all."

"Can't say I disagree with that observation. Those Cummings'll talk a blue-streak when it's gossip."

"So what am I going to do with this?" Bethann tapped the envelope on the table.

"Take it to him?" Edna Earle closed the door and rinsed the cloth in the sink.

"Make another trip in? The movers are coming."

"Since when were they ever on time? Anyway, I'm here."

"So you go and I'll stay. You know where he is and I don't."

"Sheriff's office is one block east of the square. Big sign. Cummings County Jail." Edna Earle balanced herself against the sink.

Bethann flicked the envelope against her thigh and set her mouth in a straight line. "Look, I do not intend to spend this next year arguing with you." She picked up her purse and swung it over her shoulder. "And I certainly don't expect to continually lose!" She turned on her heel and slammed out the door.

A chuckle escaped Edna Earle's throat. "Then you'd better get prepared to fight dirty." Oh, yes, this was going to be a very fun year indeed.

***

Bry swung out of his office, placing the Stetson on his head as he made for the door. "Paperwork's in the out tray," he told Corinne. "I'll be gone most of the afternoon. Need me, call." He opened the swinging glass door to the entry that separated the official office from the official jail as Bethann cautiously opened the front door. She stood there getting her bearings, as if trying to decide what to do next.

"Unless you've come to visit or make bail for the Johnson boys—drunk and disorderly again—I imagine this is where you want." He swung the door wider. "Come on in."

Bethann inched through. "You," she paused "this got mixed in with mine." She held out the envelope for him and he took it.

"Didn't want to mail it for me?"

"I didn't know what class you were used to."

"Probably not as low as you think."

She smirked. "Touche´." Turning, she went back into the entry, then quickly outside.

Bry deposited the envelope on the office desk in front of Corinne. "Take care of this. Your turn to face Evan." He followed Bethann.

She was already settled in the SUV, engine started, seatbelt adjusted. Bry tapped on the passenger window and it rolled down. "Forget something, Sheriff?"

He balanced an arm on the vehicle top and leaned in

toward her. "Edna Earle been around?"

"What a polite way to ask if I know she comes with the property. Yes, she has successfully infiltrated my quarters."

He smiled, breathed in her perfume, didn't know what he wanted to say next.

"Is there anything else?" she asked.

This is ridiculous, Bry thought. They obviously didn't care for each other. Then why did her half-smile intrigue him as much as her green eyes sparked feelings he'd laid to rest fifteen years ago?

"Sheriff?" she asked again. "Is there anything else?"

He pulled his mind back to the present. "No, I guess not." He shook his head to clear it and straightened up, watched the window rise, and the SUV back away. He stood rooted to the spot, not moving till she was on her way. Then he turned and walked to Sally's Grille for lunch.

***

Bethann paced among the boxes delivered midafternoon. Touching them was touching pieces of home. Somehow all these had seemed fewer when the movers packed. It had seemed so necessary for her year's sojourn, her enforced sabbatical. Now, staring at the boxes as the sun set, a glass of chardonnay in one hand and the packer's list in the other, the task appeared daunting. It was simply going to take a year to find a place for it all, the promise of a junk man notwithstanding. The kitchen was wall to wall with boxes. The washer and dryer were pushed into a corner. The movers had begrudgingly put the new mattress and springs on Joe Tom's bed for her, but the old set languished on the porch. The downstairs bedroom was to be turned into an office, but the carpenter couldn't have squeezed in there now with a shoehorn.

Pen and Tux were nowhere to be seen. Bethann didn't blame them. She wanted to hide, too. And Edna Earle? That darling had watched all the proceedings of the day, commented on every aspect of the afternoon's affairs, declared she'd already worked overtime, and beat a hasty retreat. At least Bethann had brought the corkscrew with her. She certainly wasn't going to be finding anything in that mess tonight.

It was a new variation of the old waiting game. It had never been her specialty, although God knew she'd had enough practice. Waiting for Marsh to get home from work when they were childless was lonely, but waiting for him when Ted was a baby was exasperating. Atlanta Divines had filled those lonely times. Now here she was, faced with an unexpected year of waiting. The cookbook would occupy her, but Edna Earle aside, she'd still be lonely.

The phone rang. Bethann hopped up on the dryer as she answered the wall unit in the kitchen.

"Mom?"

She smiled at Ted's voice, an audible piece of Marsh

still alive. Father and son—it had been difficult enough to tell the difference in their voices two years ago. Now, as Ted attained adulthood, the timbre of his was his father's reborn. Sometimes it clutched at her; tonight it comforted. "Already studied for three hours and going back for more?"

"How'd you guess?" The muffled voices and music in the background were proof he wasn't in the library. "So how are you going to like it?"

"I'm trying my best to remember all twenty million little-bitty reasons for doing so. Particularly since Cummings won't be connected to a cell tower for another month."

He laughed. "Oh, no! Tethered to a land line! How will you ever make it?" He abruptly changed subjects. "So, how's Edna Earle?"

"Funny, you seemed to have forgotten to mention that she came with the property." She heard his uneasy sigh and relented. "Unless she's changed, I'd say she was just as snappy as you remember."

"And Bry? Have you had dinner with Bry yet?"

Bethann paused. "You mean the sheriff? I've barely met Bry, but you seem well acquainted."

He stammered. "Oh. I thought maybe, you know, he's a nice man and you're a nice woman and—"

"And in one year, I'll be home. In Atlanta. Richer. I'm putting up a calendar, marking the days off."

"If you say so."

***

In the next two weeks, Edna Earle made herself indispensable as the house was feminized and put into a routine like it had never seen before. The boxes were unpacked, the computer set up, the cat door installed. The exterior doors had keyless entry locks—Lord, but that girl was picky about security! The McLeod couch sported three coordinating quilts circa 1910. Each room had at least one ceiling fan, the Navajo rugs were on the walls, and every document more than ten years old had been burned with the CPA's blessing. All potential junk was relegated to the smallest bedroom upstairs and Edna Earle was dragging herself home each night to a hot bath. Wasn't she too old for all this?

Still, each morning she looked forward to arriving to find the coffee pot/espresso machine spewing away. Bethann had chosen to start the cookbook on brunches so some exotic pastry would be in the oven. When Bethann emerged from the shower they would taste and comment and change. These were all tried-and-true Atlanta Divines recipes, but now they were wearing a gloss of West Texas. In order to conserve their waistlines, she volunteered to create goodwill for Bethann by sharing the overruns around town. She had a schedule, but she also had a plan, coming back to the sheriff's department every few days.

Bethann was working hard and Edna Earle had to admire her determination. She'd quickly surmised that the local grocery would be inadequate for her more esoteric purchases and had taken off to the warehouse store two hours away. She busied herself in the kitchen, rarely leaving the house, conducting business with Delmar on the phone. At night, she told Edna Earle, she spent her time at the computer.

Neither of them mentioned Edna Earle's unemployment again.

Chapter Six

"**E**ver go to high school football games?" It was a late September Friday morning, and Edna Earle stood at the sink, scraping the breakfast dishes and lazily watching Bethann fling flour like dust on the kitchen table.

"Sure. I was on the drill team."

Edna Earle temporarily sidetracked. "You mean Thomas and Lanelle stayed in one spot long enough for you to be on the drill team?"

"Get a grip, Edna Earle. Lanelle inherited bank stock when it meant something. Thomas was a textile engineer. We lived and breathed cotton in one place till the company was bought out. Then he took early retirement and his pension fund and they ran with it. That's when they got happy feet. After I was grown."

Edna Earle went back to her original premise. "I wasn't talking about when you were in high school. I was talking about now." She tried not to let the exasperation show in her voice. She'd decided a month was long enough for Bethann to adjust to the house and circumstances. She'd actually made it through yesterday without once referring to "that damn will." It was time for action.

Bethann was still distracted. Pen was on the floor considering a leap into the middle of what was taking Bethann's attention away from him. He jumped before she could answer Edna Earle. "Damn cat!" Bethann elbowed him out of the way and he scattered flour as he indignantly made for the pet door and the back porch. Flour was left in little cat prints the length of the kitchen. "Edna Earle, I'm sorry, I'll clean it up."

Edna Earle allowed an inward sneer but kept focused on the bigger picture. "Never mind. Needs to be swept anyway. When are you going to lock those two out?"

"I'm not and you know it." She went back to rolling dough.

"House is no place for two critters like that." Edna Earle reached for the broom and bit back more critical words. The Plan was more important than a lecture. "Did you go to high school games with Ted?" It looked like she was going to have to spell it out.

"Well, of course." It was like 'what kind of parent do you think I am, lady?'.

"Well, I have a season ticket, but I've volunteered to work in the concession stand tonight. Want to take mine and go? Nobody plays football like small town Texas."

"That's what I hear." Bethann sprinkled a brown sugar and nut concoction on the rich sweet dough. "Aren't you a little old for concession duty?"

"Senior citizens do it once a year for a service project so all the parents can watch. But we pick our game. Early in the season before it gets cold."

"Sounds smart to me." A black and white nose inched its way through the pet door. The women stomped their feet simultaneously and it was gone.

"Well, want the ticket or not?"

"Nah. I'll work at home. Give it to Sam or somebody."

"He has tickets."

"The sheriff."

"Ticket."

"Anybody not go to this?"

"No." Edna Earle stopped sweeping and stood at the end of the table, just beyond the flour-fling range.

"And you can't stand to let it go to waste?"

"Abhor waste."

"Okay, then, just tonight." Bethann began rolling the dough lengthwise.

"I wasn't offering you the season."

***

Edna Earle put herself in charge of the concession stand money, so she could sit on the high stool and maintain a constant lookout for her two unsuspecting victims. She had less than a year to get two lonely, headstrong people over to her way of thinking. She'd faced worse. Few had defeated her matchmaking ways, Sam and one of her beloved granddaughters simply the exception that made the rule.

Bry showed up before the kickoff. He was in uniform, a 'presence' at the game. He waved and smiled, went off to confer with the good ol' boys at the fence surrounding the field, then disappeared up the first ramp into the stands.

Bethann was late. The first quarter was almost over before Edna Earle looked down to find her standing at the counter.

"Clock stop?"

"Really, Edna Earle, what could have happened that I wouldn't care to miss? Anyway, I couldn't decide what to wear."

Edna Earle surveyed her. Jeans, white knit golf shirt, hair in a ponytail knotted with some sort of scarf trick, big gold earrings, sandals. Football must be a different game in Georgia. "You look fine. Take the second ramp, turn left, top row with your back against the press box. You'll have to crawl over about six people, but that's the quickest route."

"Sure you don't want me to do the money?" Bethann drummed her fingers on the wooden counter and chipped at the white paint.

"As Joe Tom's heir, you need to be seen."

"I can't believe season tickets didn't come in the will."

Edna Earle paused as she realized Bethann was being sarcastic. "Run along now!"

Oh, to be a fly on the wall of the press box!

***

"Lord, look at that!" Sam leaned back in his bleacher seat and pressed his spine against Bry's knees. He nodded and Bry followed his nod. Bethann climbed the metal stadium steps, ticket stub clenched in her hand. He watched her lips move as she stared down, counted the rows.

In one swift moment, Bry knew precisely what the empty seat beside him and the ticket clutched in her hand meant. Edna Earle had overstepped and meddled once again. He thought the matchmaking issue was settled two years ago after the debacle with that divorcee from Chapelpeace. Obviously, *someone* had a short memory and it wasn't due to her age. If Edna Earle was so set that no one should live alone, she should have practiced what she preached and remarried after Vernon died. There was one fellow who obviously got the better end of the deal by going on before.

He watched Bethann politely excuse herself down the row. Getting to Edna Earle's piece of bleacher, she stopped and stared at him. He returned her look and raised his eyebrows.

"This is Edna Earle's seat?" She pointed to the empty spot beside him.

"You know Edna Earle and I know Edna Earle. What do you think?"

"I think I should go home."

"'Lo, Bethann," an out-of-uniform Sam turned

slightly and offered her his hand. She took it to shake and was pulled down into the seat. "Let me introduce you to my wife." A sweet-faced, very pregnant girl turned as best she could to nod in Bethann's direction. "Honey, this here's Joe Tom's niece. Bethann, this is Renita."

"Nice to meet you. And congratulations on your impending bundle of joy. Edna Earle hadn't mentioned your fatherhood, Sam."

"It's the one place Edna Earle's not likely to meddle," Bry commented.

She pursed her lips but didn't pursue it as she gingerly set her shoulder bag down between them. She sat stiffly, just as he did.

Weren't they a fine pair of bookends? He hoped Edna Earle was enjoying herself in the concession stand because when he got hold of her... He dug in his pockets, producing a knife and block of wood. His knuckles reddened as he whittled with more force than was needed.

A tap on his knee and he jumped. It was Sam. "Going to get Renita a drink. Want something?"

He shook his head no, managed to murmur, "But thanks," as he continued making toothpicks, which wasn't the initial purpose of this block.

"Bethann?" Sam asked and Bry shuddered at the conversation-stopping look she bestowed. Sam touched his wife on her shoulder. "Be right back, sweetie." He beat a hasty retreat down the bleacher steps and Bry wished he were going with him.

***

"Boy, are you in trouble!" Sam put the two chili dogs, chips, popcorn, and large drinks down so he could find the money stuffed in his jeans pocket. "It's like January up there, it's so cold! Lord, Edna Earle, warn me next time!"

She smiled in return. It was going just as planned.

"Edna Earle, look at me!" She glanced up from the money box. "I don't know which one of them is going to kill you first!"

"Keep your voice down. Want the whole town to know?"

"What doesn't the whole town know now? Hell, they're sitting up there like statues in the cemetery, afraid if a breeze came along they might accidentally bump each other!"

"Hmmm," the old woman stared off into space, wondered if she could conjure up just such a breeze for just such a purpose. She handed him his change. "I hope all that isn't for Renita. She'll be big as a house by the time that baby comes!"

"Now you're a midwife!" He began gathering his purchase. "Let me have a box!"

"Gimme, gimme, gimme. And so impatient!" She handed him a small pasteboard container. "And my mother was a midwife. Birthed half this county!"

"Yeah, yeah. I'd call in sick tonight if I were you!"

Edna Earle smiled to herself as she helped the next paying customer. She wasn't going to call in sick, nosirree. Not on your life! She'd be at her weekend job as matron down at the jail. She'd always had a love of fireworks!

***

Bethann was astonished when Sam handed Renita the box and took only a drink for himself. Maybe they hadn't eaten before they came. Maybe she was carrying twins.

Delmar came over and welcomed her to the social life of Cummings. He pointed out Missy to her and a well-padded sixty-ish matron turned and waved on cue. Brother Bob circled in from Bry's side during half-time and invited her to church on Sunday. His extension of the invitation to Bry was met with a cold stare.

At the beginning of the fourth quarter, Renita turned to Bethann and announced it was time for a trip to the 'little girl's room'. Would Bethann like to find out where it was so she'd know in the future? An escape route was offered and Bethann leapt at the chance. Halfway down the stands, she figured Renita needed her for balance. But it didn't matter. She was out of there!

"Figured you needed a way out," Renita admitted as they stood outside the restroom. "That old biddy did you dirty, huh? She thinks she is some hot matchmaker. Even tried with Sam." She put a fresh stick of gum in her mouth. "I'd offer you some, but that's my last piece. You can get some at the concession, if you want to get a few words in on Edna Earle."

"It's okay. I'm not much of a gum-chewer. But I do appreciate your helping me get out." She patted her jeans pocket for her car keys and retrieved them. "I'm out of here, Renita. Just say I wasn't feeling well." She strode off toward the gate, then came back to where the girl still stood. "I left my purse up there. What was I thinking?"

Renita thought for a second before she disappeared into a stall. "I'll have Sam bring it over in the morning."

Just one more thing to do before leaving. At the concession stand, Bethann broke into the pay out line to whisper to Edna Earle, "You're so damned lucky tomorrow's Saturday!"

And she was gone.

***

Night driving was never one of her favorite things. Doing so much night catering, she had had to adjust, and Kiki was with her most of the time. At least in Atlanta, there were street lights and traffic lights and buildings lit like day. And cell phone service. The countdown in the weekly Cummings newspaper said they had three more days until being connected. It couldn't come quickly enough.

Night driving on country roads was something else again. The stadium was on the side of town opposite Joe Tom's, so she had to drive back through town. Instead of waiting for the lone traffic light to turn green, she rolled on through. Hell, she'd just left all of the county's law enforcement at the game—who was going to catch her? Cummings could be stripped bare and no one would know it till the school song was sung one more time and everyone had been down to the Dairy Mart for a celebration/commiseration ice cream cone. She was not even aware of which team was ahead. *Damn Edna Earle!*

Distinctive flashing red and blue lights beckoned in her rearview mirror and brought her up short a mile from her front gate. A quick glance at the speedometer found her five miles over the limit. That—or running the red light in town? Why not both? Cursing herself and circumstances in general, Bethann pulled over, rolled down the window, and turned off the ignition.

With the side mirror, she watched the truck door open behind her. He did it quickly, as if he hadn't taken time to run the tags. How many Georgia cars were there in Cummings anyway? She might as well have a bull's eye on her rear! The officer left the grill-lights flashing, announcing her misdeed to anyone who passed. Then seeing him approach, she knew it was Bry from the walk. She leaned back against the seat, closed her eyes, and held out her left hand for the ticket. Edna Earle could consider herself unemployed.

"Well, okay, if you can hold it with one hand, palm up."

Bethann felt the sudden weight of her purse and barely opened her eyes in time to grab it with both hands.

Bry stood there, then leaned over, crossing his arms above her car door and peering in through the window. "Feeling guilty? You were doing sixty."

"I know what I was doing. Are you going to give me a ticket and be gone?"

"God, gal, they must have fed you pits instead of peaches! I brought your damned purse to you and I don't even get a 'thank you', much less a kiss my—"

"Thank you," Bethann broke in. "Renita said Sam would bring it out in the morning. I wasn't expecting you to." Her words were clipped.

He nodded. "That's it?"

"What else do you want?"

"Sincerity?"

"I sincerely thank you for leaving the game which I'm sure you were very interested in because you whittled the whole time and never said a word to anyone while I was there. I admit I was speeding. Sheriff, may I have my ticket or may I go home?"

"Damn, woman, you are awfully hard to like."

"I didn't know you were trying."

Bry paused at her words, seemed to consider them before straightening up. "Everybody deserves a warning the first time," he said slowly. "Go and speed no more." Slapping the top of the SUV, he strode back to his truck.

Bethann sat there, a deep feeling of misery stealing over her. She reached to start the ignition, stopped just before it turned over. *Pits!* He had accused her of eating *pits!* And that was precisely what she sounded like. Even without Kiki there to remind her, she was embarrassed by her own rudeness. It wasn't his fault Edna Earle had tricked them anymore than it was hers. A glance in her side mirror showed him still there, now with the red and blues off, doing the gentlemanly thing and waiting to make sure she got on the road. Opening her door, she got out and strode back to his vehicle.

This time he rolled down his window. "Car not start, Mrs. Fox?" His voice was even, controlled.

"Car starts fine." She raised her eyes toward heaven, for inspiration, if not forgiveness, before looking back at him. "I was rude, Sheriff. No excuse."

He cocked his head toward her, his eyebrows raised in disbelief. She didn't blame him, but couldn't he *say* something?

"I'm sorry for biting your head off. I really was raised on peaches, not pits. Although I seem to be eating an awful lot of crow meat lately."

Now he smiled and she quickly looked away from him. She couldn't bring herself to look him in the eyes. Studying her finger as she ran it across the chrome at the bottom of his window, she quickly went on. "Would you like to come over for a cup of coffee? It's the best I can do by way of thanking you for my purse and apologizing for my rudeness."

Amusement lit his face as she glanced quickly at him, trying to determine if she was being forgiven, believed, neither or both.

"Coffee would be nice."

Chapter Seven

Bry pulled into the drive behind her. Bethann got out, climbed the steps, then waited for him on the porch. As he joined her, she punched in her access code on the key pad at the front door and pushed it open. She began turning on lights as she moved to the kitchen. He removed his hat as he came through and without looking, dropped it to the hat rack. It promptly fell to the floor.

"What'd you do with the rack?"

Bethann turned in the hall and smiled as she watched him retrieve it. "I don't wear Stetsons and I usually come in the back door. So it's in the kitchen. Things have been rearranged since you were last here," she called as she flicked the lights on in the kitchen and he heard water being drawn into the coffee pot.

Bry looked around. *Rearrange*d would be one word for it. The main thing was the now-quilted McLeod couch. The bookshelves were cleared, the top of the old rolltop desk was actually visible, and there was a new TV encased at the opposite end of the room. The American flag from Joe Tom's casket was displayed on the mantel. The two most notable differences were matching black and white cats whose eyes had not left him since he entered. They lay curled in opposite wing chairs by the north fireplace. Bry wondered if the defiant look in their eyes had come from their mistress or if she'd learned it from them. Joe Tom must be spinning in his grave.

He ambled into the kitchen. The table was unchanged, but that was about all. New shelves were covered in pots and pans and appliances that he had no idea what they were used for, although he did recognize a microwave. Bottled water dispenser, washer, dryer, cat food. Edna Earle must have had a fit. Spying the hat rack, he took aim and sailed the hat. It hit the floor.

"I had that maneuver down pat in the other room." He went over, retrieved it, brushed it, placed it gently where it belonged.

"Things have changed." Bethann repeated as she reached into the refrigerator and took out milk.

"Make mine black."

"Cappuccino."

"Oh."

"Know what that is?"

"I have been to the big city. It's been a while, but I've been." He stood in the center of the room and rested his hands in his back pockets. "And they let us have TV now. Cable in town. Satellite out." And if that wasn't sticking his foot in his mouth, what was? "Bethann, I didn't mean…"

She gave her head a small shake, as if dismissing the comment and the memories it might evoke.

"Open the windows for me, okay? I hate to go off

and leave the ones downstairs all open. Might as well put a sign on the gate that says 'rob me'."

Was she trying to lighten the conversation? Surely, he could do the same.

"You were safe tonight. Had all the local hoodlums spotted at the game." He moved to open the wide windows in the kitchen. The cooling night air circulated quickly.

"I love sleeping with the windows open." Bethann pushed buttons on the machine and readied cups. "There's a train around somewhere, too."

"That'd be the four o'clock three times a week. What are you doing up that time of night?"

"Gee, Rhett, sometimes Scarlett just can't sleep."

He was immediately contrite. Sometimes Rhett didn't sleep either.

The espresso machine made enough noise for three pots down at Sally's. He watched Bethann expertly handle the frothing milk and the deep dark liquid. "I'll fix it for you this time. Next time, you can adjust it for yourself."

Next time?

She carried the two tiny cups over to the table and they sat down.

"Joe Tom have these hidden somewhere?" He closed his hands gently around the china, hoping it wouldn't shatter at his touch.

"It wasn't exactly a western dinnerware concept. I had to import." She watched him out of the corner of her eye as he sipped gingerly.

"Different."

Bethann laughed and handed him a paper napkin. "You have a milk mustache."

"You've got one, too."

"Do not!" But a quick lick of her upper lip told her she did. Bry tried not to watch her tongue flick out and taste, but he lost the battle. He shifted his weight in the creaky old chair, both irritated and amused by the tightening in his abdomen.

Further conversation was halted by the appearance of the cats. Not waiting for formal introduction, they leapt in unison onto the table. "Penguin, Tuxedo! Off!" Barely phased by her words, they hunkered down, twitched their tails and stayed where they were.

"Great control. I think you did better with Ted than that."

"Yeah, but Marsh was un-trainable."

He quirked an eyebrow at her, couldn't help the slow smile that lifted the corners of his mouth. Beneath all the bluff and bluster, all the resentment and stubbornness was a woman with a sense of humor. Who knew? Would that be what got her through the next eleven months?

Something would have to because it wouldn't be him, despite Edna Earle's none-too-subtle techniques.

***

An hour later, Bry was rethinking that line of thought as they slowly walked through the living room to the front porch. He donned his hat, thanked her for the coffee, said goodnight, and went to the truck. She still held a coffee cup, and leaning against the stone column at the top of the steps, waved.

Bry opened the truck door and put one leg in, glanced up to where Bethann stood above him. He had actually enjoyed the interlude. Their conversation had continued to ease as she warmed up pastry from the morning. They'd dwelt on nothing specific, just generalities, the weather, old movies. The scent of her perfume had mingled with the coffee, and it was going to be very difficult to concentrate on the keg party that was undoubtedly being held in Wil Cummings' back pasture. He hadn't been able to banish the image from his mind of her tongue flicking to her lips, ridding them of froth. The thought of kissing her surfaced.

She did look highly kiss-able. The way she leaned against the stone column

highlighted her silhouette, and the light streaming from the open front door caught her red hair and gave it an angelic glow. Hell, he could resist anything but temptation. Joe Tom had taught him that and taught him well.

"Bethann?" He balanced, one leg in the truck, one on the gravel drive.

She pushed away from the column, set the cup on the railing and came down the steps toward him.

"What? Want a cup to go?" She stood on the other side of the door, catching the handle in her hands and balancing backwards. Her face was turned up to his. He pulled his leg out of the car and edged around the door.

"I've probably had enough coffee." He leaned on the opened door.

A man knows when a woman wants to be kissed, and the last hour had put a new slant on how Bry viewed Bethann. They exchanged sly smiles and he began to lean down. Bethann pulled up on the handle and moved towards him. He could smell her, perfume and coffee and pastry. She closed her eyes and parted her lips and Bry felt fifteen again.

The radio crackled and they both jumped. "Hey, Sheriff, better get over to the keg party. More fun than expected."

The moment was gone. Bry hastily pulled back, then sat in the driver's seat as he reached for the radio. Bethann let go the door handle and dropped her hands to her sides. Bry glanced quickly at her and thought she looked about thirteen, having been caught with the new boy in town.

He replaced the mouthpiece. Bethann was back on the porch, picking up the cup, heading toward the door. She waved and went in.

He shook his head and tried to shake the almost-taste of her from his lips.

**

Heat radiated off Bry as he careened through the doors of the department. The younger set was getting careless: the oldest Cummings grandson had put unwarranted moves on a Williams granddaughter and the melee that ensued had trailed all the way out of the pasture and down to the highway. He'd confiscated the keg, called a few parents, and watched the rest of the kids scatter at the sound of the sirens. For that he'd given up kissing Bethann!

Kissing Bethann—he licked his lips as he sailed his hat to the rack and sorted through loose papers on his desk. Damn—he was losing his mind if he was interested in kissing Joe Tom's peach-pit niece.

Wasn't he?

A cleared throat at the door brought him back to reality. Edna Earle held a cup of coffee and had an impish grin on her face. "Coffee, Sheriff?"

He turned toward her. "Since when do you offer me wee-hours-of-the-morning coffee? Aren't you usually napping in the back?"

"Tsk, tsk. And such a temper." She walked in and deposited the cup on his desk. "You left the game early."

"You reassigned my seating." He sat down and leaned back in his chair.

She ignored his comment. "Get her purse delivered?"

"Don't you really want to ask if I delivered anything else, too?"

"There is hope for you yet."

"Edna Earle, sparring with you is like going after it with a verbal grand master. Can't you just learn to mind your own business?"

She balanced her palms on his desk and leaned over. "When there's so much at stake? You need someone and she needs someone and I figure the time is right for both of you. I have experience in these matters, you know."

"I can name about half a dozen experiences I could've skipped because of you and your 'experience in these matters.' Don't you think Bethann and I can eventually figure this out?"

"Bethann, is it? What happened to Georgia pit-eater, or Joe Tom's bitch niece? At best, it was Mrs. Fox. You have less than a year before she packs up and skedaddles out of here, and no, I don't think you two would ever figure it out on your own."

"Well, thank you for your vote of confidence. Now that you have set me on the road to eternal happiness, Edna Earle-style, will you leave me alone?"

"Do you really expect me to say yes?"

He cocked his head. "Not even for appearance sake?"

She raised her right hand. "I promise not to interfere with your love life ever again."

"How come it sounds so real, but I know there's a hitch?"

"You wanted a promise, I promised."

"There's still a hitch."

"Then it's up to you to find it."

"You are one wicked old woman. You really are."

"But you love me. Not like you're going to love Bethann..." her voice trailed off as she closed the door. Bry watched through the glass as she headed to the back.

***

Bethann lay awake. The breeze blew gently over the covers, and the ceiling fan stirred pleasantly, making a soft whir. Pen and Tux were in their usual places, bedded down tail to nose, but disturbed by her sleeplessness. Even though she had brewed decaf coffee, she lay awake hours later, and it had nothing to do with the espresso.

She'd enjoyed his company. He'd graciously accepted her apology for her rudeness. After the initial embarrassment subsided, she'd relaxed. They'd laughed together. They'd looked each other in the eye and only slowly broken contact.

He had wanted to kiss her. She had felt the heat from him, smelled him. She'd watched his hands as they'd pulled on the car door, his strong fingers curling over the metal. What a waste, she remembered thinking. Those fingers should be curling over hers. Flesh to flesh. And those lips...

Bry had wanted to kiss her. That didn't bother her. She had wanted him to. That did.

Why? Because he had known Marsh? Was that any different than the latest undesirable in the Kiki and friends get-a-man-for-Bethann sweepstakes? He had been newly-divorced and in their social circle for ten years. But this was different. She'd never wanted any of Kiki's options to kiss her. But then she'd never argued with them or traded insults either. She had felt nothing for any of them. Nothing. Hardly the case with Bry. He stirred strong emotions, pleasant and otherwise.

Bethann turned over again and faced the window. The sound of the four o'clock train whistled in as the curtains ruffled. He was on duty. Did he hear it, too? Somehow, the thought comforted her and she finally drifted off to sleep.

***

Bry shifted his weight as he stood on the ramp of the deserted depot. He remembered the first time he'd been there, shaking in his too-small shoes. Thank goodness, the train no longer stopped. The locomotive just pulled its burden through three mornings a week with a regularity you could set your watch by. This morning, his gaze lingered on the disappearing boxcars.

Damn! He hadn't expected to enjoy Bethann's company so much. Or at all, for that matter. Laughter so smoothly replaced the caustic comments that he was not even aware when it happened. One minute they were at each other's throats, the next, he was contemplating kissing her. Truth be known, he was contemplating much more than that. Who'd have ever thought from all Joe Tom's negative comments, that Marsh's wife—

Marsh's wife. That's who she was. The bitch niece

that Joe Tom never let up on except when Little Tom was visiting. Then not a bad word out of the uncle's mouth about the boy's mother. Marsh's presence alone wouldn't stop Joe Tom. He'd rag on her all day if he had a mind to. Marsh would only half-heartedly defend her. He'd told Bry once that it just wasn't worth fighting the old man. Ignoring him and his comments was the best way to get them to stop. Or bringing Ted. Bry had carefully watched after that and seen the truth of it.

But she was Marsh's wife. Shouldn't make a difference. He'd never known them as a couple. Never known her till a month ago, except through Joe Tom, Marsh, and Ted. Shoot, Edna Earle'd set him up with divorcees or single women he and Meg had known before she'd—

Bry put his hands in his pockets and started back to the truck. He got in, turned the ignition, sat for a minute. Trouble was, it just didn't feel right, her being Marsh's wife and all. *Liar!* he accused himself. Trouble was, it felt too right. And she wasn't Marsh's wife, she was his widow.

He turned the truck and left the train tracks. But Edna Earle was right about one thing. Less than a year, she'd be gone back to Atlanta and the life she really wanted. She was just biding her time, collecting her inheritance… or collecting his?

Damn! Nothing was ever going to come of this. The sooner he let it be, the better for them all.

Chapter Eight

Edna Earle hesitated as she punched in her entry code at Bethann's back door Monday morning. The thought crossed her mind that the owner might have been sufficiently miffed to change it, but the door popped open.

Still, there was a difference. The sweet smells of brunch had been replaced. The coffee gurgled, the cats looked expectantly at their bowl, and a pot of something threatened to boil over on the stove. Edna Earle hurried to that trouble spot first. Some sort of soup brewed disturbingly. She cut down the flame and reached for her apron from the hat rack.

Heading toward the refrigerator, she planned breakfast and determined how best to break the 'brunch is over, soup's on' news to the beneficiaries of Bethann's uncaring largesse. "Where's momma?" she asked Tux as he jumped into the kitchen window for a better view of the sizzling bacon and eggs. "It's back to the good stuff, if she's into soup." Tux approved with a purr and ooched closer to her.

"Didn't know but what you'd be too ashamed to

show up this morning." Bethann strode into the kitchen, already dressed, but barefooted, as she seemed to be most of the time around the house. Obviously not raised with dirt floors, Edna Earle noted. She hoped the subject of Friday night would be forgotten. "None for me, thank you. When the eggs and bacon are gone, I'll not be buying more unless necessary. It's yogurt time." She pulled Tux out of the window, grabbed some yogurt from the fridge, poured a cup of coffee and sat down at the table.

"Soup's on, huh?" Edna Earle opted for light conversation.

"Sirloin and rice. I've been trying to condense it all weekend from fifty servings to two so we can put it in a special seasonal romantic cozy-up section we want in the book. But then, you'll be able to contribute to that, won't you? Romance is your specialty, right?" Curt, clipped words, punctuated with the click of the spoon in the yogurt container.

Edna Earle had considered this scene all weekend, and since the pace was unusually slow at the jail, there'd been a lot of time. Bry wasn't upset with the ticket exchange. Why should Bethann be?

"I hate seeing lonely people when it's not necessary."

"I'm not lonely. God knows, I'm rarely alone."

Edna Earle shifted her weight and deftly flipped the two eggs. "Bry is lonely. You are lonely. It's a different lonely than the void the cats and I fill."

"Did it ever occur to you that I might be happy like I

am? I don't need another husband."

"I didn't say you had to marry him!" She banged the plate down and the cats scattered out the back door. "Just a little companionship."

"Vernon's been dead for years. Where's your companionship?"

"What did I need with another old man? I had Joe Tom to look after."

Bethann's eyes widened and a look of sly realization possessed her face. She put her hand over her mouth to cover laughter. "You were fond of the old bastard!"

"Was not!" Edna Earle's righteous indignation kicked in. "He rarely said a kind word to me."

"Well, it must have been like talking to yourself."

They were silent, gearing up for another round. Edna Earle set her plate on the table and ate aggressively. Bethann refilled her cup.

"I'll be gone in less than a year."

"I'm well aware of that."

"Then leave me be! Let me pick my own companions," she said as she sat back down.

"Looks like you have," Edna Earle commented as she nodded toward the cat bowl.

"What's your interest in Bry?"

"I'm *fond* of him, that's all."

"Not related? Grandson? Nephew? Some woodpile relation?"

"I resent that. We always married before the birth."

"You're just *fond* of him." The older woman nodded.

"I don't believe that. There's something lurking in that curly head of yours and I don't trust it."

"Then you are inordinately untrusting."

Bethann looked at her over the rim of the cup. "You think you know all there is to know about me, don't you?"

Edna Earle's response was guarded. "I know a great deal that you think I don't know."

"And you think you know all there is to know about Bry?"

"Yep." She put down her fork and laced her hands in front of her.

"Then what is there about me—what is there about him—that you think we are so suited to each other that you can shamelessly manipulate us?"

Edna Earle put her plate of egg drippings on the floor for the cats. Folding her arms on the table, she looked straight at Bethann. "Why are you two so suited? Well, you're both widowed."

"Bry was married?"

"Well, if he's a widower—" Edna Earle thought better of the insult. "Meg wasn't from around here. He met her while he was an MP in the army. Sweet little thing, from Colorado, I think. He was a deputy, putting money by, and they had glorious plans for some kind of ranch." She shifted her weight and became more comfortable in the chair, delighted in Bethann's rapt attention. "She was pregnant. Thunderstorm, car rolled late at night. He was driving. They were both trapped, except he lived and she didn't. Kind of took the ranching urge out of him. He decided he'd stick to law enforcement. Next time elections came around, he ran for sheriff, and he's been doing it ever since."

Now Bethann sat very quietly. "How long ago was this?"

"Fifteen years. They hadn't been back but a couple of years when it happened."

"So he was from here."

"His mother's people are." Bethann's intense interest spurred her on. "In fact, his mother's birth was the first one my mother—who was quite a fine midwife, I might add—ever let me attend."

Bethann pursed his lips. "How old were you?"

"'Bout ten. I found it to be an altogether nasty experience."

"Let me get this straight. You saw Bry's mother being born. So she was raised here. Bry wasn't?"

"Rae—Bry's mother—and her mother never did get along. She ran off soon as she could with some cowboy she met who was passing through. Six, seven years later she comes home penniless, deserted, pregnant out to here." She made a circle with her hands in front of her belly. "Her mother turned her out, so she left before the baby was born. Fifteen years later, she dies in some fleabag motel, and as skinny a little runt as you'll ever see shows up on the Cummings depot."

"Bry?" Bethann held her coffee cup with her fingertips, balancing it inches from her lips. She didn't drink, just stared at Edna Earle.

The older woman nodded. "Rae's mother had to take him in. Vernon was doing some plowing for them at the time, so he was around the barns and all. Said she didn't treat him well. Gave him food, clothing, what education she had to. He graduated high school and he was gone. Two tours of service and then the army put him through college."

Bethann finally set her cup down. "So why did he bring his bride back to a place that had made him so unwelcome?"

"Nowhere else to go, I guess. Maybe he thought once he was educated and with a wife, things would be different." Edna Earle stared off into space. "But they weren't."

"His grandmother still alive?"

She settled her gaze back on Bethann. "May June Cummings. Wealthiest woman in the county."

"The lady in the Jeep at Joe Tom's funeral." Bethann started folding her paper napkin into triangles. "The lady who feuded with Joe Tom. About what?"

"My best guess is property. Hard as it is to believe, I don't know it all."

"Two shocks in one conversation. I may not survive the afternoon." She smoothed out the napkin and started over. "Bry is May June's grandson, but you're the one he treats like a grandmother."

"I'm the one who loves him like a grandmother. And he loves me. I know that."

"So won't he inherit when she dies? Are there other grandchildren?"

"Don't know about the inheritance. I really wouldn't put anything past May June. But Rae was an only child, Bry an only child, no more grandchildren. All those Cummingses running around are from May June's husband's family. But he was the oldest child and inherited the lion's share, and May June, to her credit, is a good manager. It's anybody's guess who'll inherit what and how much."

Bethann stopped toying with the napkin and studied the old woman. "You've tried this matchmaking business with Bry before, haven't you?"

She nodded reluctantly. "Never came to nothing. But I have honed my skills."

"You've told me this so I'll feel sorry for him and be nicer, right?"

"I've told you the truth. You wanted to hear it. It'll keep you from sticking your foot in your mouth."

"I don't think there should be a next time, Edna Earle." She wadded up the napkin and sailed it toward the sink. It skidded into the window sill.

"Girl, that's up to you."

Chapter Nine

Two weeks later, a blue norther came in with a vengeance. It took Bethann by surprise. Weather didn't change with the blink of an eye in Atlanta. Pen and Tux ran through the house for two days in anticipation of the cold. Pen took to hunting in the barn, bringing up mice and laying them neatly by his food bowl. Bethann unceremoniously dumped his offerings outdoors but knew Edna Earle praised him and took to sneaking him cream.

Edna Earle backed off on her campaign about Bry. However, Bethann knew the truth to her sudden quiet about all things sheriff. The old woman was trying to garner all Bethann's sympathy and then spring something on her. With her opening question, Bethann knew the moment had come.

"Going to the Harvest Fair?" Edna Earle appeared as nonchalant as possible as she swept the living room, forcing Bethann to raise her feet to the quilted couch where she was re-editing a string of anecdotes attached to Kiki's morning email.

"'Fool me once, shame on you. Fool me twice, shame on me'," she quoted through the red pen stuck sideways in her mouth. "You got reserved seats for it, too?"

"Very funny. I told you I was through with all that nonsense. You two want to miss the next best fifty years of your lives together, it's nothing to me." She opened the front door and continued out onto the porch. The cooler air snaked in behind her.

"Close the door, Edna Earle!"

"Wrap up in one of them quilts you're so proud of!" she snapped as she slammed the door and finished the porch. Coming back in, she stood beside Bethann, broom out to one side, like a guard at Buckingham Palace.

"It just so happens," she began and Bethann sighed and put down her pen, "that the church is in need of some workers for its booth. And since you have refused to come to Sunday services, it would be a good time for you to do something for this community you seem so anxious to get shed of."

"Are you finished?"

"Hardly. It's Thursday and Friday nights, all day Saturday. I figured you could work during the dance Saturday night since more than likely your dance card will not be filled."

"What kind of booth?"

"Food. We do chili, chili dogs, baked potatoes, and sausage-on-a-stick."

"Jeez, Edna Earle, are you sure you're a church and not just a conduit to the other side of cholesterol and fat heaven?"

"Are you implying that you're too good to work?"

"I am implying that your menu needs mending."

"Too late. It's already ordered. If you're around next year, I'll put you in charge. Now how many hours can I sign you up for?"

"Don't think I'm suspicious or anything, because after all, it's been two whole weeks and I don't think we've even mentioned the word Bry, but—"

"I am not in charge of his social affairs and he hasn't darkened the church door since Meg died."

"If I don't agree, how long will I hear about this?" She tapped on the papers with her pen.

"You leave in August, right?"

***

"Going out to the Fair later on?" Edna Earle stood in the doorway to Bry's office in the middle of Saturday afternoon. Sun streamed in through the windows, a bright, crisp autumn day with a full moon chaser. The Harvest Fair was enjoying unusually good weather, since it seemed to rain on that particular weekend three years out of four. The dance had even been moved from the old stock pavilion out to the street. The bandstand was relocated and everyone connected with the Fair seemed in very high spirits.

Edna Earle knew her query didn't seem strange. Bry had been out to the fairgrounds the last two nights.

"Thought I might. Usually do." He glanced up from the papers. Edna Earle was already turning to go, when he called her back. "All right, I'll make you happy." She raised an eyebrow. "I'll ask about her. How is your charge?"

"Bethann? Oh, she's just fine. Works all the time. Writes and cooks and cooks and writes. We're moving into 'Extravagances' next week, whatever that means, but I suppose we'll all eat well." Sarcasm only tinged her words as she turned to leave again.

"I don't suppose she's had time to go to the Fair?"

It was very hard to suppress the smile as she pivoted toward him. "No, not really." She paused. "But I have talked her into working at the church booth tonight. From six to nine. Thought it would do her good to get out in public. Going to have to make sure she's properly dressed though. This is no Junior League outing."

Bry smiled at the jail's matron. "You need time off to go get that done? Place is calm, not a wayward woman in sight."

Edna Earle smiled. "Sure. I never miss a chance to skip out while I'm on the payroll."

***

Edna Earle had told her to be ready by five thirty, so why was she surprised when the bathroom door was unceremoniously opened at five just as she was rinsing her hair in the steaming shower? "Hurry up! I'm going to find you some proper clothes!" the old woman called, then slammed the door.

Emerging from the bathroom, one towel around her head, another around her body, Bethann stopped Edna Earle in the hallway. Jeans were over one arm, one of Joe Tom's old shirts over the other. She surveyed the woman. "What the hell are you wearing?"

Edna Earle looked down at her khaki dress, complete with name tag and sheriff's department motif proudly stitched above the left breast. "My uniform."

"Did you forget to mention something to me, Edna Earle?"

"Told you I worked weekends."

"Yeah, but I thought you disturbed somebody else, not the—come here, let me read you—'Cummings County Sheriff's Department'." Bethann measured the words and cocked her head. "You sly old biddy. No wonder you can keep up so well. I just thought you were nosy and related to half the county."

"I am nosy and I am related to half the county. I also work as weekend matron so Corinne can have time with her family." She handed Bethann the clothes. "Don't you have any boots?"

"I have some ankle-high—"

"Good. Go get them." She disappeared into the Joe Tom 'discard room' once more.

Bethann held the turquoise and black plaid shirt up to herself, smoothing the tails down over her thighs as she admired the plaid in the vanity mirror. She had to admit the colors were good. At least it wasn't the McLeod tartan. She pulled it on. It hung on her. "Now what, genius?" she asked as Edna Earle stood in the doorway.

"Tuck it in and roll up the sleeves. Put your jeans on and this." She tossed a black suede vest at her. Bethann knew protesting would only delay the inevitable. "It's a little big, but you look kind of fetching. Put those big silver dangle things on your ears and let's go."

"My hair's wet, I've got to dry it," Bethann explained as she hooked the hoops into her lobes.

Edna Earle grabbed her arm as she went through the door toward the bathroom. "Looks fine. Brush it out in the car and we'll let the breeze fluff it."

"It will frizz!"

"But won't you be cute."

"All right, old woman, I'll humor you. You arc going to so embarrass us, that this is the last thing I'll ever have to do for you!"

***

Edna Earle deposited Bethann at the church booth. It was located in Food Alley, where chili competed with soft drinks and funnel cakes for the customer's money and clogged arteries. She assured Bethann she'd see she got home okay, even if it meant leaving work again.

Bethann was suspicious, but let it go. This was the last time she'd let Edna Earle push her around. In fact, she felt disaster looming. This was going to cure Edna Earle. The expense to herself didn't matter.

Business picked up almost immediately. Night came.

Bethann began to relax, even enjoying the work and the society. It seemed no one cooked on Fair nights, they just consumed from one end of the Alley to the other. It was a high-calorie, no-holds-barred fat consumption orgy.

The church booth clean-up crew came on at nine and Bethann found she could go, although she wasn't sure to where. The church members thanked her, invited her to services the next morning, and eased her out of the conversation and the booth. No telling what Edna Earle had promised them to keep their curiosity in check. Not one personal question had been asked.

The street dance was in full swing and Bethann, who had never appreciated country music, much less listened to it for longer than five minutes, found herself humming and tapping her toes to the rhythm as she stood outside the booth and watched. She was in the middle of what looked to be all of Cummings County and she was alone. Surrounded but alone, the feeling she'd been trying to escape for two years.

She took a deep breath and stopped the toe-tapping as she scanned the crowd. Some faces were familiar from the funeral or her occasional visits to the post office or grocery store, but none were known well enough to ask for a ride home. Edna Earle hadn't even told her when she'd be back. Bethann had just assumed nine. She fought a rising panic as she realized she'd left her cell phone on the dresser. Now she'd have to find a pay phone and call.

***

Bry stood on the other side of the street, seemingly involved in a conversation about cattle prices, but really watching Bethann. He saw her come out of the food booth, noticed how she stood there, looking lost. She put her hands in her hip pockets and rocked back on her heels, shrugged her shoulders and turned toward the exhibits. He hastily excused himself and followed.

Even though her frizzed red hair was as good as a beacon, he almost lost her in the crowd. He recognized the vest and shirt as vintage Joe Tom. He'd have to give Edna Earle points for cleverness.

He caught sight of her again as she started to dig in her pockets for change, read an unladylike tribute on her lips as her fingers came up empty. He watched as she caught her lip between her teeth and then settled her hands on her hips and surveyed the crowd as he walked up. The smile that flooded her face—happy to see him or just relief? He wasn't sure.

She launched right in. "Edna Earle pulled me out of the house so fast, I didn't even get my cell phone or any money! And no car, no—!" she blustered.

Her exasperation amused him and he laughed in spite of knowing he'd rue the action. He leaned on the pay phone box. "So I'm a welcome face?"

"Anybody I knew would be a welcome face!" He raised his eyebrows. "I didn't mean it that way. Oh, hell, Bry." She punctuated the air with her hands. "Open mouth, insert foot. Story of my current life."

He recovered and pushed off from the phone. "So you're a lady in distress?" He couldn't resist a dig to their first meeting. "I recall you've turned down my help before, so I don't know if I'll be safe offering it."

"I can always wait for Edna Earle." The cadence was clipped. Her eyes darted through the crowd as she crossed her arms and set her stance.

"Damn, gal, I'm just trying to be nice." He shook his head, rested his hands on his hips, let his fingers play on his holster. He caught a whiff of her, perfume mixed with food booth. Tantalizing in more ways than one.

Bethann lowered her eyes. Looking back up, she attempted amends. "After you get in a few digs."

"That you deserve." He bent toward her slightly.

"I deserve?" She pointed to herself, let the hint of a smile curve her mouth. "What about you?" She emphasized the last word and playfully poked him in the chest with a finger.

His hand shot out and grabbed her wrist, his fingers instinctively tightening, catching them both off guard. Then his hold relaxed and she pulled her hand back, protected it under her breasts.

"Hey, sorry, Bry. Didn't mean to touch you. Didn't know—well, I'm sorry, that's all. If Edna Earle would just come on." Her voice trailed off and she went back to searching the crowd for the wayward Edna Earle.

"Oh, damn, Bethann, it was reflex. Too many years—" He let his voice die out, too, as he silently cursed too many reflexes over too many years. They stood there awkwardly, trying not to draw attention to themselves.

Bethann looked at the ground, then up at him. "Let's face it. Edna Earle goofed. It's just not going to work. Not that either of us wanted it to, but—" she shrugged. "I'm the way I am and you're the way you are and I'm counting the days." She let her voice trail off again. "I'd appreciate it if you'd find me a ride home or call Edna Earle or just get me out of here." She took a deep breath. "Please, Bry."

"Bethann, I can't tell you how sorry—"

"I know." She held up a hand. "Can't you just get me a ride home?"

"I'll take you, Bethann. Okay?"

She looked at his expression, at the furrowed brow, the color in his cheeks. A part of her softened. "Okay." He gently touched her back and turned her toward the street where his car was. She walked beside him, her arms folded across her chest, trying to picture a scenario from his past that would make him react so violently to her simple touch. Nothing in her background gave her a reason for it. What had this man suffered? Would Edna Earle know?

He opened the car door for her and she slipped in. "I've never been in a patrol car before." She tried to lighten the mood.

"In this county, that puts you in the minority." He eased the car around pedestrians. Bethann was aware of the hasty glances exchanged by the populace as they watched the sheriff leave with Joe Tom's niece.

Where *was* Edna Earle?

They rode to the house in silence. Bethann muttered a quick 'thank you,' then launched herself from the car and up the steps. She punched in the code and ran up the stairs, burying herself in the middle of the family bed. She fought tears of frustration, finally giving in to them and vowing justice from Edna Earle.

Chapter Ten

The wind whipped back from the north at midnight, bringing with it the threat of rain and the autumn chill experienced earlier in the week. It whistled through the half-opened window in Bethann's room and disturbed her already restless sleep. She pulled her boots and socks off, threw the earrings to the dresser and scrambled under the covers, not bothering to undress further. Pen curled beside her, and in an unprecedented move, Tux got on the bed, too. She clutched them and fell back to sleep.

At three, Tux awakened her. He pushed his paw on her throat and meowed. "Go away, boy." She shoved at him but he came back. "I'll feed you later. If you're that desperate, go hunt with Pen." He sat on her pillow and licked at her face. She sat up and held him at arm's length. "Bad cat. Go away." He was limp, not even struggling, unusual in their relationship. Then she smelled what had him so upset.

Smoke!

She ran barefoot through the open bedroom door and down the stairs, skidding around the landing and wrenching her arm. The smell of smoke was less here, but as she flipped lightswitches, nothing happened. No electricity, although the kitchen was brightly lit. Through the window over the sink, she saw the barn in flames. Tux jumped onto the sill and cried even louder.

"Where's Pen?" But she knew. If he wasn't snuggled with her, he was in the barn hunting.

She dove for the wall phone. Dead. Her cell phone— where was it? Panic overtook her and unthinking, she ran outside calling for the other cat.

Heat propelled off the barn and stopped her advance. Sinking to her knees in the yard, she caught the remote sound of a vehicle. Turning in its direction, she saw the unmistakable outline of a Jeep, heading overland through the back of the property. She was stunned. Arson. Who feared her enough to want her gone?

No electricity. No phone. Miles from town. Nearest neighbor Edna Earle at work, not at home. The barn was aflame and the wind threatened the other out buildings. She surveyed her property. Unless the wind whirled, the house would be safe, wouldn't it? Kneeling in the ruts of the driveway, she watched as if fascinated by the flames. What was there to do? And where was Pen?

This was about as helpless as it got.

***

Returning from his respite at the depot and mesa overlook, Bry saw the fire immediately. Radio-ing the 911, he circled down toward the property. As he got closer, he was able to verify what he feared: Joe Tom's place.

Bry had shut the gates after he left Bethann, and this little bit of security now held him up as he jumped out of the truck and hastily threw them open for the volunteer fire department water truck that was on its way. Already, he heard the sirens. Rain began to pellet as he careened into the open area in front of the house. His headlights barely picked out Bethann's slumped form through the rain. Slamming the brakes, he tore out of the front seat and raced to her.

She knelt shivering, her hair plastered to her head and cheeks, her hands hugging her upperarms. He went down on one knee beside her and turned her face with his hand. "Bethann, what happened?" She gave him a blank look, as if she didn't recognize him. He shook her gently. "Bethann, it's Bry. Are you all right?"

This time, she reached out to him, holding his face in her hands, her eyes searching his, as if she could make him understand better by doing so. The barn roof collapsed and she involuntarily jumped. "P-Pen's missing. Do you see Pen?"

The cat? Her barn had just crumbled and she was worried about a cat? "Cat's don't burn, Bethann. They're way too smart. He's okay. How about you? Are you okay?" He moved a soaked lock of hair off her cheek.

"N-no. I'm c-cold." Her hands on his face were like ice. He raised her up and began peeling his jacket when she surprised him by stepping closer, placing her arms around him inside his jacket, putting her feet on his boots. She still shivered, but never took her eyes from the barn. He pressed her deeper into his warmth and, he realized, it wasn't just what he wanted to do, it was what he needed to do.

He didn't release her as the fire truck, volunteers' pickups, and deputy car arrived. He watched Edna Earle as she struggled to open an umbrella while getting out of her car. The sudden deluge had turned the driveway into a slippery mudbath, and Bry kept one eye on Edna Earle and one on the volunteer fire chief, Evan Cummings, as they both approached him.

Evan was trying very hard not to stare at Bethann. Bry could already imagine this news being relayed to the morning coffee crowd at Sally's. He pulled Bethann even closer. If that old gossip Evan was going to talk, he might as well have a good story.

Edna Earle reached them first and held the umbrella over them as best she could. "Much as I hate to break this up, Bry, I need to get Bethann dry and warm. You can look after yourself. Come on, honey, let's go in."

Bethann slowly refocused her attention. "Pen's missing. He was out hunting, Edna Earle. What if—"

"Nonsense. You can't burn a cat! Now come on!" She tugged at Bethann's shoulder through Bry's jacket.

Bry knew Edna Earle was right, that Bethann needed to be inside. Reluctantly, he loosened his hold on her and she backed off his boots. "S-sorry 'bout that," she murmured.

"You're barefoot!" Edna Earle's mouth dropped

open. "And still dressed!"

"Look, Edna Earle, don't make this any harder," Bry cautioned as he tipped Bethann's chin up. "What *are* you doing barefoot? Let me carry you." He made to pick her up.

"No!" But she stumbled after two steps and he gathered her into his arms. She didn't resist, just clung to him as he strode towards the back door. Edna Earle came behind as quickly as she could.

Sam was coming down the back steps. "No electricity, no phone. I'm going to check the lines."

Edna Earle produced a flashlight from the folds of her jacket and preceded them into the kitchen. She hunted through a drawer for candles and matches. Pinpoints of light appeared as she lit and set down candles.

As soon as candles gave light in the living room, Bry put Bethann on the couch and began wrapping her with the quilts. Edna Earle opened the fireplace damper and started the fire with logs already laid.

"You really should get out of those clothes," Bry told a soaked Bethann.

"I've g-got to find Pen." She struggled weakly against him as he continued putting quilts around her even as he suggested the change to dry.

"Pen'll find you. He's okay, Bethann." They spoke in little whispers. He stood and turned toward the kitchen.

Freeing a hand from the layers of quilt, she grabbed at him. He didn't react to her touch as he had earlier in the evening. "W-Where are you going?" Her lips trembled.

"Check out the barn, find Sam. I'll not leave without coming back in," he reassured her.

Sam stomped in from the kitchen. "Best I can tell, wires were cut at the poles. Kind of a sloppy job really. It'll have to be light and stop raining before we can get anyone out here for the electricity, Bethann. Don't know about the phone."

"I c-could've told you they were cut." She drew her hand into the quilts.

"How?" Bry knelt back down in front of her and put his hands on her shaking quilt-covered knees. "This is no lightning fire?"

"I saw a Jeep leaving, g-going towards the back land, your land. It'd stopped to watch the fire. I'd already found no lights, no phone."

"Jeep? You're sure?" She nodded and he exchanged glances with Sam. "Well, that narrows the field considerably." Hesitantly, he reached his palm toward her cheek and cupped it gently. The misunderstanding of a few hours earlier disappeared in his simple touch.

"I'll take care of it."

She snaked her hand out from the quilt and placed it over his, just as gently. Their eyes held. Bry felt an almost irresistible urge to pull her mouth to his.

Bethann saw it in his eyes. In the midst of all this turmoil, she was drawn to this man, and it didn't really matter if Sam and Edna Earle were standing right there, that the yard was full of trucks and men. But the muffled loud "meow!" and the sudden weight on her shoulder did.

"Pen!" Her attention whipped from Bry to the cat as the animal unceremoniously dumped a dead mouse on her lap. Bry jumped back, losing his balance and catching himself with a hand. "Oh!" she continued, "I don't know whether to hug you or wring your neck!" She picked up the cat and nuzzled, dismissing the distinctive smell of smoke which clung to him.

Bry stood and brushed his jacket and pants legs. "Edna Earle, why don't you stay here the rest of the night?" She nodded. "Sam, we've got business." He started around the couch toward the kitchen.

"Bry?" Bethann called as she struggled to stand, dumping cat, mouse, and quilts on the floor. "You know who did it?"

He stopped and looked back at her. "Got a real good idea."

"Who? Why?"

"Can't say who yet. But the why, well, that's usually fear, isn't it?"

She felt so helpless. Joe Tom's old shirt was molded to her, her hair was plastered to her head, her lips quivered from cold and fear. "Will you come back and tell me?" The question ended as a whisper.

"Sure." He let his gaze linger on her before he went out.

Through the front windows, Bethann saw the fire

truck and pickup brigade leave also. Morning light would soon tell the extent of the damage, but no one was hurt. Maybe that had been the intention. Just a good scare. Well, it had worked. She was scared.

"Come on, Bethann, let's take advantage of that gas water heater and stove and get you clean, dry, and fed. I've made do without electricity before. So can you." Edna Earle stood on the bottom stair and motioned her to follow with the flashlight.

"Do you know where he's going?"

"Got a real good idea. There's only three Jeeps in the county. And they all belong to one Cummings."

***

"Don't want to wait till first light for this?" Sam asked as he and Bry drove up to the imposing white wrought iron gates. Double C's entwined with cactus were closed resolutely against all outsiders.

Bry rolled down the window and pushed the button on the call box. "Don't exactly think she waited till first light, do you?" Impatiently, he pushed again.

Sam shifted his weight in the passenger seat. "Bry, listen…"

"I can leave you at the gate, Sam, if that's what you want."

"Then what happens if you need a witness?"

"I haven't ever needed a witness here."

"Bry—"

The box crackled to life. "Who's there?" The voice was young and masculine.

"You know damn good and well who." Bry hit the lights and horn. "Hear that and open these gates!"

They parted, and Bry drove onto his grandmother's estate for the first time in fifteen years.

How different it was than Joe Tom's. As manicured as a golf course, oaks lined the paved drive with solar lamps set equidistant among them. A quarter mile from the gate, the road became a circular driveway with paths leading from it for the stables and barns, the maids' quarters and the foreman's. The two-story white stone house gleamed now that the rain was over. The colder winds had quickly air-dried it, polished it.

Bry and Sam were met on the front steps by May June's foreman, Cain Stevens, a man who'd started with her as a ranchhand some thirty-odd years before. He'd hardly been a friend of Bry's when he'd been here as a boy, and the wounds had only festered over the years. With him was the man who'd chauffeured May June to Joe Tom's funeral, cowboy-tough and young-man-confident. The glow from the porch lights caught them all in a circle.

"What can we do for you, Sheriff? If it's not a family emergency, I'd suggest you not wake your grandmother." Cain Stevens stood his ground. Their dislike of each other was what made county legend.

"Cain, why don't you let May June and me settle this?"

"Before five in the morning? You get to go home. I have to live with her."

"I have noted that arrangement." The old resentment surfaced in Bry's tone. He took a deep breath and set his jaw to keep it under control. Sam shifted his weight slightly and caught Bry's eye in warning and reassurance. This time Bry wasn't alone.

"Why don't you just state your business?" The chauffeur decided to stretch his mental muscle.

"You have a name?"

"Dan Kincaid."

"Well, Dan Kincaid, this isn't between us. Yet. Either you wake her or I do. Unless, she really doesn't know what you boys have been up to."

Cain stepped closer. "Just cut to the chase, Phillips. This about the fire over at Joe Tom's?"

"This is about what started the fire over at Joe Tom's. And who cut the electrical and phone wires, burned the barn, and then was so colossally stupid as to stand there and watch and get ID'd!"

Stevens cut Kincaid a furtive, quick glance. "Don't know what you're talking about. And I don't think you do, either."

"New owner saw a Jeep headed over my land," Bry emphasized the ownership, "just as the barn was beginning to burn real bright. Now a Jeep's a distinctive shape, and there are only three in the county. They all call this place home."

"New owner? Not the way I hear it. She's just

marking time. Maybe you set that fire hoping to run her off so you could see what's in that envelope and hope it's you. 'Bout your only chance to legitimately inherit anything, wouldn't you say?"

"Nah, Cain, you got it all wrong," Dan interjected. "I think he set it so's he could scare her into his bed. Word is, she's quite a piece of work. And a McLeod hand-me-down—hell, he's used to that!"

Bry's fist caught Kincaid's jaw. The younger man stumbled and fell to the porch. Bry picked him up and bounced him against the front door before allowing him to slide down to a sitting position. Sam grabbed Bry's shoulder before he could reach down and deliver another blow.

Kincaid stood, got his balance, rubbed his jaw and then the back of his head. "Court, Phillips, I'll see you in court."

"Cut it out, Dan, you got what you deserved." Cain's tone was sharp. "He's too new to this game to be a real player, right, Bry?" Sam eased his hold on his boss as Cain continued. "I'd say you were fishing in the dark. You don't have any proof. But just because I'm in a generous spirit, you're welcome to look at our Jeeps without a search warrant. They're all sitting out by the barn. Soaked. Muddy. It'd be mighty hard to prove one of them's been on a dangerous mission. Now you still want me to wake your grandmother?"

Bry flicked his eyes over his old nemesis, took his measure again. He was the taller of the two now and the better man, despite this early morning behavior. "I can't fathom what she wants to gain by scaring Joe Tom's niece. But I'm sure there's a profit motive somewhere. And I'm also sure you two couldn't cook it up and carry it out by yourselves to save you. So let's let this be a warning. No one was hurt tonight and it had better stay that way. I'm on to you and I'll be watching like a hawk."

They turned and silently strode to the truck. Bry wrenched open the door and started the engine with a grind. He grimaced as he put it in gear. He'd hurt his hand but said nothing. Some actions had their own rewards.

Chapter Eleven

Edna Earle met him at the front door. Easing it open, she put her fingers to her lips and shushed him to be quiet. Tiptoe-ing toward the kitchen, she pointed to the quilt-covered form on the couch along the way. "Look, but don't touch! I just now got her down!" she warned as he slowed behind the couch

Bethann was asleep. One robe-covered arm was on top of the quilt, nestled on a cat that slept contentedly with her. Her hair was sprawled out on the bed pillow. Without make-up, she looked more girl than woman. Bry shifted his eyes to the fireplace. The cat he supposed was the culprit of the morning stretched his wet form out on a quilt laid down for that purpose and slept as well. No sign of the mouse.

'Look, but don't touch' echoed in his mind as he gave serious thought to leaning down and kissing her. He'd have disobeyed Edna Earle, but Dan Kincaid's jeer held on: just another McLeod hand-me-down. That hurt worse than his hand.

He went into the kitchen and hung his hat over the back of a chair as he started to sit down. Edna Earle silently pointed to the hat rack. He picked it up to try a swing, then winced and groaned, dropping it on the table.

"Let me look at that." She held her hand out, and he put his larger one in it as he sat down. "Don't suppose you caught it in the car door?" She massaged it for broken bones.

His eyes slitted as he watched her. "You should probably see the doc, but you won't, will you?" He shook his head. She placed it gently on the table, successfully sailed the hat, and opened the freezer for ice. "On my death bed, will you tell me what happened?"

"That'd be the only time. Got any coffee?"

She finished dumping ice into a bowl, put it on the table before him, and filled two coffee cups from the old pot on the gas range top. She settled down opposite him. "Did you see her?"

Bry ignored the question. "When are they going to have the electricity fixed? Saw Shep's truck out there."

"He's working on it. That's what relatives are for. And Corinne's husband'll be over with the phone company truck soon as he can. The only place I'm not connected is May June's. Did you see her?"

He grimaced as he eased his hand into the top of the ice. "No. Just got reacquainted with Cain and met the new kid."

"Pretty boy. That's what the girls at the beauty shop call him. Myself, I've not been that close to judge," she said archly.

"Well, he's a little less pretty this morning than he

was last night."

"Um-hum." She mulled this over. "I don't guess I get to know why." He shook his head again. "Are you going to get sued over it, Sheriff?"

"No. We're just all going to let it be." He sipped his coffee. "What's for breakfast?"

"Think you live here?"

"Somebody may have to."

He watched as his implication sunk in. "I've got my own place, thank you. We tolerate each other as it is. I'm not moving in. She won't allow it."

"The barn was the warning. What's next?"

"What's May June want with this place anyway?"

"Hell, Edna Earle, you tell me! You're the one that's known her all your life. She owns half this county and a quarter of the next one. How much more can she want?" He straightened, and taking a deep breath, plunged his hand into the ice. He let his breath out with a groan.

"Maybe it was just Cain. There's no reason he'd be in that envelope, is there?"

"None that I know of." Bry took his hand out of the ice and tried to move it, wincing at the pain. "I don't think Marsh even knew him. Joe Tom never would give him the time of day. Cheated him horribly if he happened to sit in on poker. Everybody knew it, played along."

"The envelope's the key to this." She got up and went to the refrigerator, studied its contents. "*We* are on a health kick. Lots of yogurt, no bacon or sausage, the last two eggs." She held them in her hand and turned to him.

"Be selfish and I'll over-easy them for you. Be generous and we'll have pancakes."

"Generous is my middle name this morning." He placed his hand on the table cloth and tried to stretch it out. Wincing, he eased it back into the ice just as the lights came on and the house hummed back to life. A truck honked as it flew past the kitchen window. No sooner had it left the yard than a phone company one honked on its way in, taking its place at the large pole.

Edna Earle pulled out a bowl and started assembling ingredients. The griddle appeared on the range. "I'm not moving in."

"How about a couple of nights a week on a varying schedule?"

"How about we make Delmar tell us what he's obviously told May June?"

"Who's moving where?" Bry and Edna Earle turned towards the door to find Bethann adjusting the tie on her chenille robe. She yawned and finger-combed her hair. "Jeez, I feel like something Pen dragged in." She shuffled over to the window and peered out to where the barn smoldered. "Going to tell me who did this?" She turned to Bry.

"I only have suspicions. Nothing I can prove."

"So give me an hypothesis."

"May June Cummings or someone who works for her. Only Jeeps in the county."

"Motive?"

He shook his head. "That's why we want Delmar to

tell us who's in the envelope."

"Will he?" She stifled a yawn.

"Probably not without a lot of legal hassle."

"That'll take about a year."

"Probably."

"So who's moving where?"

Edna Earle shot him a don't-you-dare look. He ignored it. "I think Edna Earle ought to move in."

"Really?" Bethann raised a brow. "For my protection or your peace of mind? And just what good would she have done me last night?" She poured coffee and sat down beside him at the table, took a sip of the steaming liquid. She sighed as the heat spread through her.

Edna Earle set the first plate of buttered pancakes in front of Bry and handed him a cup towel for his wet hand. He raised it out of the ice water and dried it off. The swelling was going down, but it was so stiff he wasn't able to hold a fork.

Watching his left-handed attempts to cut the pancakes, Bethann asked. "What happened?"

"Slammed it in a car door."

"Sure, I believe that. Want me to cut them for you?"

"I am not a child, thank you." He continued to saw away.

"Neither am I. You eat with your left hand and I'll stay here by myself."

Edna Earle set Bethann's yogurt before her and disappeared into the living room.

Bry's hand ached, he was hungry, and the strain of

the last few hours was beginning to take its toll on his patience. He pushed the plate back and made to rise.

"Please. Don't go." Bethann reached out her hand to him but quickly drew her fingers back. "I'm sorry. Everything we say to each other gets scrambled, doesn't it?"

"And why do you suppose that is?" He lowered himself and perched on the edge of his chair.

She shrugged. "Guess we're just on different wavelengths. We want different things."

"Really? We don't both want you to be safe here?"

"Bry..." She closed her eyes and sighed. "It wouldn't work, Edna Earle and me." She looked at him, bit at her lip. "You'd be out here investigating a murder."

He chuckled. "Okay." He studied his hand. "But the least you can do is massage the hand I hurt in your defense."

"In a car door?"

"Yeah." She shook her head, took his bruised hand, held it and warmed it between hers. Their knees touched as he turned to her and she drew his hand into her lap, further massaging it. "I haven't had a chance to say thank you for this morning. Edna Earle said you called in the alarm."

"It was visible from a long way off." Her hands felt so good surrounding his, soothing it, making the pain disappear. He was mesmerized watching the top of her head as she concentrated on gently rubbing his hand.

He reached over with his other one and pushed a

strand of hair out of her face. McLeod hand-me-downs, be damned! She raised her head and smiled to his touch. He cupped her neck and drew her to him, leaning over to kiss her, lightly pressing his lips to hers, stroking her cheek with his thumb. She melted toward him, releasing his injured hand, as he gathered her into his arms and onto his lap.

They gave into the touch of each other's lips. Her fingers toyed with his neck and the backs of his ears. This was not the schoolyard flirtation of two weeks ago.

Bry held her closely, all pain momentarily forgotten, his hands moving on her back, wanting to explore where he knew he shouldn't. Not yet, at least. The awkwardness of the night before disappeared in their mutual longing. How long had it been since he felt like this?

One kiss became several and when they finally stopped for breath, they rested their foreheads together. Her arms encircled his shoulders as they had when he'd carried her into the house just hours before. She was curled on his lap and his hands continued to trace the pattern of her back.

"You're not acting like a man whose hand is hurting," she whispered.

"What hand?" He kissed her forehead, couldn't hold her tightly enough.

"Kiss me again."

The phone rang just as he leaned to do so and they parted like scalded cats onto separate chairs. Edna Earle reached the phone before either of them were aware she was back in the room.

"Works fine, Ed, thank you." She paused. "I think we can handle that." She hung up. "That fast service will cost us an autographed cookbook, half a dozen jars of pear preserves, and your next experimental overrun." She turned her back to them and resumed her place at the stove.

Bry and Bethann faced each other. She clutched her robe at the neck, as if she had just realized what she wasn't wearing while in his lap. He'd not been unaware of her mode of dress, of how little fabric there was between the two of them.

"Edna Earle, why don't you get Bry some fresh pancakes. I'm going to get dressed." Her eyes lingered on his, then she left, her bare feet a rapid staccato on the stairs.

"Don't say a word," he admonished the old woman, as she put a fresh plate in front of him and took the other away. His hand was better able now to manipulate the fork.

"Not much to say, far as I can tell." She sat down across from him and nursed her coffee. Her eyes sparkled.

He stopped chewing and pointed his fork at her. "Okay. Ask, say, do, whatever you have on that little mind of yours. I'll not have peace till we get this all out."

"Well, was it worth it?"

"Worth what?"

"All the agonizing and arguing and hemming and

hawing, I've been seeing go on around here?"

"That is a mighty personal question." She sat silently, daring him to not answer. He finished chewing and took a swallow of coffee. "Yes. Now are you satisfied?"

"Not as well as you are, I hope." She got up from the table and started clearing it. "Lord, long day ahead. Clean this mess up, go back to work, hunt down Delmar. Woman's work is never done."

"Busybody. Old snoop."

She smiled at him. "Yeah, but you love me." She pulled on latex gloves. "She talked me into these to keep my hands soft and young-looking." She cackled and turned the faucets.

Bethann appeared back in the kitchen, a tee shirt and jeans hastily thrown on, her hair combed and back in a still-damp ponytail. Bry eased his chair from the table and stood. Retrieving his hat from the rack, he held it as he went to Edna Earle and kissed her on the cheek. "Now be sweet and consider moving in no matter what she says," he whispered as he leaned down. She let him kiss her, then shook her head.

He went past Bethann and into the living room. She followed silently. At the front door, he turned to her as he put his uninjured hand on the doorknob.

"We'll try to pin Delmar down this afternoon. Not that it's going to do any good, but we have to give it a shot. I'll let you know when so you can be there. He's a pretty slick old character." She stood two feet from him, just out of reach. "Think about letting Edna Earle move in?"

Bethann shook her head. "No way." Her tone was all business.

The heat of the kisses had worn off and, suddenly, they were as awkward as the night before. "Get some rest."

"You, too. At least I've had some sleep."

Their eyes lingered on each other, but neither moved. Reluctantly, Bry pulled the door open, settled his hat on and left, closing the door silently behind him.

***

Bethann stood uncertainly in the kitchen doorway, her hands in her pockets. "Need something else to eat?" Edna Earle asked.

She shook her head but didn't move. Edna Earle walked towards her, wiping her hands on her apron. "Contrary to what most folks think, I'm not a mind reader. But what I do know is human nature, Bethann. Get that guilty look off your face. Nothing wrong with what you were doing."

Bethann looked toward the ceiling. "I know. It's been two years. Kiki and our friends have been working on me for quite some time." She blinked and crinkled her eyes. "But, he knew Marsh, Edna Earle."

"So? You haven't dated other men who knew Marsh?"

"A few. But," she hesitated, "he knew a side of

Marsh I didn't really want to know. Does that make sense?"

"Not really." She untied her apron. "I'm going back to work. Tell me, did you enjoy it?"

Bethann felt her face grow hot. "Jeez, that's a little personal."

"I figure you did or you wouldn't be going through all this angst. That is the word, isn't it?"

"Yeah, that's the word." She smiled slyly. "It was really very nice."

"Then get on with it and go from guilty to guilty pleasure. Lord, girl, you're young enough to enjoy it all over again. If I were you, I'd go for it." She opened the back door. "Be glad he knew Marsh. Gets all that mess about what the first one was like out of the way. Moves up your calendar. See you at Delmar's." She disappeared through the door.

"You mean, it moves up *your* calendar." Bethann sat down at the table in the chair vacated by Bry. She pulled up her bare feet, hugged her legs. A smile drew across her lips and she rubbed her cheek on her knees. She'd enjoyed those kisses, just as much as she'd enjoyed the way his hands moved on her back, the way his touch promised so much more. Something in him had changed as he had placed his hand in hers. Maybe lawmen were just more cautious about who touched them than other men were. Or maybe—Bethann stopped that line of thought. It didn't matter. His lips had been warm and inviting. She had lost herself in those lips and hands, in that lap. Guilty pleasure—and wouldn't it be a wonderful one?

But—that's all it would be, wouldn't it? Just pleasure? There was nothing wrong with that really, but she was only here until August. What was the point of pursuing anything that didn't have the possibility of being forever? Without a future, could it even last a month?

She straightened her legs and put them over in the other chair. Crossing her arms, she tilted her head back and studied the tin ceiling. Sometimes it paid to live only for the moment, only for the day. But if your heart was going to want to stretch itself into the years…

Damn! It really didn't matter if guilty pleasure had never looked so good, because in the frame of Bry Phillips, it was an impossibility.

***

"How come I feel like I'm surrounded by wolves?" Delmar hustled to get around his desk, leaving Bethann, Bry, and Edna Earle on the other side. "And what is she doing here anyway?" He pointed to Edna Earle, who cantankerously sat down.

Bry stood his ground in front of the desk. "We all inherited from Joe Tom. The arsonist last night used Edna Earle's property or mine to enter and leave. I'd say we were all involved in this."

"Arson, is it? I didn't hear that in church this

morning."

"What you heard was lightning striking because May June was in church. What's it been since she last darkened the door? Twenty years?" Edna Earle held forth from the comfort of the leather chair.

More like fifteen, Bry thought. She had come to Meg's funeral.

Delmar just looked at Edna Earle and pointed a finger. "You're one to talk."

"I work Sunday mornings."

"Can we keep this to the subject at hand?" Bry was brusque, his temper in bad need of sleep, his hand needing more painkillers. Or another massage. "Yes, arson, Delmar. Evan said there was a kerosene can boldly left in the center of the barn. Amazingly, there were no fingerprints. We need to figure out why May June wants that property. Bethann saw one of her Jeeps leaving the scene so we know it was her. Now why don't you share that envelope with us the way you've shared it with your aunt?"

"I resent the implication, Bry. If you can prove it, go arrest May June. Personally, I'd say looking through the smokescreen of a burning barn is hardly identification adequate enough to hold up in court. As to the contents of Joe Tom's envelope, we'll just see!"

He moved to the ancient safe in the corner of his office. Crouching, he spun the dials, miscalculated, and started over. Successful at last, he reached in and retrieved the cause of the commotion. Flinging it on his desk, he dared them to comment.

It was a legal-size white envelope. Joe Tom's signature scrawl and the two-year-old date graced the front. Delmar flipped it over. Yellow and black McLeod tartan was sealed into the flap. A wax blob was at the point, with JTM drawn in. There was wax at various points along the seal. Delmar held it up to the sunlight streaming in the window. The paper inside was folded so thick that nothing could be read.

"He brought this into me when he came to sign that accursed will two years ago. Told me to put it in the safe. Open it when and if necessary. She may be my aunt, but I am not going to break the trust Joe Tom or any other client has in me. I do not know who the default heirs are. I do not care. If May June knows, then Joe Tom told her and we all know the odds against that!" He sat down, his summation argument given.

Bethann leaned over the desk, balancing herself with her palms. "Get out the checkbook, Delmar. I'm going to rebuild that barn." She looked at Bry over her shoulder. "Do you own any horses, Sheriff?"

He wrinkled his brow. "Two," he answered cautiously. Where was this going?

"You have your own stable for them?"

"Keep them at Edna Earle's son's."

She turned back to Delmar. "Sheriff's going to be keeping his horses in my barn. Be a pity for anyone to be burning it now." She straightened up. "You have my permission to tell your aunt that. Coming, Edna Earle?"

The old woman got up and grinned wickedly at Delmar and Bry as she followed Bethann from the room.

"Well, well, Sheriff," Delmar started as he reached into the humidor and withdrew two cigars. "Looks like we have a player on our hands. I'll give him

this—Joe Tom always was a good judge of horseflesh and women."

Chapter Twelve

Work on the new barn progressed at a rapid pace. Whether this was due to the assurance of ready cash, Edna Earle's contacts, or just plain Cummings County curiosity, Bethann was not sure, but the day after she'd told Delmar to open the checkbook, workmen showed up at the door. She was presented with three different floorplans and chose the one in the mid-price range. She also arranged to have the dilapidated out-buildings bulldozed, the windmill shored up, a double garage built onto the house, and motion-sensitive security lights added around all the buildings. Delmar complained about the cost only once and then Bethann felt he'd done it just for form's sake. After all, whose money was she spending other than her own and Ted's?

Two weeks after the fire, the barn was finished. It was basic, but insulated and keyed to lock. Bethann left Edna Earle fussing with the laundry and drove to town.

No longer hesitant, she breezed in through the jail doors, then slammed to a stop when she didn't immediately see Bry. Spying Sam, she went over to him before Corinne could stop her. "Hi, Sam. Sheriff in?"

"Nope." He leaned back in his chair and smiled. "Can

I help you?"

She paused. "No. Just tell him I came in." She started for the door, then turned back. "Better yet, don't mention it." Sam smiled more broadly at her nervousness.

"Want to leave him a note?"

She chewed on her lower lip. "Nah."

"You can just put it on his desk." He indicated the open door to Bry's office. "No problem." He held out a piece of paper and nodded as she took it.

Circling Bry's desk, she noticed how neat it was, papers stacked and pens arranged in a row. A carved cougar crouched on the front edge next to his nameplate. Retrieving a pen from the end of the line, she balanced herself on the edge of his chair and began to write.

"Now not just everybody can sit there." Startled, she looked up to find Bry leaning in the office doorway, his arms crossed over his chest, his grin broad. He removed his hat and carefully placed it on the rack. Approaching the front of the desk, he leaned on it and balanced on his palms. "Writing me a note?"

She picked it up and read it aloud to him. "'Bry—Barn is ready if you want to take me up on the offer for your horses. B'" She handed it to him. "No good ol' boying around here. Money talks and things get done."

He took the note. "Not to mention that Edna Earle's related to most of your contractors and none of them would dare cross her."

"It's all in who you know. Or, in my case, who Edna Earle knows." She smiled at him.

He'd been scarce since the fire. Since their kisses. Had he come to the same conclusion she had—it couldn't be forever, so why bother? But if she really believed that to be true, why couldn't she stop grinning now?

"Very clever, Mrs. Fox." He came around the desk and sat on the edge of it, facing her, placing one leg on either side of the rolling wooden deskchair. She started to get up, but he shook his head. "No, stay. I've wondered what a lady sheriff would look like in that chair."

His legs had her hemmed in. Despite his two week absence, he must have come to a different conclusion, she thought. They didn't take their eyes from each other. He folded the note over and over, making it into a tiny square.

Finally, he took a deep breath. "It's been a long two weeks."

"I've been busy." She rubbed the chair arms with her thumbs, a nervous little gesture that reminded her of her hands on the back of his neck. She stopped it. "Phone lines work both ways, you know."

"Evan's been having quite a field day with his account of finding us in the rain. There's even a pool down at the lunch grille for when we're going to—" he searched for appropriate words "—going to—"

"Finish what Evan thinks we've started?"

"That's close. Edna Earle's in it."

"Tell me something that will surprise me."

"That's easy." He tossed the note into the wastebasket and leaned over the chair, balancing himself on its arms, further enclosing her. "I wish I'd closed the office door because I don't think there's an innocent way to do it now."

"Sheriff, be careful, or you'll make me blush." *Or my heart beat out of my chest.*

"I don't ever want to do that." A smile edged his mouth. "Least not in public."

She placed her hands over his and rose to meet him. The resolve she'd worked on for two weeks melted as she placed her lips on his. It was a kiss of urgency, of mutual longing. His ardor surprised her but only slightly less than her own did. Bry raised his arms and with them, her. Caught in the vee of his legs, she gave herself over to the guilty pleasure she'd sworn to deny herself.

Emerging from his embrace and kiss, she pushed back on his shoulders and reached to the floor for her purse. "Maybe two weeks wasn't long enough."

"Guess it just depends on what you see as the big picture." His face was flushed under his light beard, and he stood, trying to surreptitiously straighten his uniform pants.

"Bry, I—" she stopped as she read the look on his face. It was fear of rejection mixed with hope. Her resolves about guilty pleasure took over and she knew she had to be honest. "I've never been a 'for the moment' type of person. October's almost over, and I'm out of here in ten months. I don't want an affair," she whispered, "but it's the wrong time for anything else." He raised his eyebrows. "But then, that's presumptuous, isn't it?"

"Yeah, I'd say so." He stood less than a foot from her and she felt his heat. "This is hardly the place to discuss anything, providing there's anything to discuss." He studied the tips of his boots and Bethann searched the desktop for answers. "Why don't I bring the horses out tonight and we'll talk then."

"I'll stay in my wing chair and you'll stay in yours?"

"If that's what you want, I'll bring the pot of glue."

***

Dusk was fast approaching when Bethann heard the pickup and trailer wheels grinding in the drive. She finished the glass of chardonnay in one swallow and left it sitting on the table in its proper place. She'd planned a light supper for them, even though it hadn't been mentioned. They could always eat while sitting in the wing chairs. She could always freeze it as leftovers.

She'd spent the afternoon in jumbled thought. Presumption? Hell, she'd presumed herself into his bed—into an affair! She'd presumed a few fervent kisses far beyond a one night stand. That might be all he wanted—might be all he ever had need of. And she'd as much as told him that wouldn't do for her—talk about presumptions! She'd presumed from Edna Earle that Bry was a forever-type man but had not been able to find the nerve all afternoon to ask if she was right. Lord, she thought Edna Earle would never go today. How did that woman always *know*?

Now she was practically skipping down the back steps, presuming he'd even still come in. She must have taken leave of her senses!

***

Bry skillfully backed the trailer to the double barn doors. Nice job of construction. He noted the corral was mended also. Looked like Edna Earle's nephew's work. He was handy with wood, but always in need of employment because he was also handy with the bottle. The William's family black sheep. That must be what he was to the Cummings.

He saw Bethann at the kitchen window. Part of him couldn't believe he'd still come. He was astonished at their abrupt honesty with each other this afternoon. He'd not been so candid with a woman since Meg. He'd taken Bethann's ardor as assent to a longer lasting relationship. Only to be told—what?—that she was out of here in ten months. Well, ma'am, he wasn't a one night stand either. Best to get this worked out and be on a purely business level. If he hadn't already agreed to stable the horses here, he'd have backed out.

Bethann reached the cab of the pickup and opened the door for him. "New vehicle?"

"Traded with Sam for the night. It was Joe Tom's. I swear it knew the way here." Light conversation. Everyday things. The deep would come later. He got out and headed for the back. "Borrowed the trailer, too." She unlocked the barn door as he led the first horse in, then swung on a stall gate as he worked.

"What are their names?"

"Range and Rover," he called as he went back to get their gear.

"Like the car?" She laughed.

"I always thought it'd be a nice vehicle to have, but figured two horses was as close as I was getting."

He installed them in the barn, carried in bales of hay, the harness, saddles. "Jeez, it's like moving a baby," she commented. "I didn't know they had so much stuff."

"Well, they don't just take care of themselves. I'll have to be here everyday to see to them." He watched for her reaction. There was none other than a nod. "Don't suppose in good weather you could let them out into the corral?"

"I just open the door, they'll go?"

"Basically. I'll come by and show you in the morning."

She brushed her hair out of her face. "Come on in when you get them settled, okay?"

***

Twenty minutes later, Bry knocked on the back door and eased it open without waiting for a response. Bethann stood at the stove, stirring and tasting from a small black pot. One of Edna Earle's aprons was tied around her. Spinach salads perked up the table, two bottles of wine were open, and the aroma of fresh baked bread permeated the house. Perhaps he had misjudged the evening.

"Expecting someone for supper?"

"Yeah, and if you don't hurry up and leave, he'll see you." He almost mistook her teasing tone for dismissal. His ego had not allowed the possibility of another player.

She hurried to correct any mistaken impressions. "I'm sorry, Bry, I was teasing!" He hesitated before placing his hat by the door. "Wash up, we'll have supper."

He moved to the sink, turned the hot water on, noticed it responded quicker than before. Some internal workings of the house must have been spiffed up, too. He wanted to ask if supper came with his evening care of the horses but figured he'd know soon enough.

They sat down to crisp salads with a choice of homemade dressings, some sort of beef and rice soup, and rolls that rivaled Edna Earle's, although he certainly wouldn't be the one to point it out to the old woman. It was followed by poached pears for dessert. They didn't talk much, just the basics of conversation.

"Make us a fire while I fix cappuccino?"

"After a meal like that, I'm not about to refuse you anything." It was the first part of the conversation that hinted at the purpose of the evening. He went into the living room as she cleared the table, leaving the dishes for later.

Carrying the tray in, she found the wing chairs arranged three feet apart with the coffee table's edge drawn up between them for the coffee. A bottle of white school glue was placed near the edge of the table. The fire was just catching, and Bry was smiling at his cleverness.

They sat opposite each other. Bethann drew her legs up into her chair, Bry crossed his. They both fiddled with their cups. The fire found a friendly log and whooshed into full blaze. Pen and Tux sauntered in and laid full-length before the fire.

"Got plenty of firewood, I see."

"We traded pecans for it. Edna Earle brokered the deal. Anything else I need, she calls, I write the check."

"Pretty easy life to get used to, huh? Have a wish, write a check. Joe Tom must be spinning in his grave."

"If Joe Tom had had a few more wishes, I'd have less means to write checks. On the other hand, the Marsh Fox family was and is far from destitute. Marsh was a very hard worker, an excellent provider. Atlanta Divines just provided the icing on our cake."

They lapsed once more into silence. He licked his lips, tasted the coffee on his tongue. What if they just let well enough alone? What if they just let themselves fall into whatever this could be? Did they have to plan for it not to happen? "I know this was my idea," he coughed, cleared his throat, "but do we really have to have this conversation?"

She took her gaze from the fire and nodded. "What

we—" she moved her hand between them. "There has to be a solution. I can't... don't want to... go on like this. I want all the cards on the table."

"So deal."

The fire provided the only light in the room. Dusk had dissolved into dark, and it seemed at cross-purposes for what they wanted to accomplish, an enlightening of their situation. She got up and turned on the Mason jar lamp that sat on the couch end table.

Returning to her chair, she stared at the fire, as if gathering all her arguments. Finally she set down her empty cup, folded her hands and looked squarely at him. "I said it this afternoon. Ten months from now, I'm gone, history to Cummings County. Kiki and I are taking my four million and opening a tearoom, maybe eventually a full-blown restaurant. I have a future beyond this place. I can't deny the obvious attraction we have for each other. I just can't live with it and then be gone."

"If you're not going to live with it, what are you going to do?"

"Ignore it. Ignore you."

"Really? You've invited me to stable my horses here, take care of them twice a day, and yet ignore you in return? Lord, lady, you must be used to men with more willpower than I've ever encountered." He set his cup by hers and crossed his arms. "Let's talk about this afternoon. What makes you think I want to have an affair with you anyway?"

"Pardon me." She crossed her arms in imitation of

him. "What usually comes after what we've been doing? Even though I was married for twenty years, the game has not so changed that two people who are as physically attracted to each other as we are stop at kissing!"

"So you admit you're attracted to me?" She rolled her eyes and he wagged a finger at her. "Peach, your pit is about to show."

She leaned forward. "You are making my pit show!"

He laughed. "Tell me, did Marsh come out here to hunt or for a vacation from you?"

"That does it!" She stood up and pointed to the front door. "Out!" He didn't move, only smiled more broadly. "Out, Bry! Or I'll call the—the—"

"Yeah, who you going to call? Sheriff is sitting right here, not laying a hand on you."

She was wearing her frustration like a badge. She sat down with a flounce and crossed her arms again. "I don't know why I ever kissed you in the first place."

Bry leaned forward, clasping his hands and balancing his elbows on his knees. "Sure you do. You find me as irresistible as I find you. You've just admitted it."

He had nothing to lose, everything to gain in this relationship, so he leaned back in the chair and patted his knee. "And we could get a whole lot solved if you'd just come sit on my lap again."

She narrowed her eyes at him. "Does the word insufferable mean anything to you?"

Not like hand-me-downs does, he thought. He stared at her, auburn hair sparking gold in the firelight, green eyes shooting daggers, nostrils flared. They'd last one month or one lifetime, there'd be no in between. But she wasn't even willing to let it go far enough to test. Once, his heart had been wrenched from him, too. Maybe that was the real crux of the matter.

"What are you afraid of, Bethann? That we might actually move beyond an affair to where we cared and loved and then you'd have to make a decision to stay or go? I've had my heart broken, too. I can't imagine that Edna Earle hasn't filled you in on all the sordid details. Deciding to care about someone is deciding to put yourself at risk. For the first time in fifteen years, I'm willing to take that risk." And he was baring his soul to prove it.

"It's not the risk, Bry. There is no decision. I'm here under protest." She measured her next words. "I am going to leave when the year is up. I have no schoolgirl fantasies about happily-ever-after. Atlanta is not going to move to the middle of West Texas. You are not going to find the mountains of northern Georgia enchanting. Emotionally, I am not a short-timer. I either play for the possibility of forever, or I don't play at all."

Their eyes locked. He felt that if he held out his arms to her, she'd come, but it would solve only a moment's need, not the real question. It dawned on him that he'd already held her for the last time.

He stood. There was nothing else to say. "I'll not disturb you when I tend to Range and Rover. I don't think their presence will be a deterrent to further mischief, but it won't hurt." He stepped around her chair and strode into the kitchen.

Bethann felt his heavy tread in her soul and blinked back tears before setting her jaw and following. "I'll still be glad to learn about taking care of them. It'll save you time. Just because I'm not willing to be lovers, doesn't mean we can't be friends."

He reached for his hat. "Doesn't it? You play for forever or not at all. I don't know if I can just be friends with a woman I want to give so much more."

Tears brimmed again in her eyes. "I'm so sorry I've hurt you. I was just trying to save us both from any more pain than we've already had."

He opened the back door and stepped through, settling his hat on his head. The movement triggered the sensors and the path to the barn was lit like day. "I'm sorry, too. Maybe if I had all that big city charm, I'd have handled this better and we wouldn't both be miserable." He turned and strode to the truck.

She shut the door, locked it, refused to allow herself to watch him drive away. Hell, she thought, if I'd liked big city charm, I wouldn't have married Marsh.

The pickup and trailer made a noisy exit. Bethann took the half empty bottle of zinfandel to the living room, tugged a quilt off the couch, and sat down in the chair vacated by Bry. She tipped the bottle's mouth to hers and drank. Pen leaped up to her lap and she desultorily stroked him.

Somehow, this was all Joe Tom's fault. Tomorrow

she'd go to the cemetery and tell him all about it.

***

Daybreak was an hour away the next morning when Edna Earle drove over the pasture and into the McLeod yard. She tripped the sensors but was pleased to have the light for getting up the steps and through the backdoor. The dishes from the night before were still in the sink and the morning coffee wasn't brewing. Tiptoe-ing into the hall, she caught sight of Bethann in the living room.

The fireplace was only embers. Pen and Tux curled together in front of the hearth. Bethann was slid sideways in one of the old chairs, her head on its arm, her feet under her. The quilt was twisted about her and resembled a strait jacket. An empty wine bottle stood next to some school glue and two empty coffee cups.

Edna Earle moved to the chair and shook Bethann's shoulder gently. "Hey, girl, wake up now! Lord, what made you spend the night down here?"

Bethann grimaced before she even opened her eyes, blinked to clear her vision, and started struggling out of the quilt. "Let me help you." Edna Earle reached behind Bethann and pulled at the corner. Slowly, the quilt unwrapped. Bethann was still dressed from the night before.

"Do I even need to ask if the wine or the coffee came last?"

Bethann raised bleary eyes. "Why don't you just

configure your worst case scenario and play it in your mind. It would come close to last night."

"Um-hum." She tucked the quilt back onto the couch. This was not a time for subtlety. If she wanted to find out what had gone on, she'd best attack. "There are still dirty dishes in the sink. I told you I wouldn't clean up after your entertaining. Might as well march in there and do it."

Bethann's mouth dropped open and the tears followed in streams down her cheeks, then a sob. *Good Lord!* Edna Earle rushed to her and tugged her over to the couch so they both could sit down. "Bethann, I'm sorry. I didn't mean it to sound so—"

"B-bitchy." Bethann supplied the word between sobs, her head in Edna Earle's lap. The older woman smoothed the fabric in Bethann's blouse over her shoulders, patted her, made soothing sounds.

"Okay, what happened?"

"He wants to have an affair."

"He said he wanted to have an affair?" She settled her mouth in a firm line and mentally fixed Bry in her sights.

"Not in so many words."

"What did he say?" She continued to pat her shoulder, rub her back.

"He wants us to see each other."

"And?"

"If we do, we'll have an affair."

Edna Earle weighed the merit of this. They were both

widowed, over forty, damn lonely, emotionally wrecked. Of course, her mother—God rest her soul—wouldn't have approved.

She pulled at Bethann's shoulders, made her sit upright. The younger woman's face was red, tear-streaked. Her nose was running and she wiped it on her shirttail. "Well, what's so wrong with that if you're both in agreement?"

"You're on his side. You always have been. And who said we were in agreement?" She was settling into a state of petulance.

"On a purely moral basis, I agree that affairs are wrong." Edna Earle's Southern Baptist background held up. "However."

"There is no 'however', Edna Earle. It's not like I'm the new schoolmarm looking for a rich rancher to hook. I'm out of here in ten months. I won't stay. He won't go."

"Whose assumptions are these? Most affairs burn themselves out in six months. All the ladies' magazines say so. There's no stay or go to it. You're assuming the two of you might actually fall in love!"

"You don't see that happening, huh?"

It was all Edna Earle did see happening. They were a perfect match. And Bethann must see it, too, or she wouldn't be so stubborn at denying herself. "Afraid you might be hurt again? Afraid you might put your heart on the line and love him, and he wouldn't return the favor? Afraid he'd leave you? Marsh didn't mean to leave you,

Bethann."

"I know." She rubbed her hands between her knees. "I'm just thinking too much. When he kisses me…" her voice trailed off, then she looked sheepishly at Edna Earle. "They're forever kisses. He's pretty damned presumptuous himself."

"Did he say they were forever kisses?"

"No." She sighed. "He says as little as possible. Except we can't be friends, if we can't be, you know, friends with benefits."

"I bet he didn't say that either." She patted Bethann's knee. "But we've got a mess in the kitchen to tend to first. C'mon, let's do it."

Chapter Thirteen

Edna Earle would have liked to shoot them both. Or hog-tie them and toss them into a room where they'd have to work together to get out.

Bry came twice a day to tend to Range and Rover but didn't come to the door unless hailed. When he was off-duty on a morning or afternoon, he would pointedly saddle one of the horses and ride back towards his land. If he thought he was issuing a challenge to Bethann, she was ignoring it. And him. Edna Earle never told him about finding her asleep in the chair, and for all he knew, she'd had a perfectly relaxing night after their argument. It had taken the better part of the next day, but Edna Earle had wormed out of Bry how he'd spent that night: sitting on his porch and drinking straight bourbon till four in the morning. She'd figured as much since he had been late for work the next day and in a surly mood for three.

Bethann's mood lightened as both Thanksgiving and Ted's arrival approached. Edna Earle carefully broached the idea of the two of them spending Thanksgiving Day with her and her brood over at her son's. She no longer was in charge of the big to-do, preferring to be the guest of a daughter-in-law. "You can't do a proper Thanksgiving for two people," she admonished Bethann the morning the call came from Kiki stating the Wright family couldn't make it. Her mother-in-law had demanded a command performance holiday, thanks to the wedding of a niece on Saturday night.

Bethann protested Edna Earle's invitation. "I haven't seen Ted for three months. I'd like to look at him and cook for him."

"If you think that boy's going to want to sit around here and look at his mother, you have lost touch with reality."

"What else is he going to do?"

"Hunt. Can't tell me he didn't mention it."

"It breezed through the conversation." She cast Edna Earle a sideways glance. "Starting with talking you into cooking up all the quail and teaching me how to do it 'right'."

Edna Earle made no attempt to hide her pleasure. If Ted were hunting with Bry, then Bry would be around for dinner. As Bethann and Bry had spent the last three weeks acting as if they were on separate planets, this would only work for her. "Be glad to on Saturday."

"You work Saturday."

"Thanksgiving vacation. I take it every year."

"I'll ask Ted tonight what he wants to do about Thanksgiving," Bethann said.

"And then you'll do it?"

"Yes. Of course, Edna Earle."

"Good, I'll tell 'em to prepare for two more. I'll let you know what to bring. It is covered dish."

She didn't mention that Bry never missed Thanksgiving with the Williams.

***

Ted arrived late the Tuesday night before Thanksgiving. He changed planes in Dallas in order to get the commuter hop, but it was still a two hour drive for Bethann to meet him at the small airport. His smile told her he had missed her just as much as she had him.

The drive home passed quickly as they caught up on the details, and as they pulled into the drive, every sensor flashed to life, illuminating the house, new barn and garage. "I'm impressed. Looks like you're putting the place over to your way of thinking, Mom," he commented as he pulled his bags out of the back. "Why did you rebuild the barn if you're not going to stay?"

They walked up the steps. "For you, if you decide to keep the place. And stubbornness." She had told him the barn had burned but hadn't mentioned arson. "And Bry keeps his horses here."

"So you've met Bry? Nice guy. You like him?"

"He's all right." Bethann flicked on the kitchen lights and caught Ted's broad grin. She ignored it as she read the note on the kitchen table. "There are sandwiches in the fridge from Edna Earle."

"Just all right? Mom, you don't *really* like him?"

Was no one immune from matchmaking?

"I don't really know him, Ted." She started into the hall, avoiding this line of questioning. "Or should I call you Little Tom now that you're here?"

He followed her, bags still in hand. "Found out about that, huh? What was I supposed to do? He was an old man and I was just a kid!"

"Your father should have done something about it." She stood in the middle of the living room and spread her arms. "What do you think?"

He looked it over solemnly. "Joe Tom's spinning in his grave."

Pen and Tux stretched a welcome from the couch. He went to them, lifting Tux and nuzzling. "They didn't feed me very well on the plane. I'll eat a sandwich before I go to bed." He plopped the cat back on the couch and headed for the kitchen, two black and white bodies trailing.

Bethann stood in the kitchen doorway and watched him raid the refrigerator, set out snacks for both of them. She had always thought him the perfect blend of his parents, Marsh's dark hair and firm jaw, her green eyes with just a hint of her smile. She answered his questions about her life at Ranch McLeod, and he indulged her with more stories of college, eventually turning the conversation back to the subject which seemed to interest him most. "I don't suppose you checked with Bry about hunting tomorrow?"

"I am not your social secretary. You could have

called from school."

"Think he's still up?"

"It's midnight, Ted. Think of it as sparing the poor birds till tomorrow night. You need your sleep anyway. You look so tired." She reached to smooth his hair out of his eyes.

"Only the place has changed. You're still mom." He dodged her hand and took his dishes to the sink.

"Let me tell you what else hasn't changed. You made this mess, you clean it up. I'm tired. See you in the morning." She pushed back from the table but had to stop in the doorway to watch him, her son, with her at last. Then with a shake of her head, she saw him dump all the leftovers into the refrigerator, not taking care to cover them. She knew Edna Earle would be there in six hours and would take care of him just like she always had.

***

Bethann found Edna Earle and Ted with their heads together the next morning, huddled over coffee mugs, egg plates already pushed aside. "I can't believe you didn't opt to sleep late," she commented as she filled her mug. It was seven o'clock and she felt as if she'd overslept.

"Too much to catch up on," he said as he reached towards another biscuit and the jar of preserves.

She studied him. "What are you wearing?"

He leaned back and touched the lapels of the striped

bathrobe, his green eyes shining. "Joe Tom's old robe. I always wore it. 'Cept it fits me better now than it did last time I was here." He stretched his wide shoulders. Marsh's shoulders. Marsh's height. "And you sure had it hidden. It was in that third bedroom up there. You're not going to throw all that away, are you? I want some of those things."

"Just what I told her," Edna Earle interrupted. "Thought it best not to throw anything away that might have sentimental value for you."

"Like the rifles and guns and scopes." He sighted down his arm and took out the kitchen clock.

"They're still in the cases. Why one person needs so many…"

"Just do, Mom." He looked at her. "Can I have the truck? Need to get ammunition and a license."

"Sure, take it. I'm spending the day cooking for Edna Earle's family Thanksgiving tomorrow. You seemed awfully anxious to go. Edna Earle got a granddaughter I don't know about?" She winked at Edna Earle as she said it.

"Nah, I got a girlfriend." He paused. "She's a freshman, too, from Dallas, a Classics major."

"What is she going to do with that?"

"It makes you well-rounded and that's important in business." He grabbed another homemade biscuit. "This is the one."

Bethann finished her yogurt. "Four years is a long time. Things'll change."

Edna Earle looked delighted. "Yeah, I remember giving that advice to another young man at this very table. He'd come home from college back East and said he'd met the sassiest peach of a Georgia gal. Your grandmother Annie Lee was alive then. None of us had much faith in that four year deal." She reached over and patted Ted's cheek. He didn't move away from her hand. "Shows how much we knew. Got you out of it."

Chapter Fourteen

Late Saturday afternoon found Bry and Ted in slow pursuit of a quail dinner. Their saddlebags were full to the legal limit, but they were in no hurry to reach the house. Range and Rover followed the two borrowed bird dogs over Bry's land and onto the McLeod property.

The Thanksgiving break had gone well, Bry thought. He and Ted had hunted Wednesday and Friday afternoons as well as today. Ted had threatened to not return Christmas if his mother fancied up the quail or didn't freeze enough of them for a Christmas break treat. To Bry, he'd been talkative about school and his newest romantic pursuit and about his plans for the future of Ranch McLeod if his mother could stick it out. Still there was something he wasn't saying. This was Bry's last chance to ferret it out.

"I've known you since you were five, Ted," he began. The boy nodded, but kept his eyes straight ahead, as if he knew some special conversation was about to begin. "I think there's something you want to say, but you just haven't yet. I've heard most everything. I doubt you can surprise me."

Ted sighed. "It's Mom."

"Okay." Bry had figured as much. She was the one

154

component of Ted's life they hadn't discussed at all.

"When I went to buy my hunting license, Evan implied you were sleeping together." He pressed his lips together and stared at Bry, waiting confirmation and ready to defend his mother's honor?

"And you believe Evan?"

"I saw you holding hands at Thanksgiving dinner."

"During the prayer. At the Williams house, if it's prayer time, you hold hands. You know that."

He seemed unconvinced. Had he seen Bry's thumb trying to persuade Bethann's hand to stay put and not leave after the 'amen?'

"Well, are you?" Ted faced ahead. "Sleeping together?"

"Did you ask your mother?"

"No." He snorted. "Like she'd tell me."

"And I will?"

"Bry!" He pulled on the reins and stopped. "I think you two would be great together, but to be gossiped about at the feed store?"

Bry reined in beside him, whistled for the dogs to stop. "What your mother and I do, or do not do, is no one's business but ours. But because I love you like a son, I'll be straight with you." He leaned toward Ted. "No."

"Don't you think she's attractive? Aunt Kiki and that crowd sure do. They're all the time trying to fix her up with all these smarmy men. She just hates it! Fake charm and hair plugs and no one's being themselves. No one's real." He took a breath. "You're real."

Bry smiled and shook his head. "Ted, I think your mother is a most attractive woman." And stubborn. With a bit of a temper. A definite attitude. And now he knew a dislike of smarmy, big city men. The horse moved beneath him, anxious to return to the barn and dinner. He put them back in motion before continuing. "So, I have your blessing to pursue your mother romantically?"

Ted didn't answer.

"Ted? You can't have it both ways. She's your mother, but she's an attractive single woman also."

"Well, she does like you."

"I think she's a bit attracted."

Ted snorted. "I expect you to be honorable. And responsible."

Bry laughed. "Like you are with your girl?"

"I've been getting The Talk. When mom quits, Edna Earle starts."

The roof of the barn appeared on the horizon. "You know, Ted, your mom says that she's leaving in August and nothing can change that. Her life's in Atlanta with Kiki and the business."

"Then I guess you're just going to have to work faster, aren't you?"

***

Bry's whole being hummed with the knowledge that Ted approved a relationship between Bethann and himself. It was like getting permission to court the favored daughter. What had he been thinking? He'd run away from only one challenge in his life, and she was sitting on the other side of the county in a lonely fortress of her own making. Damn Bethann's rhetoric! He'd go for it, as Ted said.

They stabled the horses, brushing them, giving them fresh feed and water. They worked as a companionable team, all the tensions of the week gone. Together they cleaned the birds, presented them to the cooks, went to wash up.

Dinner turned into a celebration with the telephoned news that Renita was in labor. Edna Earle mumbled that given that girl's body build, it'd be tomorrow afternoon before they got a baby, but everyone ignored her.

Pushing back from the table, Ted excused himself. He headed for the living room, only to appear back at the kitchen door and announce his intentions to have a double fire before he left. "Where's the firewood? We're low."

Bry winked at him, then folded his napkin and stood. "Your mother and I'll get it."

Bethann rolled her eyes. "We have a log carrier."

"That's right. Us!" He pulled on her chair, giving her no choice but to rise, pitch her napkin into the middle of the table. "I need to help Edna Earle with the dishes," she continued to protest.

"You allergic to wood? I bet you'll have time to do both." He opened the back door for her. She walked through first, waving her hand to turn on the light sensor. Bry grabbed her wrist smartly before the lights came on and turned her to him, shutting the door as he did so.

"Bry?" Enough light fell through the kitchen windows to allow them to see each other's face. She drew her brows together. "I was just going to get us more light!"

"Maybe I don't want more light." He started to draw her to himself, but she pulled back.

"What's going on?"

"This." He circled her waist with his left arm and made her come to him. Pulling her into his body, he released her wrist and brought his mouth down on hers. The kiss was hard, impatient. She responded by pushing at his shoulders and struggling. She did not kiss him back.

He withdrew his mouth but didn't let her go, continuing to hold her tightly while she tried to step back.

"Bry, what has come over you?" she hissed. "My son is inside. Don't make me call for him!"

Bry smiled a slow, widening smile. "I don't think he'd come."

"What?" Her voice was still low, and though her hands were still on his chest, she had stopped pushing. "Let go of me!"

"No, Bethann, I like you right where you are."

"Why don't you think Ted will come?"

He leaned over and kissed her forehead. "Your son

gave me permission to court you this afternoon." He relaxed his hold on her waist but didn't release her.

"What?" Her voice raised considerably.

"Shhh." He brought his right hand around to cup her jaw, stroke her cheek. "Ted thinks we'd make a hell of a couple. And since I have long held that point of view, I have decided to announce my intentions once again and not take 'no' for an answer. I must have been in a real slump to let you get by with that next August business." There was laughter in his eyes and voice now.

She pushed against him again. "You are not going to court me."

"You can't stop me."

"Hell, I can't!"

"Bethann, you've got a trashy mouth. Let's sweeten it up!" He settled his lips on hers, this time gently, let his left hand slip over her blue-jeaned bottom. She gave a little involuntary cry, but parted her lips at his insistence. Her fists relaxed and she arched to him, winding her fingers around his neck.

Bry drew back. They were both out of breath, hearts pounding, entwined so closely the cold night air couldn't inch between them. "You are not going to court me."

"Then what was that we were just doing?" He looked at her with half-closed eyes, a smile still playing at the corners of his mouth.

"You know damn good and well—"

"There's that trashy mouth again. Thought I sweetened it up." He leaned over again to kiss her.

159

She pulled back. "I'm not ready to be hurt again."

"Who guaranteed hurt?"

"I leave in August."

"I could die tonight on the way into town. Hell, Bethann, none of us knows our fate and of all people, you should know that. Would you have thought a year ago that you'd be spending Thanksgiving in Cummings, Texas?"

She smiled then. "Good Lord, no."

He loosened his hold on her. "Can't we try?"

"No," she whispered.

"I could love you, Bethann. I could love you so good."

"Please, Bry, I know you could, but don't. Don't say anything else." She moved out of his arms and he let her go. Moving to the woodpile, she knelt to stack the split wood in her arms.

He came up behind her, knelt down with her. "I'm not giving up. Not only do I have the whole town's blessing, now I have Ted's."

She turned to him. "The whole town? What is the whole town doing involved in this?"

"Small towns are family. Like it or not." He brushed the back of his fingers over her cheek. "I have stated my intentions to Ted fully and honorably. But to you, I'll just serve this warning: Mrs. Fox, not only do I plan to love you, I'll see you in my bed before the spring is out."

She rose, an armload of wood balanced precariously. "If I were you, I wouldn't be giving any quilts away."

Chapter Fifteen

Every morning for the next week, Bry knocked on the back door at seven o'clock and asked Bethann to lunch. She refused but as she couldn't leave him standing there hat in hand, she invited him in for breakfast. Edna Earle had the game figured out by Tuesday and began to import food past Bethann's watchful eye. So while Bethann had coffee and yogurt, Bry and Edna Earle feasted on biscuits and eggs and bacon. By Wednesday, Bethann came downstairs already dressed, and by Friday, she opened the door for him even before he'd set foot on the first step. She was every bit as stubborn as he was, and two could play this game just as well as one.

"I won't be here tomorrow so you'll have to make do with yogurt," Edna Earle told him. "Or does this little campaign stop on weekends?"

"I have the weekend off," he announced. Bethann's betraying heart thumped a tattoo. "Sam's coming back from paternity leave and I'm taking some hours off for the double shifts I've been working. I think he's actually looking forward to getting away from two grandmothers, five aunts, and a post-partum Renita. He'd bring his new daughter with him if I let him."

"Jail may actually look good to him," Edna Earle commented. "He's probably still suffering from that twenty-hour labor."

"Edna Earle, you have no shame." Bethann sipped her coffee and pondered the possibilities of the weekend off with the sheriff. Bry's breakfast campaign amused and flattered her. She refused to think of it as courtship. He wanted to sleep with her and that was that. Well, the horny little devil could just find it somewhere else as far as she was concerned. He'd not made another physical move toward her since the Saturday of Thanksgiving. She acknowledged the cleverness of it, making her wonder when and how and where. Damn, damn, DAMN! He infuriated her.

Bethann had started two calendars in the kitchen, one counting down the days till Ted returned and the other showing how long it was till she spent three days between Christmas and New Year's with Kiki. She didn't know which event she looked forward to the most: to get back to Atlanta, to see the girls, to work at what she loved—or to coddle her son, knowing full well his chief playmate over the holidays would be the sheriff. She'd just have to take the bad with the good. She smiled at Bry when she rose from the table, but he only looked perplexed. At least he wasn't a mindreader.

Saturday, Bry didn't show up, so she worried about him, made up an excuse to call Edna Earle down at the sheriff's department, learned nothing. She tried to work.

Couldn't. The final draft of the cookbook was due the end of January. The cover had been designed, the paper stock and fonts selected, and she and Kiki were having their portraits done when she went back. How dare he worry her by not showing up!

Sunday morning Bethann was awakened by a noise at her window. Rising, she watched as Bry evaded the falling pebbles he was aiming up at her. Next to him, Range and Rover were saddled and waiting. An ax was tied to one saddle and a travois affixed to the other.

Bethann raised the window. "What the hell are you doing?" She looked back over her shoulder at the bedside clock. Pen jumped in the window and looked down scornfully. "It's seven thirty! It's Sunday!"

"You still got that damn trashy mouth. Layer up, get down here, and let me take care of that for you." She started to close the window. "Let's get a Christmas tree!" She stopped the downward motion of the window and leaned back into the screen. "Don't you want a big, well-shaped cedar for Ted?"

She was laughing. "Is there any such thing around here?"

"Well, all right, they're really junipers. But we call them cedars. How about a big, well-shaped juniper?"

"I hadn't really thought about it. Thought I might go in to town and find a fir."

"But that wouldn't be any fun."

"What about breakfast?"

"Got it all packed. We'll go a little ways and I'll fix it

for you. Owe you one."

"Or two. Give me a minute and I'll be down."

Well, why not? She browsed through Joe Tom's castoffs, grabbing a leather vest and an unopened package of long handles that would be too big for her but would have to do. She got her parka and gloves. Her heart lifted and she felt relief that he was here after his absence yesterday. Twenty minutes later, she opened the back door and found him sitting on the steps whittling.

"Don't you do anything with that knife besides make toothpicks?"

He ignored the question as he stood and smiled crookedly at her, propping one leg on the step above. As she approached, he reached out an arm and looped her to him. "First things first. We got unfinished business." Bethann's heart picked up its beat. "Matter of your trashy mouth." He pulled her to straddle his leg, leaned over and kissed her. She was uncertain which part of her body felt the greatest jolt—her lips or between her thighs. She was stunned when he finished the kiss, dropped his leg down and grabbed her hand, while leading her to the saddled duo. "You can ride, can't you?"

Bethann was having a hard time recovering herself. "Some."

"Up." He gave her a boost into Rover's saddle, nonchalantly pushing her rear. If it had been his intention to totally flummox her, he'd succeeded.

Leaving the yard, they rode toward his land. Bethann took the opportunity to clear her mind, try to control her emotions. If he thought he was going to seduce her on a Christmas tree hunt, he was sadly mistaken. On the other hand, her body had not reacted that way since she and Marsh were dating! She only half-listened as he pointed out landmarks, showed where the coveys of quail were, mentioned how he might try to draw in some wild turkeys or ducks next year.

Half an hour later, they pulled up beside a pool and Bry dismounted. "Breakfast time." The campfire was already arranged, a picnic cloth spread on the ground, weighted with rocks so it wouldn't blow in the morning breeze. Good Lord, Bethann thought, what time did he get up to do all this?

She slithered off the horse, dropping rather inelegantly to the ground as he put the waiting coffee pot on the grate over the coals. From the saddle bags, he produced bacon and eggs and proceeded to fix breakfast for her. She wandered to the water's edge, so still in the morning air a slight mist rose from it. The aroma of bacon made her mouth water. He brought her a cup of coffee and they stood together, sipping silently. Bethann didn't know what to say. She was still dazed from the kiss and feelings she thought she'd packed away forever.

It was a beautiful day, full of a clear blue sky and companionable silences. Neither felt compelled to fill the time with chatter. They visited every pool and fence break on his property before he brought her to his perfect Christmas tree. It was as well-shaped as a native juniper could be, and it was huge.

Bethann stood in awe of its size. "Where do you suggest we put it?"

"What about in the middle of the living room? Then we can decorate it all, not just one side."

'We can decorate.' The sentence echoed in her head. Well, why not? She'd never do it alone. He chopped it down, tied it securely to the travois, and they slowly dragged it back to the ranch house.

He busied himself caring for the horses and making a tree stand. She prepared an afternoon snack. He carried the tree in, put its trunk in a bucket of water, and set it where he thought it should go. It was perfect, almost touching the ceiling but allowing a walkway around it at the back of either couch. "What do you suggest I decorate it with?"

"What about the attic? Surely Marsh's mother or grandmother left Christmas decorations. Wasn't there anything in the attic when you cleaned out?"

"There's an attic?"

He grinned. "Where do you think they found Joe Tom?"

"In the attic in August?"

"At the foot of the ladder. Looked like he'd been up there and got overheated, collapsed on the way down, hit his head. Edna Earle found him when she came in the next day. He'd been dead for hours."

"She never mentioned it."

"Probably didn't want to upset you." He gave a short laugh. "When I show you the attic, you'll realize it's probably because she didn't want to clean it out."

***

Buried in the closet in the Joe Tom room, above the boxes of old shoes, was a pull string looped up over the doorway. She'd not have found it herself. Bry reached for it easily and pulled on a trap door. A ladder slid down from it. "After you, ma'am."

"Not on your life."

He grinned and started up the ladder, his head and shoulders disappearing from view with two steps. He lifted a hand over his head, and Bethann heard the distinctive click of a pull-chain light. He finished his climb. She followed.

"Dear God in heaven," she said as she stood in the room. It covered the entire house. A porthole at either end supplemented the dim light bulb. Between the two light sources, she could make out an attic crammed with family memorabilia. "It's like a museum."

Trunks, paintings, boxes, an old rocking chair and one made of cowhide and horns, an artificial aluminum Christmas tree, empty frames, game trophies, bedspreads, curtain rods, metal toys, a military uniform hanging from the rafters. Little insulation. No wonder the house was always so cold. "Close your mouth, Bethann. You'll let flies in."

She almost asked if he was offering to close it for her but thought better of it. "I thought I had this place cleaned up. Clever old Edna Earle."

"Gives new meaning to spring cleaning. I mean, what were you going to do when the book goes in?"

She flapped her arms at her side. "Hadn't given it much thought. Till now." She turned around. "How did you know about this?"

"He had me hauling things up and down from here all the time. Mainly a game trophy circulation. This ol' buffalo," he patted its shaggy and moth-eaten hide, "and I have been ladder-buddies for years."

"And there are Christmas decorations?"

"There's that old aluminum tree over there. Bound to be decorations."

Starting by the discarded tree, they lifted lids and quickly shut them if all they held was paper. Glass ornaments were uncovered first, then tinsel, a set of reindeer, melted candles, tree candle holders that clipped on, ancient tree lights shaped like Santa Claus.

"Marsh used to talk about these. I thought he was kidding!" She gently pulled them out of the box. "I can't believe they'd be safe to use." She held them up for Bry's inspection. He checked the end of the cord. It was whole.

Bethann bit her lower lip. "Marsh said there was an angel on the tree when he was a little boy. On the top. Instead of a star. Let's find it." They began to scrutinize the boxes more carefully. At the bottom of one, they found an ancient tree skirt, heavily embroidered and set with sequins and velvet. The back was in tatters. But in all the Christmas loot, there was no angel.

"Maybe it broke, Bethann."

"We'll find something else." She glanced towards the portholes and saw there was little light remaining from outside. "When it's light tomorrow, I'll come back up. This will be fun. For now, I'll make us some dinner."

She sat on her knees amidst the old and the tawdry. Her nose was as dust-covered as the boxes and the bottom of her jeans looked like she'd dusted the floor with them. Bry stared and smiled. "What?" She looked from him to herself. "Why are you smiling?"

"You should see yourself. You look like a dust bunny."

"You've cleaned house, too." His hair had enough dust in it to give Bethann an idea of what he'd look like in ten years and it was quite attractive. His shirt front had gone from blue to steel gray. He reached down and brushed himself off, scattering even more into the air. They both sneezed.

"Let's get this stuff down before we get sick." He picked up boxes and moved them to the hole in the floor. "Go down and I'll hand them to you." She did, and they worked together to deliver all the attic treasures below.

Bry tested the tree lights and they worked. Bethann found more broken glass ornaments than whole ones. She produced a bottle of wine. He raided Joe Tom's good liquor cabinet.

As many ornaments as there were, the large tree, all sides exposed, still looked bare. She put her fork down on the empty omelet plate and rolled the wine glass against her cheek. They perched side by side on the back of the McLeod couch, admiring and criticizing their handiwork. "I can put a new backing on the tree skirt, so we can still use that."

"Then string popcorn and cranberries and get more lights. Evan keeps pine cones down at the store. You could tie them on, go for a natural look."

She tilted her head and visualized. "I'll think about it." She stood abruptly and downed the rest of the wine. "Finished?" She held her hands out for his plate.

He set the plate on top of hers, then balanced himself and swung his legs around to grab hers and pull her in slightly. She gave him a warning look.

"You're assuming that because I've shown you a wonderful day in the country and you have your hands full, I'm going to take advantage of the situation." She raised an eyebrow. "I've thought about it." He finished pulling her in by her elbows, only the plates separating them. "I just thought I'd kiss the cook." He smiled and pecked her on the lips. "I've had a great day, Bethann. Can we do it again?"

"I don't need another tree," she answered coyly.

He let his hands drift down to her bottom and now he hooked his thumbs in her back pockets. "I'm sure we'll find something you need."

Chapter Sixteen

Edna Earle was speechless the next morning as she stood at the woodstove and gazed into the living room. Damn biggest, ugliest cedar tree she'd ever seen. It actually stood there kind of proud of itself. Oh, but the decorations brought back memories. She'd seen those Santa lights before, recognized the glass ornaments, shook her head at the frayed tree skirt. The attic had not served these things well.

"What do you think?" Bethann stood on the bottom stair. "Although I must admit it looked better last night when Bry and I finished than it does this morning. Must be the lights." She plugged them in. Half lit, half flickered, and then all quit. "Should have known it was too good to be true." She unplugged them, plugged again, and they all shone brightly.

"Bry helped you with this?"

"It was his idea really." Bethann launched into a complete description of the previous day and Edna Earle listened with slackening jaw. He was going to do it, she concluded. He was going to win her over. This was hot insider information and she needed to update her bet in the pool down at the Grille. Bethann was neither

171

embarrassed nor too happy, so Edna Earle knew it wasn't too late. "Did you know about the attic?"

Edna Earle snapped back to reality. "All houses have attics. You didn't clean this one out?" Bethann glowered at her. "Girl, I was tired of cleaning. Let's get breakfast going. You can finish telling me the Christmas story while we contemplate doing just that."

***

They put cleaning out the attic and completing the book on the back burner while they finished decorating the tree with pine cones and berries, small ornamental birds Bethann found on a trip into the mall two hours away and new strings of lights. She kept the old ones on for looks only. The treetop stayed bare. Nothing seemed adequate to crown this particular seasonal tribute.

Bry still showed up at breakfast, his presence now accepted, anticipated. Bethann enjoyed their give and take, their word play, their innuendo. But they didn't touch. He was biding his time and, as Edna Earle pointedly and repeatedly told her, costing the old woman money. Two of her chosen dates at the Grille had slipped by. Did she, Bethann asked, expect them to sleep together as soon as they said a polite hello? Edna Earle had humphed off, muttering that this had better not turn out to be a platonic relationship. *She* would be sorely disappointed. Of all the pool participants, only one had chosen the option of abstinence. Damned that she wanted

Evan to win. And, as Bethann warmed to Bry's ways, she'd be damned that she wanted Evan to win either. Still...

That week Bry talked Bethann into going to lunch down at Sally's Grille. They sat in a front booth and Bry visited with everyone who entered. They all had a Christmas greeting for him, a curious look for her. As he handed her back into the truck, he leaned over and whispered, "Want to watch the fur fly?"

"Sure, Sheriff. What do you have in mind?"

"Kiss me. Skew the pools. You know we're not going to sleep together. They don't." He paused. "I don't."

She smiled at him, touched his cheek, pulled him to her. She kissed him deeply, asked his lips to open with her tongue, got her request. She drew back in time to see heads disappearing back down into the booths and the store fronts. "Damn, Bethann, let's do that again."

"Nah, Sheriff. You've got to get back to work. Remember?"

"Can't remember a thing when you kiss me like that."

***

Three days later, Bry looked up from his second pile of paperwork that day as his office door slowly opened. "Can I come in?" Ted asked.

He motioned him to sit as he dropped a set of papers in the 'out' tray. "How was driving in?" He clicked the pen closed and leaned back in his chair.

"Long, but I had company." He flashed a grin. "Dropped Gina off in Dallas. Spent last night with her family. Like 'em a lot." He winked. "And they like me."

"It works better that way."

"See you finished the cougar," Ted commented as he toyed with the carving on the desk. "I like the sign over the gate, too. What's Mother think about it?"

"I don't believe your mother has ever mentioned it."

"Doesn't she know it's yours?"

"I've never told her."

Ted rolled his eyes. "I'll fix that for you. So, how's it going?"

"Cold outside with mischief enough to go around."

"Not in the workplace, the home place. My home place. How goes it there?"

"Did you see the tree?"

"Hard to miss the tree. That your idea?"

"Yeah. Scouted it out in November."

"It's ugly."

"Looks better at night with the lights on."

"Been there at night with the lights on, have you? How about with the lights off?"

Bry quirked an eyebrow. "Worked out all those conflicts, have you?"

Ted ducked his head.

"Well, you just stick around," Bry rose, "and you'll see how it's going." He came around the desk. "Now scoot. I've got work to do and your mother's invited me to your homecoming dinner."

Ted looked back up and smiled broadly. "Good. Then you can help me tell her I want to go skiing after Christmas with Gina and her family."

"Why is that a problem?"

"I told her I'd spend every holiday with her."

Bry shook his head. "I'll be interested in seeing how you handle this."

***

Bethann and Edna Earle fixed the Thanksgiving quail for Ted's homecoming dinner. She watched him squirm around some question he wanted to ask, noted the surreptitious looks he cast Bry's way. With the last piece of quail on his plate, he finally came clean.

"Gina's family is going skiing after Christmas. Up to Vail."

Of course, that's where this was going, Bethann thought. Gina. Skiing. Gina. To make him squirm a little more or not?

"That's nice," she said. "More wine, Bry?"

He shook his head, gave Ted his attention.

"So, Mom, they've invited me to go along."

"You want to go?" She picked the last biscuit from the basket.

"Well, yeah, I thought it would be, you know, nice." His quail was shredded.

"So what am I going to do while you're on the

175

slopes?" If she couldn't make him suffer, she could at least see if he'd listened to any of her plans.

He gave her a crooked smile. "Be in Atlanta with Aunt Kiki."

"You *were* paying attention."

"Mom—"

"Will you pass through before the semester starts?"

"Promise." He winked at Bry.

With Ted in residence, they settled to a new routine. They slept later, walked to the road and back, admired Bry's handiwork on the Ranch McLeod sign, took Range and Rover out for daily stretches. While it was peaceful for Bethann, she knew it was boring for Ted, so every once in a while, she'd lean over and whisper, "Vail."

Besides bringing the usual box load of presents from Thomas and Lanelle, the mail brought a Christmas party invitation from Delmar and one from Edna Earle's Sunday School class. Bethann declined both. However, she accepted Bry's invitation to the combined county law enforcement party. They danced to a country band. Unsurprisingly, he was an able dancer. Her abilities were more along the ballroom line. They managed however, finding, that for all the city-sophisticate skills in her possession, she could enjoy herself in Cummings, Texas.

As he brought her home he pulled up in the front drive, stopping the truck just short of the security sensor range. Leaving the engine running so that the dash dials lit the interior dimly, he reached to the glove compartment, opened it and pulled out a small box, gaily wrapped for Christmas. He put it in her lap.

"I didn't know we—"

"Shhh, Bethann. It's not a matter of exchange. It's what I wanted to do for you."

"Among other things." Her decision to play along with his game allowed her the innuendo, and she winked at him as she pulled on the ribbon. Gingerly, she unwrapped the gift and shook the top loose from the bottom of the box. Inside, she curled the papers away and lifted a silver bracelet inset with coral and mother-of-pearl. "Bry—" she breathed his name as she turned it in the lights of the dash.

"It just looked like you. Bought it the day before we found the tree." He took it from her, fitted it on her right wrist, kissed underneath it as he did.

She slid easily into his arms. It wasn't that she'd changed her mind about August, but she needed the kiss, needed his touch, had actually grown to anticipate it. This time, his hands brushed the sides of her breasts and when she didn't object, he cupped them and rubbed his thumbs over her nipples.

"You know, of course, this isn't why I stopped out here." He was breathless, and he withdrew his hands and gently pushed her towards her side of the seat.

"Could've fooled me." She stayed where she was, knowing he had the advantage of her. How long was she going to allow herself to be teased?

***

Bethann accepted the Christmas Eve invitation for dinner at the same Williams son's as Thanksgiving. Bry, however, wasn't there. He'd agreed to work a double shift so the family men could have the time off. After a dinner that put Thanksgiving to shame, Bethann and Ted enjoyed a wonderful Cummings tradition as the firetrucks and ambulances drove Santa through town and countryside preparatory to bedtime. In truth, Edna Earle whispered to her as they finished gathering the dishes, there were three Santas actively working the county, setting little boys and girls on their knees, getting last minute orders just right. The Santa that arrived at the Williams' household bounced each grandchild and great-grandchild, made a blushing Edna Earle tell him what she didn't want, then proceeded to hug every woman in the room. When Bethann's turn came to be hugged, Santa sat in the dining chair she was leaning on and pulled her into his lap, holding her there. She gasped in surprise.

"I think this little girl needs her present early," he declared to a roomful of laughing relatives. Then Santa winked familiar blue eyes at her and in the words of the seven-year-old, "Lookit Santa lay one on Miz Fox!" Her struggle had been perfunctory; Santa's beard did itch. They parted to applause with the host wanting to know just who did hold the sheet and money for the barber shop pool.

Ted's voice rang out. "Hey, Santa, you will be

stopping by Miz Fox's later to give her something special, won't you?" The adults collapsed with laughter. The children didn't think it fair Mrs. Fox might get two personal visits. The host deposited a check in Santa's hand. The food bank would be supported for a year on what the Santa visits brought in on Christmas Eve.

Bethann looked sharply at Ted and Edna Earle. Had they known? One ducked head, one unbridled smile.

***

Bry didn't made it back that night. Bethann lay in bed, idly stroking the cat curled beside her. She looked at the window, its curtains drawn so she could see the full moon. When had her attitude about Bry changed? She couldn't really put her finger on it. Just subtleties. Like anticipated kisses. Or breakfast together. Finding herself listening for the sound of the truck tires, raising her head every time the door at the Grille squeaked open. He was running a marvelous campaign. She still felt his hands on her breasts and that had been over a week ago. Only two things stood in her way of giving in, having an affair: Bry wanted more and August would be here before she knew it.

She turned over, putting her back to the Santa Claus moon. Next week she'd be in Atlanta with Kiki and the business. Next week she'd renew her faith and get her head on straight. Next week she'd do without Bry.

***

The Atlanta airport between Christmas and New Year's, an adventure in and of itself, took on new significance to Bethann. She scanned the waiting faces for Kiki, found Jon instead. "She was swamped!" he explained as he bussed her on the cheek and took her carry-on. "This all?"

"I have all of three nights, how much can I bring?"

"Good. Luggage pickup would have taken even more time."

He hurried her to the parking lot. Tossing the bag in the backseat, he drove the large Lincoln at an unsafe speed out of the lot. "Jeez, Jon, where's the fire?"

"End of year inventory clearance. I've got to get back to the dealership."

Bethann held on as they zipped toward north Atlanta through heavy midday traffic. An hour later, he deposited her at the familiar door of their small rented kitchen space and squealed off.

"Mister Hospitality brought me," Bethann announced to Kiki.

"Babe, you look great!" Kiki was all flour and cinnamon as she started to hug Bethann, then thought better of it. "Texas must agree with you. Or is it the sheriff?"

"Same song, second verse." Bethann laughed as she grabbed an apron and wrapped it around herself. "What kind of mess do you have us into?"

Kiki launched into a detailed discussion of three cocktail parties and four brunches. "I overdid it. Without you to say no, all I did was say yes. And I knew you'd be home. I sent you a copy of the schedule."

"It looks worse now that I'm here."

"Spa time in the West is over. It's work, work, work for you now."

They settled easily into the old routine and Bethann found it exhilarating once again. She'd forgotten that she'd often felt herself on a treadmill, going from engagement to engagement. She'd forgotten that some nights Marsh and Ted had both been asleep when she'd arrived home. She'd forgotten how tired she'd get, how cross she and Kiki would be with each other. She'd forgotten the pleasure of a job well done and a clientele well satisfied with their caterer.

What she didn't forget for four days and three nights was Bry. Through the running around, the sitting for the book portraits, the renewal of old friendships, the promise that August wasn't that far away, through it all was Bry. She'd push the image down, try to forget what he looked like standing in the doorway Christmas morning, a sheepish grin on his face, an awkwardly wrapped present held out to her. She'd twisted her bracelet silently in front of him. He'd pushed the present on her even more. Reluctantly, she'd accepted it.

As they sat in front of the fire, coffee cooling in their cups, Ted and he watched as she opened it. Buried in hay was a hand-carved star. It had seven points, and a bottom just hollow enough for the top bough of the tree. "Till you find Marsh's old angel." Ted dragged the ladder in, took the star, affixed it to the top. It brushed the ceiling and bent the top branch.

"In keeping with the ambiance of the whole room." Ted's comment fell on deaf ears. Bry was cradling Bethann, rubbing his chin on the top of her head.

Now, standing in her own business surrounded by friends she dearly loved, doing work she found fulfilling, Bethann came to the realization that a voice was missing, a presence not even near enough to see within a half hour's time.

She fought this inner battle for three days and gave up on the fourth. Much as she hated to leave Kiki and all the events she'd booked, it was a problem of Kiki's own making. The overbooking would never have happened had Bethann been there. But she was going to escape. While Bethann couldn't put it into words—wouldn't really allow herself the thought—she was going home.

Chapter Seventeen

Icicles threatened to overwhelm the Ranch McLeod sign as Bethann drove under it on New Year's Eve. The wind had torn the gate open and it swung erratically back and forth. The truck tires crunched on the icy ruts as she slowly made her way to the house.

The groceries swayed and bumped in the back seat and rear compartment, but the frozen meat gave her traction. She turned on the fog lights and slowed her progress even more. If the road had been this bad at the warehouse store, she might have been tempted to stay in the city. After all, Joe Tom's will didn't make a specific provision for her untimely highway death due to what the radio was touting as a once-in-a-century ice storm.

She reached the driveway between the house and barn. Her security floodlights didn't come on and a tingling began at the base of her spine. Coupled with this weather, no electricity was not an option, plus the cats would be terrified. She reached for her cell phone, read 'no service.' Had the storm taken out the tower? Just as she clicked the phone off, the SUV's headlights illuminated the front grill of Bry's truck on the far side of the barn.

She eased the truck over the ice to the back steps. The security light over the back door blinked on. She watched as Bry approached, arms outstretched to balance himself on the ice.

Catapulting his bundled frame through the passenger door, he stretched out his gloved hands to the heat vent, involuntarily shivering as he rubbed them together. Bethann sat in silence, too stunned to move or say anything. Catching his breath, Bry leaned back in the seat but still kept his hands near the vent.

Bethann began. "I think I'm in shock. No security lights, an ice storm, you on the other side of the barn. Do you have car trouble? Radio not working?"

"So many questions, so little time." He raised his eyebrows at her. "How was Hot-Lanta?"

"Whole lot warmer than this place. Why don't we finish this conversation inside?"

"No, you need your options first." He moved his boots nearer the vent and took his hands away. "I came out about six to check on Range and Rover and see if you were back. No security lights came on. None. But the electricity in the barn was working, so I knew the problem was a little more personal. All your bulbs had been unscrewed just enough to not contact. Using a BB-gun would have been too obvious." He let that sink in. "They're back, Bethann."

It took a moment for the import of his words to register. As if ignoring the conclusion, she peered through the driver window at the house and the beaming light. "I thought you said all the lights were out."

"I re-screwed that one so you wouldn't be frightened out of your mind when you pulled in and I came up. The cell tower is iced or I could have called you."

"I wonder how long they've been unscrewed."

"They were all right last night."

She pulled her hands off the steering wheel and locked them between her knees. "So what do I do?"

She felt vulnerable. His schedule had kept him from seeing her the two days before she'd left, and she'd been gone four. "And don't even suggest I spend the night with Edna Earle."

"Why not?" he asked.

"Five nights away from the ranch, Bry. I just finished using three. The next two are in June, if there are no emergencies."

"This isn't an emergency?"

"No. You've been watching for six hours, I assume?" He nodded. "But no one's been back. This weather, I wouldn't think they would be. Even arsonists have their limits."

"What if they've changed to murderers?"

"Is your constituency capable of that?"

"'Fraid so." He put his hand on her seat back and leaned towards her. "Please don't stay here, Bethann. I'll do nothing but worry."

"I have to, Bry. I have electricity and a wood-burning stove Edna Earle was supposed to have begun for me this afternoon. She thought—I thought—I'd be home hours ago."

"The fire's going. It was really hard sitting in that cold truck, seeing smoke from the woodstove, but the last place I needed to be to catch our friends was inside. So why weren't you home earlier?"

"The plane was late, and I stopped at the warehouse store for supplies for the final tests in entrees and desserts. And I'm not much good at driving in this kind of weather. I switched to four wheel drive over an hour ago." She put her hand on the door handle. "It's almost midnight, Bry. I'm going to unload the car and go to bed."

Leaving the keys in the ignition, she opened the door and stepped out into the bitter cold. She held onto the railing as she climbed to the porch and punched in the code. The door opened and she went in, flipping lights as she progressed through the downstairs. Returning to the kitchen, she found Bry stacking sacks on the table. Her luggage sat by the hall door. "You don't have to stay and help."

"Hell, Bethann, I'm already cold. Check out the house, stoke the fire, and start putting the damn stuff up. I'll bring it in." He clomped out and she went to the hall and added wood to the stove.

She glanced once more into the living room. Both fireplaces were laid with logs, and Pen and Tux snoozed contentedly together on one end of the McLeod couch. There was a slight meow from one of them in recognition of her return. Obviously, Edna Earle had taken good, if begrudging, care of them.

She took her carry-on and went up the stairs, hearing them ring hollow. The upstairs hall was barely warm. She looked in each room and shut all the doors but the bath and her bedroom. She deposited the bag on the bed, turned on the electric blanket, and stuffed her nightgown under the covers to get it warm. She might just change into it under the sheets.

Back in the kitchen, she found Bry standing at the sink, running the hot water. "I see Edna Earle left this dripping and the cabinet doors open so the pipes won't freeze."

Bethann checked the sacks. "Where's the meat?"

"Left it in the truck. It was frozen already. It's five degrees out there. God only knows what the wind chill is. It'll keep till morning. I wasn't going to."

She shrugged out of her coat and hung it on the back of a kitchen chair. Her eyes flicked from the car keys on the table to Bry and back. "You put the truck up?" He nodded. "Thank you."

He still stood at the sink, then slowly removed his jacket and hat and hung them on the rack by the door.

"Did I miss something here? It's really not necessary that you stay and help me put these things away. Most of it will keep till morning." Just a trace of sarcasm tinged her voice.

"Good. Then we'll have something to do after breakfast. I'm staying the night. The truck's keeping the SUV company."

"What?" The word exploded out of her. "I don't think so!"

"Well, I do." He surveyed the contents of the sacks, then opened the door of the refrigerator. "Got anything to eat? I'm starving."

"Aren't we being just a bit presumptuous here?"

He turned and closed the refrigerator door, a large grin spreading on his face. "Presumptuous?" He grasped the top of a ladderback chair. "Were you presuming I wanted to literally stay with you?"

Had her absence of four days changed so much between them? Whatever intimacy they had shared before Christmas seemed gone. Bethann felt her face flush and her mouth dropped open. "No."

"Really?" He rummaged in a sack and brought up a cello bag of apples. "Believe it or not, I can sleep on your couch in front of that nice big fire you're going to start for me and never even think about you."

She doubted that, and from the nervous tic at the edge of his mouth, she knew he doubted it also. Damn whoever was after her. Damn them for putting a wedge between them.

"Some protection you are from the beasties, if you're asleep."

"I'll look mighty good to you, if the beasties come." He rubbed an apple on his sleeve and took a bite. She reached around him and jerked open the refrigerator door, silently unloading a sack of cheeses, creams, eggs, and butter.

He started on a second apple. She grabbed the bag out of his hand and dumped the contents into a fruit bowl on the table along with a bag of oranges. She slid the rest of the sacks to the end of the table to await unpacking in the morning. Dusting her hands, she went into the living room and Bry followed.

He'd expected more of an argument. Now it looked like the silent treatment. Maybe there was a reason he'd never remarried.

Then he stood in the archway to the hall and watched her. She leaned over to whisper to the cats, nuzzle them, get a lick from a scratchy tongue. She opened the damper on the fireplace, took down the matches, removed the screen, and flicked warmth into a cold room. Replacing the screen, she ignored him entirely, as she repeated the procedure at the other end. Now two bright spots glowed from opposite ends of this very masculine room. Somehow, Joe Tom had never seemed as at home here as did his disgruntled niece-in-law.

She disappeared down the hall into the computer room and returned with an armload of quilts. She threw them into a wing chair and made for the downstairs bathroom. She brought Joe Tom's robe out from where Ted had left it and let it float down on top of the quilt pile.

"Personally, I don't care which couch you use, but the cats would probably prefer you took the other one." She turned off the lights in the kitchen and hall and announced on the way up the stairs, "There's a new toothbrush in the medicine cabinet. Sweet dreams."

Bry heard her move around upstairs. Heard her bedroom door slam shut, heard the water running in the shower, the sound of the hamper as it closed. Pleasant woman sounds. Just slightly upset, but not furious. More upset with the situation than him.

"Right, fellas?" Bry asked the cats as he sat down beside them and removed his boots. "Just a little upset. Atlanta must not have been as divine as she remembered. May be she missed me, and when I didn't ravage her the minute she got here, she got mad." They eyed him cautiously, too warm and comfortable where they were to give him even an inch of their warmed spot. "Maybe she's upset because May June's on the warpath again." He thought that one over as he unfolded a quilt. "Well, too bad, I'm going to sleep where I want to. And that's here!"

He tossed the couch pillows to the other end and stood and stretched. The water had shut off in the shower. The door to her bedroom opened and the three of them listened for footsteps on the stairs. There were none, only the sigh of the bed as she got in. "Guess she's telling you you can go up now." Pen understood, eased himself away, arched his back, and bounded up the stairs. Bry heard his running footsteps as he jumped on the bed. "Lucky cat," he muttered under his breath.

He padded down the hall in his stocking feet, checking the fireplaces and wood stove as he went. He was stiff from sitting in the truck all that time. A shower would feel good and get the hot water coursing through the entire house. He indulged himself and then put on Joe Tom's robe, which fit him admirably. After a final inspection of the doors, he settled with Tux to listen to the wind and watch the glow of the fire.

Tired as he was, sleep eluded him. Bethann's faint perfume hung on the pillows under his head. His hastily said 'I'll do nothing but worry' still rung in his head. Where had that Freudian slip come from? Of course, he'd worry! He'd been worrying for hours, ever since he'd called the airport to find that the plane had landed safely but late. He'd calculated three hours to travel instead of the usual two and gotten more nervous with each passing minute. It hadn't helped that every time the wind had changed directions, he'd seen a shadow. Maybe it was time to stop sheriffing and start ranching. But not alone. He was no Joe Tom. To his way of thinking, ranching was a companion sport. He had the right companion in mind. Trouble was, she came with a calendar already marked off.

Why not just go upstairs and appear at her doorway? Why not sneak under the covers after she slept and hold her, nestle together, see if they fit? If they couldn't just sleep together, there was really no sense in pursuing this. He and Meg had fit just right. He still missed it after all these years. Bethann had molded herself to his arms so well. They'd fit, he just knew it. And the passion, the tenderness that comes with age and experience—good Lord! it was hard to lie still and know she slept above him.

***

Upstairs, Bethann was warm enough but worried about Bry. "Tux keeping him warm?" she asked the soft bundle of fur beside her. 'I'll do nothing but worry.' The phrase ran through her mind. She'd only been gone four days. Why did it seem so much longer? Why hadn't he opened his arms to her when he'd gotten in the truck? Why was he so stiff, so defensive? How could so many things seem to change in less than a week? Maybe he was jealous of her time in Atlanta. He had no right to be. It was her home. Her business.

Oh, hell! Sure, she'd missed him while she was gone, but things were simpler there without a man involved. What if she just made up her mind to settle it once and for all? What if she just walked downstairs and said 'Let's do it'? One quick tumble under the quilts and no one ever the wiser. It might be awful. The chemistry they felt might be just so many wayward middle-aged hormones. All this angst would be for nothing. Over. Done with. Soul search no more.

She flipped over, greatly disturbing her bedmate. But how could those strong arms feel awful? How could that warm mouth be bad? It wasn't wrong chemistry that had made her feel like a teenager again when he kissed her, her pulse racing, her personal chemistry kicked into high gear.

But she wasn't a teenager again nor a young virginal wife. She was over twenty years married, experienced and well-loved. She'd spent her married life in a very satisfying situation. Her instincts had put her there once, why not trust them again?

But only eight months of exile remained. Was it worth the inevitable heartbreak?

***

Bethann fell into uneasy sleep disturbed not only by a racing mind but the blowing sleet striking the house. She heard the old trees creak and the house settle itself again and again. She pulled the electric blanket up to stifle the noise, but the crash in the front yard and the sudden ceasation of the wind had her sitting up and wide awake. She jumped out of bed and ran across the hall, jerking open the other bedroom door and running to the front window. Using the sleeve of her gown, she wiped off the damp and looked into the yard. Against the white of the icy driveway, she saw half of the old bois d'arc tree had split and landed within feet of the porch. She breathed a sigh of relief that the house was untouched. Still, she was shaken and had no intention of going back to bed without going downstairs first.

She met Bry as he turned on the stair landing. He was still tying his robe. Two stairs above him, her stocking feet stopped, and she balanced, held her breath. "The tree."

"I know, I saw it. Barely missed the porch." Their eyes held.

"Bry—"

"Beth—"

They spoke at once, then recovered and did it again. She held up her hand and rushed on before common sense stopped her. "This is ridiculous and I can't sleep."

"I can't either." He put his hand on the banister and pulled himself up a step. "Can't we just hold each other?"

A smile played on her lips. "Really? That all?" She slid her hand down the banister to his and he covered it. "I'd been contemplating something else," she whispered. They were nose to nose.

"I'm open to suggestions." They leaned into each other and kissed. The hall wasn't quite so cold as she pulled him to her and their absence from each other melted away. "I like your game plan better."

"Do you?" she whispered. "You realize it has an expiration date."

"Just got to last to morning." He encircled her waist and held her ever so gently as they kissed again.

There was mischief in her eyes as she kissed the tip of his nose.

He smiled back. "Your place or mine?"

"I never turn down a roaring fire."

He lifted her in his arms and carried her to the McLeod couch.

Chapter Eighteen

The miracle wasn't that they were at long last doing this, Bry thought as he carried her down the stairs, but that he didn't stumble with her. She wasn't heavy, but his mind had already leapt beyond the act of kissing her. Gentle pecks, long breathless entreaties. He sat down heavily on the couch, Bethann in his arms. His left hand circled her waist and she arched to him. He pulled his mouth away and gave her a half-smile. "What if I told you this old couch and I could show you a trick or two?" He raised his eyebrows.

"I thought men stopped talking like that when they ceased being boys."

"You know better than that." He put her from his lap, setting her down on Tux's half of the couch, gaining a twitched tail for his trouble. Rising, he grinned as he faced the other half of the couch, bent down and lifted from near the bottom. The seat slid forward and the back slid down and backward, forming a bed, now covered with rumpled quilts.

Bethann laughed. "An old futon! I had no idea." She jumped over to it. "Does the other half do it?"

"Think you're going to be needing more space?" He dislodged Tux and made the other half do the same, then joined her on the twelve-foot long bed.

They knelt facing one another, the fires in the background, the wind now silent. Bry put his hands on her shoulders, gently massaging with his thumbs. "Flannel?"

"I was cold upstairs. I always sleep in a flannel gown."

He glanced behind her. "And socks?"

"Can't sleep with cold feet." She flounced down on her rear and stuck her legs out. "And pajama bottoms!" She looked up at him.

"And an electric blanket?" She nodded. "And two cats?"

"One." She ran her left hand up his bare chest where it showed through the robe. "You sleep nude?" The light from the fire made her eyes twinkle even more.

"Been known to." He sat beside her with his legs out. "Not tonight." Long handle underwear showed beneath the robe.

"Looks like we've got our work cut out for us." Bethann wiggled out of her bottoms, tossing them on the floor, pulling her gown to cover her knees. Bry let out a long breath and laid down, a far more comfortable position for his aroused condition. "But I have to warn you," she whispered as she leaned to him, auburn hair trailing over his chest, her right hand balanced on his robe knot, "I have no intention of taking off my socks."

She worked at the knot and released it, then pushed the robe open so she could see his torso. His belly was taut and his arousal obvious. She ran her hand over his stomach and, catching his breath, he put his hands behind his head. Hiking up her gown, she straddled his hips. Leaning down, she kissed him tenderly, barely moving her face from his when she drew back. "Bry, I have a middle-aged woman's body."

He smiled and reached to peck the tip of her nose. "Thank God, it's not an old woman's."

"You know what I mean. This is not a hard body you're about to fool with. If that upsets you, we'd better stop now." She sat up and put her weight on him, smiling teasingly. Even through the long handles, she felt so good, so soft, so woman.

Her hands rested lightly on his chest. He picked them up and kissed the palms. "I couldn't stop now if I wanted to. Well, I guess I could. I'd have to really, really want to." He pressed against her. "And I don't."

He undid the gown button at her throat, then the one below, and so on, letting his hands rest on the fabric and body encased therein each time he moved farther down. He slid the gown from her shoulders to her elbows, revealing her breasts. He couldn't stop looking at her. Pale skin, peachy in the firelight, soft to his eyes. He smiled and finished pulling her gown from her arms. The flannel pooled around her hips, over his. A woman's body, pleasing to his eyes, to his senses.

He sat up, edging her backwards slightly, took her

breasts in his hands and gently kissed them. They were full, warm, the nipples hard. She arched her neck and he kissed her there, nestling their bodies together.

"Bethann," he breathed against her hair, encircled her with his arms and held her as close as he could. His hands found her hips, and he moved her toward him to dislodge the gown. She wiggled out of it as he laid her on her back and divested himself of his garments and found his home between her thighs. So long, God, it had been so long for him. She moved her hands over his back and his hips, clung to him, arched to him. They filled each other's need as they filled each other's body, whispering, kissing, releasing.

He lay on top of her, but her hands held him in place, and she wouldn't let him move. "I'm heavy for you, Bethann."

"No, just let me hold you." She squeezed down on him and he grinned.

"Tease! If your body's middle-aged, so is my stamina. You're going to have to wait a while."

She frowned playfully and released him. He rolled off, immediately taking her in his arms, holding her, stroking her back, her arms, her hair. She kissed the hollow of his throat, his Adam's apple, his chin. She nuzzled his chest, then turned in his arms, and they nested like spoons, watching the fire lose its vigor. He moved his chin against her hair, held her breasts in his hands, cradled her legs with his. They were twined together and very content.

"Well, which is it going to be?" Her delivery were deadpan.

"I'm almost ready now." He moved his hardening self against her.

"Not what I meant. A quilt or another log on the fire?"

"You are really a mood-blower. Is this your subtle way of saying I'm not hot-blooded enough for you?" He blew on her ear and she squirmed. "You're closer to the fire."

"Putting another log on the fire is such a manly thing to do."

"I have no objection to you showing your masculine side."

"One roll in the hay and you're giving orders."

"I've been trying to do it since we met, but you've got a damn stubborn streak."

She stretched forward and grabbed her pajama bottoms off the floor. Flipping to her back, she started putting them on. "Oh, no, you don't!" He flung them behind the couch into the middle of the room and threw her a quilt from the chair before he began to poke at the fire.

"You got cold out there," she whispered as she welcomed him back under the quilts.

"Then warm me up."

The frenzy of their first lovemaking gave way to the slow passion of their second. Bry savored the definite advantages of experienced loving. Trial-and-error eclipsed years down to hours.

They slept nested together. Bry's left arm cradled her body, his hand absently stroking from her breasts downward. She turned to her back, hooked her legs over his and they slept contentedly.

***

The crunch of tire chains on the ice of the driveway broke through Bethann's dreamless state. The morning was unbelievably still, making the noise doubly loud. Her eyes flew open as the sound permeated her senses. She grabbed Bry's left wrist and twisted it to see the time on his watch. Nine o'clock! Bright white light fell through the cracks of the shades. She sat bolt upright as the implication of where they were collided with the possibility of who was in the driveway.

"Bry! Bry!" She shook him and only got her thigh contentedly stroked. Desperately, she threw the cover off both of them, hoping that exposure to the cold room would rouse him.

Instead, she found her eyes drawn to the top of his left hip. A triangular birthmark met her gaze. Her fingers traced it, and all thought of their imminent exposure by Edna Earle or whoever else had the nerve to travel on ice, was drained from her mind.

Bry finally opened his eyes, looking startled, then quite happy as he remembered the circumstances.

"And I thought I'd just had the most wonderful

dream." He reached for her, but she moved out of his range.

"What's this?" She pressed the triangle.

"Birthmark, Bethann." He sat up. "My mother said she had one like it, so at least I know my legitimacy on one side." He smiled crookedly. "It shouldn't upset you."

Bethann sought to compose herself. "It doesn't," she lied. "The tires outside on the ice upset me." They both heard the back door open and Edna Earle's you-hoo, followed by two sets of feet. "And *that* really upsets me."

Bry's language was succinct and blasphemous. He pulled the quilt to their chins, and they looked at each other, whispering. "We're deer in the headlights. Think if we get under, she'll ignore us?"

"I'm more concerned with who's with her."

"Maybe if we're real still…"

"Bethann, you home? Girl, the lines are all out." They heard her voice as Edna Earle went to the bottom of the stairs, then watched as she approached the woodstove, came slowly into the edge of the living room and put her hands on her hips. She stopped in the doorway and shook her head. "The only thing that makes this better is that I brought a witness. Couldn't get here on my own and I sure was worried about you. Guess I needn't have been." She was turning to call.

"Edna Earle, please, don't!" Bethann hissed, but it was too late. Sam peeked around the corner.

"Hot damn, what a start to the new year!" He looked from one of them to the other. "Tell me you didn't start till after midnight 'cause today's the day I put down in my little girl's name."

Edna Earle elbowed him. "I have New Year's Eve. You know I'll be generous with the child."

Bry and Bethann looked at each and were silent. "Edna Earle, how about a little privacy?"

"Sure, sure, girl." She pushed on Sam and they retreated toward the kitchen. "I'll just be getting breakfast ready. Sam, thanks for the ride, you can go on home now you know where the sheriff is."

"You promised me breakfast, Edna Earle," they heard him protest. "I think I'll stay."

Bethann turned to Bry, the quilt still pulled to their chins. "I don't believe we have to go socialize."

"Whose house is it, Bethann?"

"You tell me. You want to kick her out?" She put her feet over the edge of the couch and searched for her nightgown. "If memory serves, you stashed my bottoms over there somewhere." He retrieved them and they redressed into their nightwear with their backs to each other. Facing one another over the couch as they flipped it back into shape, Bethann finally continued. "I didn't plan on getting caught red-handed."

"How about red-faced?" he grinned.

"Aren't you the least bit embarrassed?"

"Why should I be embarrassed for making love to you? You think we were going to be able to hide this for eight months?"

"What makes you think I was going to do this for the

next eight months?"

"That's not what you were implying a little earlier today."

"Once is all I intended. Maybe I just wanted to get you out of my system."

"Well, did it work? Did you get me out of your system? Was once enough?"

She stood her ground at the end of the couch, then turned and stoked the fireplace back to life.

"I'll take that as a no, since you can't bring yourself to say yes. I'm going to eat breakfast. I worked up quite an appetite last night."

"Oooh-h-h!" she fumed as she went to the other fireplace. She threw logs on, poked at them furiously, slammed the screen back in place.

She looked down at her fingers that had touched the birthmark. *Oh, hell, oh, hell, oh, hell!* She rubbed them together, wiped them on her robe. Tears sprung to her eyes that had nothing to do with Edna Earle's glee in the fruition of her plan. What secrets there must be! And the only way to their discovery was through Edna Earle.

She wiped her eyes, smoothed her robe, kissed her own fingertips as she'd kissed that same birthmark on Ted's baby bottom and Marsh's adult one.

She held her head high as she went into breakfast.

***

"I need to talk to you." Bethann met Edna Earle on

the landing, deftly turned her and headed her back to the kitchen table. The men had left them after breakfast, the details of the evening having been hazily shared. Edna Earle had conceded the pool at Sally's to Sam, but what to do about May June still remained unanswered.

Bethann poured them each a cup of coffee and sat down. She fidgeted, pulled her legs under her, stirred the hot liquid with the tip of her finger.

"Bry has a birthmark."

Edna Earle was cautious. "Lots of people have birthmarks."

Bethann spoke through gritted teeth. "Lots of people do not have birthmarks where my husband and son have birthmarks. The McLeod birthmark, Edna Earle! What the hell is Bry doing marked as a McLeod?"

"Oh." Edna Earle set her cup down and started pulling it in a circle by the handle. "Does he know you're upset?"

"No." Bethann watched Edna Earle as the old woman furrowed her brow and chewed on her lower lip. "Spill it. I've got a right to know with whom I've slept."

Edna Earle met Bethann's gaze and nodded. "I'd expected to take this with me to my grave. After all, it's been seventy years, and the need to share has never arisen." She wet her lips.

"Edna Earle, you are trying my patience."

She held up a hand. "I was ten years old…" her voice slipped into the singsong of the storyteller, "and Joe Tom's little sister, Annie Lee—Marsh's mother—and I were best friends. We were all the time sneaking away from our chores down to the Blackerby farm. They had an old barn back in the upper pasture, and Annie Lee and me'd made a playhouse up in the loft. There was hay stored in it and some emergency supplies in case someone got caught in a storm. Wasn't used for nothing else." She took another sip of coffee, closed her eyes.

"It was a Sunday afternoon and we had decided to play that day after church. I didn't know it at the time, but Annie Lee got sick, and so never showed up or there'd've been two witnesses." She opened her eyes and shook a finger at Bethann. "I do not intend that you should ever tell anyone this, particularly Bry. You understand?"

Bethann nodded and put her cup down. She hugged herself.

"So I was up in the loft, playing house, waiting for Annie Lee when the barn door flew open and Joe Tom McLeod walked in. He glanced around but never looked up where I was. I was burying myself in hay, let me tell you. He was twenty then, strong as an ox and had a reputation for a terrible temper. He'd whupped my older brother Jed two weeks before in a fight, and I wasn't about to announce my presence. I just hoped Annie Lee didn't come in and get us both in trouble. He had no more business being there than we did, but he was bigger and meaner and it wouldn't matter she was his sister. He paced up and down, then finally stopped and went into one of the stalls and made a bed of hay."

She sipped her coffee. "Well, I was pretty naive, let me tell you. Never occurred to me that he intended to do anything other than spend the night, and I was sure unhappy with that prospect because I didn't know how I was going to get out of there without being caught. Well, my worries were put to rest when May June Bright slithered through the door. She runs over into his arms and they get all tangled up quicker than I ever saw. He bounced her into that hay and she didn't protest one little bit. I just couldn't take my eyes off them. They stripped down buck-naked and went to acting like farm animals, far as I was concerned."

Bethann got up to replenish their coffee. "You saw Joe Tom's birthmark. Marsh told me it was common in the family."

"Yes, I saw it. Saw it on the backside of May June's baby nine months later, too. Well, I think that between the two experiences I had a real good notion of the way things were."

"But you said May June had only one child, Bry's mother. Was she born out-of-wedlock?"

Edna Earle accepted the fresh coffee. "May June was way too smart for that. She was always looking to better herself. That bunch of Brights weren't any good. They'd been poor farmers in East Texas and they were even poorer ranchers here. She'd lusted after Joe Tom for years, but her family had bigger things in mind for her than a McLeod that was just as dirt-poor as a Bright! Anyway, he left for the army a week after I saw them in the barn. Damned if a month later, she isn't paying close attention to the oldest Cummings, who'd been lusting after her since they'd both got all their equipment. She wouldn't give him the time of day till Joe Tom was gone. Month after that, she's getting married to the heir of the richest family in three counties. And little Edna Earle sees her first 'premature birth' seven months later."

"Marked like Joe Tom."

"Even at ten, I didn't have to be a rocket scientist to figure this out. Of course, I couldn't discuss it with my mother. She just politely said May June must have misread her notchin' stick."

"So May June Bright Cummings raises Joe Tom McLeod's daughter as a Cummings. What did Joe Tom have to say about all this when he got back?"

"He didn't get back for five years. By that time, after the War and all, there was more than a little water under all those bridges. Cummings had inherited and May June was living the good life. And she did have a knack for increasing and multiplying. Everything but children. Rae Bright Cummings was it."

"Mother and daughter didn't get along?" Bethann put her elbows on the table and nested her chin in her upturned palms.

"May June probably resented the constant reminder of her roll in the hay. Uneasy that any day Joe Tom might show up and expose her."

"Or his birthmark." Bethann considered all this information. "So their little dispute that kept them at odds for seventy years had nothing to do with property like you told me."

"Depends on how you want to look at children."

"Bry—from Bright? What's his full name?"

"How's this for a corker? Rae and May June hate each other. May June kicks her out not once, but twice! And when she has a son, what does she name him? Bright Cummings Phillips."

"What a mouthful—but clever. A nod at guaranteed inheritance."

"She knew May June better than that. Anyhow, she shortened it to Bry when he was a baby." She set her cup down. "Now you know, what are you going to do about Joe Tom's grandson?"

"You mean Marsh's cousin? Oh, hell, Edna Earle, I feel like some tragic figure from the Bible."

Edna Earle smiled. "Girl, that just might be a good place to start looking for answers."

Chapter Nineteen

The rest of the day passed in relative peace. Bethann and Edna Earle busied themselves keeping the house and themselves warm. The phone lines stayed iced. The temperature never reached twenty, but the wind didn't start up again either, and there was no more precipitation. Edna Earle puttered incessantly, getting on Bethann's nerves to the point that she finally hid herself in her room with a paperback she'd picked up at the airport.

But she couldn't concentrate, her mind full of Bry, his body, his kisses, his warmth. She indulged herself with detailed memories of their night together, snuggled deeper inside the quilt wrapped about herself as she had snuggled in his arms. Only when an hour had passed, and she'd not turned even one page, did she allow her mind to wrestle with Edna Earle's story and its implication for her.

Bry was more than Marsh's friend and Ted's hunting buddy, he was a cousin. By being Joe Tom's grandson, he was a closer heir than Marsh, certainly than she and Ted. But if Joe Tom had ever suspected the truth, surely he would have left his estate to him.

Damn! What had she said to Kiki months before? 'When did my life stop being normal?' Whenever she got around Joe Tom. That was why she'd so rigorously avoided him all these years. Devil of an old man. Just when she thought she had him licked, he'd sneaked back up on her. What else could there be?

***

The crunch of tire chains on ice brought both their heads up. Edna Earle stopped in mid-spoonful of soup. Bethann looked at the kitchen clock. Six in the evening, already dark, company unexpected. "Probably Bry come to check on us," Edna Earle said as she stood and set another place at the table. "Hope you got all your thinking straightened out."

"It's a little hard to see him in the same light. He's gone from tragic figure to very tragic figure."

"That said, you'd better be prepared to either kiss him hello or tell him why you won't."

"It's not like it's incest."

"Precisely and don't you forget it!"

The vehicle stopped at the back door and heavy tread came up the steps to the porch. Edna Earle answered the door before a knock could sound.

"I've always wanted an automatic door."

"Hell, Sam, where's Bry?" the old woman groused as she put the dishes back in the cupboard and sat back down.

"Well, I'm just fine, thank you, Edna Earle," he answered sarcastically. "No, I don't want you to ask about me or my day."

Bethann got up and retrieved the dishes. "Have some soup, Sam, and tell us what's been happening in the big world of ice and Cummings."

Disgruntled, he sat down across from Edna Earle and waited while the steaming bowl was put in front of him. "Well, at least it's a holiday, and the place stands still anyway."

"No wild drivers out. Good. Where's Bry?"

"Edna Earle, you are getting more cantankerous the older you get. You know," he warmed to the subject, "one of these days you are going to be so old, you won't be able to be any ruder, and then you'll just frustrate yourself to death!" He took a couple of bites. "Bethann, I imagine you made this. It's excellent and not too spicy."

"Other than dinner, what did you need, Sam?" Bethann ventured the question, cutting a look of warning to Edna Earle.

"I can eat at home, but this sure is good." He wiped at his mouth. "For some strange reason that I can't think of right now, I actually came over to get this old woman and take her back to her house so she could get some clothes and her police scanner. That way we could at least talk to you and keep you up on things. Looks like the weather's going to fair off tomorrow, melt some of this, then the phone lines can get back together and those old folks who think they can drive in any weather, can get back to menacing the roads."

"Very funny."

He tore a piece of cornbread in half and rimmed his soup bowl, stuffing it into his mouth before continuing. "It was a peaceful day till an eighteen-wheeler tried to jog up the mesa road and skidded back down, jackknifed. That's where Bry's been all afternoon, routing highway traffic, keeping flares lit. Other than that, I don't guess there's any action till Sally's opens tomorrow and all the pools pay off." He smiled at Bethann. "Thank you for starting my darlin's college fund."

"You're quite welcome. Do we have to announce this?"

"If we don't, Evan'll win in August."

"Well, I'm not fond of that prospect, either. Can't we just be quiet about the announcement? I'm not going to be able to show my face in town."

"Girl, people've been sleeping around out here for generations. At least in your case, nobody's still married."

"Words of wisdom, Edna Earle. Gee, if I were Bethann, I'd be comforted." Sam finished his glass of tea. "You ready to go or you content to live in those clothes for a few days?"

"I'll do the dishes, Edna Earle. Go on."

Reluctantly, she rose and followed him out to the car. Bethann shut the door behind them, smiling as she heard yet another spat begin. They sounded like an old married couple, their patter so well practiced each of them actually needed it.

She cleared the table, refrigerated the leftovers, took another piece of cornbread. The dishes were washed before she heard the tires again. Record time for a roundtrip to the next place. The heat of their argument must have melted the ice.

She opened the door, only to find Bry standing there. Bethann fought the impulse to reach for him, pull him into the comfort and warmth of her arms. Instead, she moved away from the opening and he entered. Watching her carefully, he put his hat on the rack, removed his heavy coat and hung it. It was as if he expected her at any moment to ask him to leave.

"Have you had supper?"

"I didn't even have lunch."

She indicated the table. "Have a seat. I'll reheat some soup."

He scraped a chair out and sat down, watching her as she poured a hearty portion and microwaved it back to life. The cornbread was still warm. She set butter beside it, poured his tea. As she served him, his hand shot out and grabbed her wrist. "I'm not going to live like this, Bethann. Out with it! Was once enough? I really thought we'd make it for at least a month." There was both anger and desperation in his voice.

She gnawed at her lower lip. Were those McLeod lips that asked that question? Had she been drawn to him for some slight familiarity that she strained now to see? Nevermind that everyone on both sides of the family had always sworn Marsh Fox couldn't have looked like a McLeod if he'd tried. He'd acted like them, and that was quite enough for all concerned, thank you. She stood there, her wrist held firmly in Bry's grasp and had to make the decision she'd avoided all afternoon. Was it to be 'yes, Bry, once was more than enough' or 'how long do you think we have before the dueling duo get back?'?

His eyes bored into hers while his hold on her wrist tightened. He expected an answer from her, and he expected it now.

Her words were caught in her throat as it closed around them and her chest tightened. The instant he had touched her, her decision had been made. "The deal was eight months at the outside."

"I know that." His grip relaxed and he gently tugged on her. She came willingly, straddling his lap as he moved the chair away from the table. "Woman, that's a position that'll get you in trouble."

"I'm already there." They kissed, their ardor intensifying significantly with each breath.

"All I thought about all day was you, was your not wanting me again." He stopped kissing her, held her face with his hands, rubbed his thumbs on her cheeks. "I thought my time had run out."

"Your time—our time—*is* going to run out. August, Bry. Please don't think this can last past August." She bent to kiss him again and little sobs broke through her breath.

"Bethann, don't cry." He held her gently away from

him. "It'll be a rip-roaring spring and summer." He quirked a smile at her, then pulled her to him, edged the slit of her lips with his tongue, took her breath away.

She drew back and gave him a half-smile. "The biggest question on my mind is how long Sam and Edna Earle have yet to be gone."

"I guess it depends on what kind of loving you have in mind."

"Given how slow my day has been, hard and fast would do."

"Damn, but I can handle that."

He stood, taking her with him, her legs encircling his waist. They rubbed noses. The tears disappeared in a laugh as she realized just exactly what he did have in mind.

He dropped her with the first sound of tire chains.

Edna Earle made more noise coming in than both she and Sam had going out. She called a 'thank you' to Sam as she opened the kitchen door. They sat side by side, Bry sipping soup, Bethann idling destroying a piece of cornmeal. Pen and Tux had finally been drawn out of their stupor and sat in a chair, peering over the table top. Edna Earle swatted them out, excused herself, and made for the guest room, pulling a duffle bag behind her.

Bry grabbed Bethann's hand. "Let's go feed the horses."

They grabbed their coats and ran like children, jumping from tire track to tire track to the entrance of the barn. It was warm inside, Range and Rover looking none the worse for the cold weather but ready to have more hay distributed their way. After he had tended to them, Bry turned to Bethann. "Why don't we stay out here a while?"

"Why, you devil, we'll get cold."

"We'll think of something." He caught her around the waist, brought her to him, pulled her hips to his, moved against her slowly. She was a willing participant, pulling his mouth down to hers, exploring with her tongue, while her hands slid under his coat and removed his shirt from his pants.

"I want you," escaped her lips.

He scooped her up and carried her to the dislodged hay. Stripping off his heavy coat, he put it beneath her as he gently laid her down. They pulled back slightly from each other. "Hard and fast is still fine with me, Bry."

"A decision, no doubt, influenced by the temperature."

"My internal thermometer." She drew his clothed body down on top of hers and began undoing his belt. "I—"

He stopped all explanations with a kiss as he undressed her. She kicked off a tennis shoe and pulled one leg out of her jeans.

Hard. Fast. They didn't disappoint each other or themselves.

Lying in one another's arms, their clothes back on, the hay scattered around them, Bry slowly traced her ribs with his hand. She pecked a kiss on his neck.

"You seem distracted. Regrouping for another go at it?"

"I always knew women were insatiable if they'd just let themselves admit it." He kissed the tip of her nose. "Bethann, in our middle-aged wisdom, we've just had unprotected sex three times. You'd shoot Ted for less."

She raised her head to look down at him. "Let's leave Ted out of this, although I'm not so naive as to think he hasn't at least come up on this decision. As for us, I last had sex over two years ago with a man with whom I was monogamous for twenty years. I have not just given you any disease."

He pulled her body onto his so they lay full length. "I last had sex about six years ago. One of Edna Earle's near-misses. She was a spinster. It was more of a desperation thing for us both. She married about a year later and has two kids now. I'd say you weren't in any danger either." He rested his hands on her hips and looked her squarely in the eye. "You're not too old for babies, are you?"

"Impending fatherhood got you down?"

"Unexpected would take some getting used to. Truth is, I've pretty well conceded to myself that I'm the end of the line. So, the only thing fatherhood might complicate is your leaving in August."

"Clever man. No dice. I developed severe endometriosis after Ted was born. Fought the good fight. Kept trying. Had a hysterectomy ten years ago."

"Well. Looks like we're back in business."

"Maybe yes. Maybe no." He raised his eyebrows in question. "When Sally opens for business tomorrow…"

He smiled at her naiveté. "You think this is still a secret? I hear they're working on double or nothing in two of the four pools."

She knitted her brows. "Double or nothing, what?"

"Depends on which side you take. But basically, it's whether or not my sexual prowess is enough to make you stay past August."

"You have got to be joking." But of course he wasn't. She slid off him and stood up, brushing the hay from her jeans and shirt, pictures of May June and Joe Tom's romp catapulting through her mind. The more things changed…

"I wish I were." He stood. "It's a terrible burden to put on an aging Lothario. I don't think my sexual ability was ever up to that." He shook the hay from his coat. "Not even when I was sixteen."

"Whose idea was double or nothing?"

He looked at her in disbelief.

"You're right. Stupid question. Only one mind really capable of it." She chewed her lip. "We're in a fish bowl."

"Basically, small town life is a fish bowl. You can't tell me you're not scrutinized by your friends in Atlanta. You're in a fish bowl there, too."

"Not where my sex life is concerned. Least not till Marsh died." Her hands were on her hips and she patted her right foot. "Well, you're not moving in."

"Damn, Bethann, I don't want to move in!" He put his coat on. "Nor do I intend to argue with you for eight months. Get it straight in your mind what you want and then be sure and tell me, okay?" His anger didn't surprise her.

She shrugged into her parka. "I'm sorry, Bry." She fiddled with the zipper, unable to get it to catch. He took the front of her jacket, got the placket started and zipped her up. She caught his hand as it came under her chin. "What do you really want, Bry?"

"It's not just sex. You know that." His eyes searched hers. "I love you. It's no secret. I want you to fall in love with me. I want you to stay."

"I don't want to hurt you."

"Unless you love me, you hurt me. Unless you stay, you hurt me. But I've accepted this affair on your terms—just until August. You made this bargain last night on the stairs. I suggest you stick to it as long as it's mutually satisfying."

She shut her eyes. "I'm not going to fall in love with you," she whispered. "I'm not going to let myself."

He kissed her eyelids. "Then just enjoy me and what we have. Think of me as an interesting chapter for your autobiography."

***

Bethann tapped her fingernails on the kitchen counter and watched the wall phone, as if staring would elicit a ring. Ted's quick in-and-out from the ski trip and back to college had produced in her the old hollow alone-feeling. She knew what would fill it. Who could fill it. Now was the time to take stock of all these feelings, to put her mental house in order, to realize that the phone wasn't going to ring. It wasn't Bry's place to make it do so. It was hers.

She took the cup of decaf cappuccino to the table and sat down. Nursing it, she sought to come to grips with her emotions. She had been so cavalier when she'd told Bry only till August. In return, he had been nothing but honest with her—his love was open, on the table, there for the taking. But she wouldn't let herself take without giving in return. She wouldn't be a one-night stand. There was too much at stake.

Take, but don't fall in love. Purposefully hurt him? She couldn't do that—but hadn't she already?

Damn! She looked back at the phone, its silence a mute testimony to how he proposed to deal with the problem. It was her decision—when to love, when to leave.

Then there were the complicating factors. She twisted the silver bracelet, recalled the birthmark and Edna Earle's story. Did the knowledge he was a McLeod affect her at all?

Of course.

Would she tell him? No. Why hurt him even more?

She laid her head down in her arms. Almost on cue, Tux jumped on the table, rubbed her forehead with his nose, meowed. She stroked him absently-mindedly as he sniffed the cappuccino. "What do you think, boy? Think we need some more constant male companionship now that Ted's gone?"

Pen joined them, biting at her hair, one of his favorite games. She sat up, petted them both. "You're right. Put up or shut up." She went to the phone, lifted the receiver from the cradle, dialed the sheriff's office.

Corinne put her through immediately.

"Bry?"

"Yes?" Was that disinterest, disgust, or wariness in his voice?

"Lunch at Sally's?"

He gave a slight laugh. "And flaunt our misbehavior?"

"Ass."

"Gonna' have to sweeten that mouth up again for you."

She grinned. "Gonna' have to catch me first."

"Oh, I can catch you."

"Still haven't said yes for lunch."

"Yes."

"Bry, I haven't changed my mind about August."

"Bethann, let's just pretend August doesn't exist, okay?"

***

What a lie. What a wonderful, sweet lie. Edna Earle

watched Bethann give herself over to it, throw caution to the winds, indulge. Bry came to breakfast. Bethann joined him for lunch at Sally's where they ran separate tabs and paid weekly. Supper consisted of what Bethann had been honing all day. Edna Earle excused herself as soon as he showed up at the back door. He didn't stay the night—or he left earlier than her morning appearance.

Through all this, Edna Earle kept her comments and speculations to herself. She'd worked for this, asked for it. Now here it was in her lap, the culmination of four months of scheming. Bry loved Bethann. She saw it in the way he looked at her, touched her, spoke to her. Everyone else saw it too, commented on it liberally. It was the talk that kept the town warm during a frigid January. The sheriff was in love with Joe Tom's heir. It looked good on them both.

Chapter Twenty

Bethann left for the package service office in Chapelpeace immediately after breakfast the last day of January. Her trust of the postal service in general, and Evan in particular, did not extend to her cookbook. She was getting it to unbiased hands, as the publisher wanted a hard copy as well as the chapter attachments already emailed. Edna Earle made her eat a hearty breakfast. Bry kissed her good-bye at the gate and she sailed up the road for a day of shopping. All attempts to persuade Edna Earle to come with her for a girls' day out had failed. Edna Earle was going to babysit at Renita's and let the new mother have a half-day to herself. After all, the baby was now two months old and manageable. Bethann had smiled at this logic. She was sure Edna Earle just wanted to check on Renita's mothering skills.

The cookbook on its way, Bethann spent the day shopping for items other than food. She ventured into a western store and bought new jeans and a shirt, a belt with a silver buckle, and earrings inlaid in a pattern similar to her bracelet. She bought six extremely fine steaks, two for the table, four for the freezer, put them in the ice chest, and headed for Cummings in time to arrive by nightfall. She checked with Bry on the cell phone as she reached the halfway point.

In general, she felt pleased with herself and her current mood. In about a month she'd proof the cookbook, in three, hold the finished product in her hands. Her exile in Cummings would not have been wasted in the least little bit. In the meantime, she'd occupy herself in the attic and read all the books on the bedside table. At night, she'd have Bry. She'd be well occupied for the next seven months.

The sensors clicked on as she rounded the house. Bry wasn't here yet. The garage door opened, she parked the SUV and grabbed about half the packages.

On the top step, she pulled up short. The flap of the pet door was missing. Pen and Tux huddled on the woodpile. They never greeted her outside. "Been up to something bad, boys? Unexpected visitors? Raccoon?" She put her packages down on the porch and gingerly touched the back door. It wasn't completely shut and swung open without her code.

Bethann stood in the doorway and muttered epithets unfit for a daughter of the South. The water dispenser was smashed, the kitchen floor shiny from the water's path to where it pooled under the washer and dryer. The cat pan was upturned. All the cabinets were open, their contents discarded on the floor. The freezer was emptied. Through the kitchen door to the hall, she caught a glimpse of similar destruction in the living room.

Backing away from the door, Bethann turned and

looked around the yard. No one else seemed to be around. She returned to the car and grabbed the cell phone from the front seat. The sheriff's department couldn't answer fast enough to suit her. "I need Bry."

The night deputy was already on duty. "He should be headed out to your place, Bethann."

"Find him and make sure he is." Too shaken to continue, she pushed the end button and settled in the front seat to wait. Pen and Tux came over and she pulled them in with her. The noise must have been extreme, Bethann thought as she stroked them to calm them down, since they considered the car their enemy, feared for trips to the vet, good only for paw printing.

Ten minutes later, Bry flew up the drive, Sam's car roaring behind. The cats leapt back to the woodpile as Bethann ran to meet them. Bry was barely out of the car before she was dragging him up the steps, pointing through the back door. He stood there as she had. Sam looked over his shoulder. "Jiminey…"

"I didn't go in, Bry. Didn't want to destroy evidence. Didn't want to find anybody." He held out an arm to her and she sheltered herself next to him. "Pen and Tux actually got in the car with me. It must have been terrible."

"Least we know where Edna Earle was all day," Sam commented dryly. "Renita kinda' took advantage time-wise." He seemed embarrassed. "I'll circle round the house, see where they got in first."

"Thank God, you weren't home." Bry drew her even

nearer.

"They were waiting for me to be gone, Bry. They knew when. This took some time."

"I know." He nuzzled the top of her head. "At least you didn't forget something and come back. Strong enough to go in?" He stepped into the kitchen, the water on the linoleum squishing under his boots. "Try and touch as little as possible. We'll get some forensic help."

Together they ventured into the hall, peered into the living room. Both couches were overturned, the books off the shelves, the rugs torn from their new sites as art. The mantles were cleared, one wing chair slashed, its old filling spilling onto the quilts thrown to the floor.

Sam reappeared just as they found the original window of entry in the computer room. "My backup hard drive is gone. More power to them. My files are password-protected."

The fax and computer were on. "Not a good sign. I turned everything off before I left." She touched the pad and the opening screen showed. "I think we're talking unsophisticated computer thieves."

"Vandal was the word I had in mind," Bry answered. "Let's check upstairs."

The story was the same in each of the bedrooms. Drawers were emptied, mattresses pulled off the frames, contents of closets thrown into the middle of the rooms. In the Joe Tom room, both Bethann and Bry checked the attic entrance. It was undisturbed.

"What do you think?" Sam asked as they met in the

kitchen. "Did they find what they wanted?"

"First impression—no." Bry continued to look around the room, as if a definitive clue to the vandals would show itself. "This looks more like a search mission gone sour. When whatever they wanted didn't appear, they wreaked havoc." He looked at Bethann. "Anything missing besides the back up?"

"Not on first glance. It'll take putting it all back to know for sure. But the Remington is here, the Navajos are unhurt, even those tacky horseshoe rodeo figures are all accounted for." She shook her head. "This would be a lot easier if May June'd just call and ask for whatever it is she thinks I have."

Sam raised his eyebrows. "Why don't you go ask, Bry?"

"Not a bad idea." Edna Earle appeared at the back door. "Called to check on something and the deputy said from Bethann's tone, all hell'd broken loose out here." She apprised the kitchen destruction. "No lie. Well, are you just going to stand there, or are we going to take pictures and then clean this mess up?"

Bry stared at her. "Why don't you just run for sheriff next time, Edna Earle?"

"Well, I could do it. Now why don't you do as Sam suggested and go bury the hatchet with that old bitch and find out what she wants?"

"You honestly think she'll tell me?"

"No. Didn't tell you where I thought you ought to bury it!"

***

Three hours later the destruction was properly recorded on film. Fingerprint dusting around the entry window revealed nothing. "Could have told you they wore gloves," Edna Earle grumbled from the kitchen where she vigorously mopped the floor after getting permission to do so.

Bethann sullenly checked the contents of the freezer. "They must have come early this morning, Bry. Most of this is ruined." She tossed chicken, vegetables, and frozen homemade broth into a large garbage bag.

"Why don't you two stop right there and finish this in the morning?" He tied the bag for her. "You go sleep over at Edna Earle's."

"No, Bry. Edna Earle can sleep here."

"Only way I'll sleep here is if Bry goes and sees May June. Even then, I'm putting Joe Tom's sawed-off shotgun by the pillow."

"Hold it right there! All we need is you shooting something up in the middle of the night." He held up his hands and turned to Bethann. "Damned if you're spending the night here—"

Bethann settled her hands on her hips. "Sam has put plyboard over the window and the pet door. You think moving out for a night will solve anything? Think again. They knew the place was empty. They meant *me* no harm! I only have two nights away left. This isn't one of them."

"You won't have any nights left if they hurt you."

"No use, Bry. I have to stay here."

He turned to Edna Earle. "What good do you think my going to May June will do?"

"Lord, boy, check your uniform. You're the sheriff. Anyway, someone has to start somewhere. What harm will it do?"

He shook his watch clear of his sleeve. "You stay tonight, I'll go in the morning."

"I'm not much in the way of protection, especially if you won't let me use the shotgun." She finished the floor with a flourish. "Why don't you stay?"

Bry looked over at Bethann and drew a deep breath. "Because..."

"Edna Earle's right, Bry. What's she going to do I can't? I'm quite capable of staying by myself, but if you're scared for me, you stay."

Bry studied Bethann, but spoke to Edna Earle. "I'll stay the night, see May June in the morning."

"Good. I'm pooped." She put the broom and mop in the corner, took off her apron. "What with watching that kid all day while Renita had the complete to-do at the beauty shop—I hope you get my five hours' worth of babysitting's good tonight," she commented acerbically to Sam. "I'll be back early, Bethann. Be up and dressed and let's get this place fixed. Can't stand a messy house," she grumbled as she went out the back door.

"Need me for anything else, Bry?" Sam stood by the

door, hat in hand.

"No, go on."

"How 'bout in the morning? You need me to go to May June's with you?"

Bry looked at him steadily. "I can handle it. I have all night to adjust my attitude."

Sam left, carrying out the spoiled food as he went, to dump it in Sally's trash bin.

They stood apart, not looking at each other till Bry moved to her, tipped her chin up. She slid into his arms, the first tears of the day splashing down her cheeks as she released her fear. He held her, stroking her back, smoothing her hair. "If you'd been home…"

"Shhh." She put her fingers to his lips. "I'm so tired. Let's go to bed."

They remade her bed with clean sheets. Nestling close to each other, she finally slept. Pen and Tux pushed her off her pillow to his. Bry laid awake until two, hearing every creak of the boards and whistle of the wind. He'd promised to see May June in the morning, and there'd be no peace from Edna Earle until he did. Whatever would he say? How could he bridge a lifelong gulf?

Bethann stirred in his arms, turning to face him, bury herself deeper in his embrace. He bussed her forehead. He'd find the words.

***

He could not have felt more awkward when he was fifteen. Standing in her glass-walled garden room, her stiff back to him as she sat in that old wicker chair at the breakfast table, all the years washed away. It didn't matter he was a grown man, an elected official, a respected member of his chosen community. He was fifteen again, an orphan, and the woman he came to see was a phantom grandmother.

She spoke first, the bun of white hair moving with the cadence of her words. "Cain said you wanted to see me. I don't usually receive visitors this early in the morning. He said you were insistent."

That was one way to put it. He hadn't turned on the sirens this time, but he had misused his elected office a bit. It was nine o'clock, for Chrissakes, she could damn well see him!

"Cat got your tongue?"

That line hadn't changed. He took a deep breath and stepped further into the room. Millie had taken his hat at the door or he'd have been twisting it in his hands.

"Come where I can see you."

He moved to stand on the other side of her breakfast table and watched her as she looked him up and down. Her blue eyes were paler than he remembered. Her nose seemed larger, her cheeks sunken. Her fingers lay lightly on the china plate in front of her and the veins on the backs of her hands were prominent. May June was a frail imitation of the woman he'd last seen fifteen years before. "You look like your grandfather."

"May June…"

"Well, I guess I haven't deserved the title of grandmother, have I?" She indicated a chair. "Coffee?" Her voice was taut.

"I'll only be a minute, May June. I've come about the break-in at Bethann's." He refused to sit, instead leaned with his hands on the back of the wicker chair she'd indicated.

"Joe Tom's squatter niece-in-law. Those Eastern gals always did think they were better than everyone else. Just move in."

"You know that's not the case. Joe Tom insisted she live there as a term of inheritance."

"I hear there were many inheritors."

"May June—"

"You'll not call me grandmother even once?"

Bry shifted his weight. Why had he let Edna Earle talk him into this? Nevermind that it was what he was supposed to do. "Grandmother—"

"You inherited off that old scoundrel?"

"You know I did."

"And that Taylor boy. Well, that was fair enough. But Edna Earle getting back what that popinjay of a husband of hers lost in a poker game. Joe Tom must have been senile when he did that." She buttered a piece of toast, broke it, slathered it with homemade jam from a mason jar.

"I am not here to discuss the terms of Joe Tom's will."

"Well, you should be." She turned faded blue eyes on him. "You going to quit being sheriff? Ranch?"

"I haven't decided."

"Can't very well decide until that Georgia gal goes home, can you? Hear you're practically living together." He expected 'blood will tell' to follow, but it didn't.

Bry leaned onto the table. Enough of this game. "May—Grandmother, what do you want from Bethann? Is there something in Joe Tom's house? Tell me, I'll get it for you. Do you just not want to see her inherit out of spite? Did you hate Joe Tom that much?"

"Too many questions. I have no idea what you're talking about."

"Bull!"

"Don't cuss. Your mouth always was dirty."

Well, Bry thought, Cain beat that out of me thirty years ago._Okay, one step at a time._ "You had the barn burned."

"Proof?"

"Your Jeep was seen on the property."

"That was months ago. Where are the charges?"

Bry flexed his right hand. "She didn't pursue it."

"Sure you don't want coffee?"

"All the motion lights were tampered with New Year's."

"Proof?"

"None. Harassment. Just to keep her on her toes."

"Did it work?"

"House was vandalized yesterday. Place looks like

hell. But I don't think they found whatever they were looking for. Still, her backup hard drive was stolen." May June jerked slightly at the news, as if it was unexpected. "It just contained her recipe book. If you're that hard up for a new menu, wait like everyone else and buy a copy in this spring."

Her composure returned. "Again, proof it was me?"

"None. No fingerprints."

She dabbed at her mouth with a linen napkin. "I'm sorry your friend is having so much trouble adjusting here. I never thought of Cummings as being unfriendly." She looked at him. "Perhaps you are not as conscientious in your job of sheriff as you should be. When is the next election?"

"May June, let's get something straight. She's not leaving till the terms of the will are fulfilled. She's shown that. Hell, she married a McLeod-Fox mix. That's stern stuff. So if this is just harassment, something to fill your empty days, give it up. Leave her be." He measured his words. "If there's a piece of Joe Tom memorabilia you want, let me know. I'll get it for you." He turned to go.

"Tell her I'll take two copies of the book."

Bry opened his mouth to retort, thought better of it and strode out the front door. Millie stood there with his hat. Outside, Cain Stevens was by the truck.

"Pleasant visit with your grandmother?"

Bry bit back the words, got in, and drove away.

Two days later, the hard drive was returned by first

class mail. The postmark was Dallas.

***

It took a week to get things back right in the house. The insurance adjuster puttered around for five hours the day after the vandalism. Pictures notwithstanding, he chastised them for cleaning up the kitchen and Bethann's bedroom. Edna Earle was all set to put him straight until Bethann silenced her with a look. They didn't offer him lunch.

As the month progressed and the days lengthened, Bethann and Bry took to riding over the ranch in his off hours. They'd sit on the hill, draw the houseplans in the dirt, measure off a driving range, decide the size of the putting greens. There was a somberness to all this. She would see it to fruition through the spring and summer, but she'd not be there to enjoy it with him in the fall.

She talked less and less to Kiki and Ted over the computer, spending her evenings with Bry, but not her nights. After his talk with May June and the return of the hard drive, they felt surely the incidents were over.

***

Edna Earle kept her prediction that affairs only lasted six months to herself. There would be no self-fulfilling prophecies here. She saw the small line of bitterness on Bry's face, the sadness in Bethann's eyes. It was March and they were already mourning August.

She wasn't the only one who felt it, saw it. The populace of the county had benefited early on from his increased good humor. A sheriff in love is much easier to deal with than one whose attitude constantly bordered on 'out of sorts.' Bry, who had had to fight for their respect, now for the first time, unexpectantly garnered their love. No one wanted him to be hurt, the betting pools at the Grille and elsewhere notwithstanding. But he was going to get his heart trounced on in August. While this possibility had held a certain amusement for them in the fall, their newfound empathy with him made the inevitable outcome sobering. As spring warmed, the citizens of Cummings took stock.

No one had a solution. Not even Edna Earle.

Chapter Twenty-One

It was the week before spring break. From the tone in Ted's voice, Bethann knew what was coming. "Mom, about next week…"

"Um-hum?" Let him suffer a little. She wasn't that easy of a mark. She finished filing the nails on one hand, shifted her weight as she sat on top of the dryer, and began filing the other.

"Gina's sorority and my fraternity have these condos rented down at Panama City and, of course, I didn't sign up, but there's an opening…"

"And you want permission to leave your poor old mother alone again?"

"Mo-om," he drew the word out, let a touch of exasperation creep in.

"Be honest, how long have you known about this opportunity?"

A pause, then, "Christmas."

"Um-hum. Theodore Thomas, when did you sign up?"

"Mom—" She clicked her nails on the receiver. "I put down a deposit in February."

"Thought an end run was best?"

237

"Sorta'."

"Sure you're not wanting to run off to fun in the sun because Thomas and Lanelle are due through sometime in the next three weeks and you just might run into them?"

"Really, are they coming?"

He probably knew the exact day. "Go to Florida. Don't do anything there you couldn't do here." She rushed to get the rest in before he hung up in triumph. "And I expect you here three days after your last exam— no excuses!"

"Yes, ma'am." His relief was evident as he rushed to change the subject. "How's Bry?"

"Fine."

"Just fine?"

"If you want a detailed analysis, I'll put Edna Earle on."

"You are still seeing him?" A touch of genuine concern showed itself in his voice.

"Breakfast, lunch, and most nights dinner."

"You just don't sound real happy, that's all."

She hadn't told him about the vandalism. After all, there was nothing he could do. "No, sweetie, I'm as happy as I can be. I've seen the proof of the book—it's a winner—and the weather's warming up. I'm going to tackle the attic any day now. Only little cloud is T and L's imminent arrival. I don't know if Cummings is ready for them or vice versa. Come on, give mom a break. When did they say they'd be here?"

"'Bout the time I hit the beach."

"You're a peach. Don't sunburn too badly."

"Love ya', Mom."

***

"Darling," the voice sang its way over the line. "Guess where we are?"

"Where, Mother?" Bethann freshened her coffee and prepared for a siege.

"At your jail! Can you imagine? Ted said your housekeeper worked here on the weekends and I think we've met her. Ella, is it?" She lowered her voice as she obviously tried to whisper into the phone. "Isn't she a little old for the job?"

"Edna Earle, Mother. You'd be surprised at what she's young enough to do. Shall I come get you?" Bethann had hoped to keep Edna Earle and her parents separated for as long as possible. As to Bry...

"Oh, no, she's given us very good directions. Don't you want to come have lunch first? That's what Ella said you usually do. With Barry somebody?"

"Bry, Mother. His name is Bry. And sometimes we have lunch. Put Ella on, will you?" She heard the phone changing hands. "Listen, Ella," she emphasized the name, "what are you trying to do to me? Thomas and Lanelle in Sally's right off the bat? Are you nuts? And with Bry? Where is he anyway?"

"Putting the finishing touches on the Wilson boys

next door. When can we expect you?" Her voice ranged into a sweetness Bethann had never heard.

"Why don't you take about a week's vacation? Like you used to do for Joe Tom when I'd come?"

"Wouldn't hear of it. Haven't had this much fun since September."

"You're fired."

"I don't think so. See you in fifteen. Shall I send them on down?"

"I'll get them there."

***

Lunch with Thomas and Lanelle at Sally's Grille, noon, a Saturday, front booth the only one available. Might as well have sold tickets. Business picked up steadily as word spread that the two responsible for Bethann had shown up. When Bry came late, slid in by Bethann and put his arm on the booth back behind her, Bethann watched Lanelle's lips purse. Thomas, on the other hand, merely raised an eyebrow when Bry told Sally he would just have coffee and pie on account of a late breakfast. "Yeah, that's what Bethann said, too," was the owner's dry comment, topped off with a wink at Thomas. Bethann's stomach dropped and she smiled weakly at her parents.

"Well," Bry began, "how long you folks planning on staying?"

Lanelle delicately wiped at the corners of her mouth

with the thin paper napkin. Putting her fork down from chasing the peach half around the diet plate, she answered. "The bluebonnets weren't quite ready when we came through the Hill Country so we thought we'd give them at least another week, then circle back south. It's been a long time since we've stayed with Bethann a week." She smiled.

Thomas cut another piece of chicken fried steak and glared at Bry. "Too damn long."

Bry took his arm off the back of the seat as Sally served him coffee and coconut cream pie. Bethann had finished hers but was occupying herself by slowly turning her mug in circles by its handle. Bry ate with his right hand and rested his left on Bethann's knee. She crossed her legs and deftly moved out of his polite reach.

Bethann spied Sam in a back booth, his cell phone clutched to his ear. He would pause from time to time and arch his neck her way. Giving Edna Earle a blow-by-blow play of the action undoubtedly. Just like the other phones being passed around for the same purpose.

"Is it usually this noisy in here?" Lanelle asked.

***

If Bethann thought it would be one very long week for her, Bry was convinced that one would seem like two. Thomas and Lanelle pulled the Pace Arrow into the area in front of the barn and plugged in. Bethann's attempts to have them stay in the house were to no avail.

They insisted on being as little trouble as possible. This way, in the RV, they had their own bedroom already fixed and no luggage needed to be moved. But they would love to eat the Atlanta Divines way again.

Saturday was benign enough. Bethann gave them the Grand Tour of Cummings County. Bry showed up in the evening to care for the horses, inquired if they wished to ride on Sunday. They did. Wonderful. Bethann would fix them all a picnic lunch.

He arrived bright and early Sunday morning with Sam's pickup and a borrowed trailer and horses. Lanelle surprised him by being quite cognizant about the animals and their gear. Halfway through their tour of his land, he let Thomas and Lanelle take the lead, made Bethann hold back. He brought Range over close to Rover. Nodding in the direction of Lanelle's disappearing rear, he commented, "Well, I see where you get your form."

"Such a wit, Sheriff."

"Ooh, pit time again. Thought I had that worked out of you." He grinned and raised his eyebrows.

"You know, this is how to make a week seem like a month." She narrowed her gaze at him. "No late nights. No late breakfasts."

"They don't know we're sleeping together?"

"Hell, no!"

Thomas and Lanelle turned around as if the vibrations from that hit their ears. Bethann waved and smiled and they sauntered on.

"Let me sweeten that mouth up."

Bethann stopped Rover with a quick turn. Bry followed suit. "Let's get something straight. This week we are friends. Only friends."

"You're kidding. Ted knows we're sleeping together. The whole town knows."

"Precisely. I am keeping them out of town. There's nothing to do there anyway. They like to play cards, read, putter. They love to play golf. Maybe you could call over to Chapelpeace and get them on the course. I've offered Edna Earle a vacation, but the old witch won't take it!"

"Southern belles don't have affairs, Scarlett?"

"Bethaaannn." Lanelle's voice carried on the still air. They were stopped on the house site. The surveyors had been out the week before and it was staked off. They'd picnic in the kitchen.

"Coming, Mother," she called back. "They don't have to know. There's no reason for them to." He sat silently. "Please, Bry. It would only hurt them."

"They loved Marsh so much they couldn't stand for you to be happy again?" There was derision in his voice.

"No." Her tone softened. "I mean, they loved Marsh. They've encouraged me to find someone else. They'll be disappointed if I don't. But how do I explain to them about an affair with a time limit?"

"I don't know, peach. You haven't been able to explain it to me yet." He urged Range on, leaving Bethann to follow.

***

243

Day to day survival. Monday, Edna Earle arrived early. "Well, what's on our agenda for today?" She sounded as chirpy as a tour guide.

"I thought we'd stay home and be bored. If we had silver, we'd polish it."

"There used to be some. Probably in the attic. We could look there."

"Oh, no, I'm not playing explorer with T and L in tow. Bry's supposed to get them on at Chapelpeace."

"Then I'm sure he will." She looked out the kitchen window. "Well, here come the dynamic duo now. They're both so astonishingly white-headed. Hard life raising you, dear? Where does that red come from anyway?"

"Lanelle's grandmother. Skipped two generations." She greeted them at the back door. "I believe you've met Edna Earle."

"Yes." Lanelle semi-ignored her, Thomas smiled brusquely and kissed Bethann on the cheek. "Sensor lights kept going on and off all night."

"Coyotes," Edna Earle volunteered as she poured the coffee and joined them for Bethann's cinnamon rolls and fruit compote.

"There are coyotes this close?"

"I've never seen any by the house," Bethann explained as she shot Edna Earle a warning look.

"Maybe it was the motion of the trailer. You two moving it any, Thomas?"

Lanelle blushed.

A very long week indeed.

***

Monday afternoon, at Lanelle's insistence, they drove to the nursery to get plants for the long neglected flower beds. Tuesday they would plant them, except Bry called with a tee time at Chapelpeace. They zipped out like the start of a marathon. "You know," Edna Earle commented as Bethann watered the ten flats of flowers, "I think they were glad to be rid of you, too. Where's Bry been?"

"That's an abrupt change of subject."

"Well?"

"At work, I guess. Range and Rover are in the pasture. They don't need much care right now."

"Um-hum. Whatever it is, you'd better call and straighten it out."

"He can straighten it out just as well as I can."

"Well, who's wrong this time?"

"He is."

"About?"

Bethann turned off the water faucet. "He doesn't see anything wrong with T and L knowing about us."

"And you do?"

"You don't?"

"Do you love him, Bethann?"

She was caught off-guard but quickly recovered. "That's neither here nor there, and certainly none of your business. Count the months. Five and I'm out of here!"

"If I were you, I'd go have lunch with him."

"Well, you're not me." She marched into the kitchen.

"Five months is a long time to do without what you've grown to like so much!"

***

"Sam, where is he?"

"In his office, Edna Earle. What's up? T and L giving you fits?"

She sighed. "Put him on."

He transferred the call. "Trouble at Chapelpeace?" Bry asked.

"Nah, they left outta here like jackrabbits. I don't think they'll make it a week. Why don't I go home now and you come on out here and straighten out this mess with Bethann?"

"Why don't you mind your own business?"

"You know I'm not going to do that. You two need to kiss and make up. Do it and get it over with, okay?"

"She knows where I am."

"I worked so hard this fall for you two. Truth is, Bry, I just don't have it in me anymore. I'm going home. Hopefully, I'll see you for breakfast tomorrow."

***

They met at the front gate, the SUV going out, the truck coming in. They got out, stood facing each other under the sign he'd carved. "Going to town?"

"Yeah. Coming to see to the horses?"

"Yeah." They stared at the ground then spoke at once.

"I'm sorry."

"Me, too."

"I'll tell them, Bry, if you want me to. God knows, I'm not ashamed."

"No, don't tell." He moved toward her and she came easily into his arms. "How could I face your father across the dinner table if I know he knows I'm sleeping with his baby?"

She grinned. "How long does it take to play a round of golf at Chapelpeace? They left an hour and a half ago."

"Oh, it'll be mid-afternoon before they're back. It's a beautiful day. Course ought to be crowded." He moved against her. "Why? You got something in mind that takes time?"

She moved her hands up his back. "Edna Earle got tired all of a sudden. Went home. Just me and the cats. I need a little amusement."

"Well, I can be a very amusing fellow."

***

Edna Earle mentally crossed the days off the calendar. Wednesday, the flats of flowers were planted. Thursday, more golf. Friday, Bethann took them riding once more. Bry joined them for breakfast and dinner each day.

Saturday morning, Edna Earle watched them double park the motor home in front of the sheriff's office.

Thomas came in alone and asked to speak to Bry. Edna Earle hustled out of the jail and into the main office where she could hear what was said.

"Yes, sir," she heard Bry start. "How may I help you?"

Thomas shut the office door firmly. She moved to the front windows and watched Lanelle sitting nonchalantly in the front seat of the motor home, filing her nails. How bad could it be if she stayed out there? Probably just a thank you for the golf and horses.

Thomas came out in five minutes, turned, shook hands with Bry, nodded succinctly in Edna Earle's direction and went to join Lanelle. Bry stood with Edna Earle at the window and watched them leave.

"I can't stand it. You have to tell me." She took his elbow in a vise grip.

He didn't look upset, only slightly pleased with himself. The grin began at one corner of his mouth and slowly spread across his face. "He told me he and Lanelle approved. Seems Ted has been easing them into the idea since Christmas. They aren't as thrilled with the affair as they would be marriage, but when I explained, he understood. I am, in Thomas Tyler's words," he couldn't help the smile that spanned his face, "to go for it."

Chapter Twenty-Two

Bethann stood on the top rung of the attic ladder and got the lay of the land. With Thomas and Lanelle gone, it was time to explore the attic. Bright April sunlight filtered in through the portholes. She reached up and exchanged the old dim bulb with a more powerful one, then dragged the droplight and one hundred foot extension cord to the far corner. Might as well be systematic. This was her April challenge, how she was going to work off the frustration of the cookbook being held up at the printer's.

Edna Earle called up at noon. "Lunch!" As Bethann's heels reappeared, she started in. "Why don't you drag some of that down here and do it in the light?"

Bethann slapped at her jeans and shirt, throwing dust everywhere. They both sneezed. "Why, you get lonely without me? Or are you just afraid I'll find something and not tell you about it?"

"I want you, I can stand on the step and yell. And you wouldn't know what to keep secret if it jumped up and—"

"Okay, okay. Let's get Bry to help us tonight."

Slowly, the attic emptied into the third bedroom. The

contents spilled into the hall. They bought a hundred heavy-duty trash bags and Bethann started separating into trash, museum, who-knows piles. No matter where she put an item, Edna Earle was likely to reclassify it.

It was slow going. More than a mere matter of throwing out with the CPA's approval, this was a history lesson. The original land deed emerged at the bottom of the trunk holding Annie Lee's mother's wedding dress. Letters of Civil War vintage had been carefully tied with pale pink ribbon and demanded to be read word for word when they were found. Original Sears Roebuck catalogs were stacked in a corner.

Two weeks into the clean out, only one trunk remained. They had already dispensed with the old light fixtures, the empty frames, the unmarked photos, the circa 1900 dresses. The aluminum Christmas tree was gone, the old shipping bills preserved in an album, the clothing declared unredeemable, burned. The Conestoga wagon lamps were back in the living room. The metal toys were lining the hall waiting refurbishing.

Bethann sat down to the final adventure on a Sunday afternoon. According to Edna Earle, several items of McLeod heritage were still missing: Marsh's Christmas angel, some silver pieces, the heirloom wedding rings Annie Lee had wanted to wear but hadn't been able to find. This was the last chance for any of this to appear.

She'd saved the largest trunk till last. The lock on it was new and wouldn't give to her impatient pulls. She remembered the set of keys on Joe Tom's dresser she had almost thrown away and retrieved them. The third small key slid in and sprang the lock. She opened the trunk carefully.

Unlike the others, the inside lining was still intact. On top, nested in a World War II army uniform was the Christmas angel. She was porcelain, her wings still whole, gossamer thin. Someone had lovingly rescued her and given her a respectful home. Bethann gingerly carried her into her bedroom and put her on the dresser. Next to her in the trunk, Bethann found the silver service, teapot, creamer, and sugar bowl wrapped in silver cloth. Bethann set them aside also.

The rest of the trunk was just as lovingly handled. The old army uniform that had cradled the angel and silver showed signs of frequent refolding. Someone had cared for it and the flag underneath. Joe Tom? Below it was a suit of men's dress clothes of the same vintage, silver cufflinks, a braided leather and silver bolo tie. Special clothes preserved for what?

The answer revealed itself in a folded piece of paper, tucked into the McLeod family Bible that Edna Earle had said she'd not seen since Annie Lee had died some twenty-two years before. Bethann opened it to the marked spot, reverently allowing her fingers to trace the old fountain pen ink that detailed the lineage of McLeods back to the 1820 arrival of one Jonathan Angus McLeod in New York City. She followed to the birth of Joe Tom and then Annie Lee, through to the marriage that gave her Marsh.

Her fingers stopped. New ballpoint ink marred the faded blue lines. Next to Joe Tom's name was another, written in an old man's scrawl Bethann recognized as his. Next to Joe Tom's name on the marriage line was that of May June Bright.

"Oh, hell." Bethann involuntarily shivered and opened the yellowed document that had been the marker. In fading letters, dated some seventy years previous, an Oklahoma marriage license declared Joe Tom and May June to be married. Stamped, legal. This was the object of May June's desires. The reason for her fear. The vandals must have been searching for the family Bible. May June knew this damning piece of evidence existed.

Bethann returned her attention to the Bible. Pencil marks now drew her attention. Rae Bright Cummings, followed by Bright Cummings Phillips.

"Oh, Joe Tom." He had known. And never told? Never threatened May June with exposure? Was the mere threat of it his revenge for her bogus marriage?

Bethann sat there for an hour, fingering the documents. The sound of Bry's tires in the drive drove her into action. He'd been foraging in the attic ruins with her at night. He couldn't see this. She hastily put everything back, slammed the lid and met him at the back door.

***

Ill-gotten knowledge led to no sleep for Bethann that

night. It burned within her. She met Edna Earle at the kitchen door Monday morning.

Edna Earle raised her eyebrows as she tied the apron about herself. "Shoot."

"May June's a bigamist."

"What brought you to this revealing conclusion?" Edna Earle poured their coffees, set them on the table, sat down herself. Bethann still paced.

"The last trunk. No wedding rings, but Marsh's angel, the family silver, the family Bible, Joe Tom's wedding clothes."

Edna Earle spewed her coffee. "What?" She wiped her mouth. "No." She drew the word out, the realization coming to her.

"You said Rae was born in winter. Exactly when did you see Joe Tom and May June in the barn?"

"April."

"When in April?"

"Well, I know I'd already worn my new Easter coat. A little research would narrow it down."

"Okay, we'll do that." Bethann thought outloud as she sipped her coffee. "I figure they eloped and you more than likely viewed the consummation. He goes to the army, she has second thoughts about her hasty behavior and the rest is history."

"You still haven't told me the evidence you found."

"The marriage certificate."

"Ooh. Let's see May June squirm."

"It gets better."

"It couldn't possibly."

"Joe Tom knew—or at least heavily suspected—about Rae and, therefore, about Bry. He wrote them into the family Bible. From the change of ink, I think he waited till Annie Lee died, maybe even until Marsh did, because the scrawl and ink for Marsh's death is the same as Joe Tom's marriage. Rae and Bry are in pencil." She finally sat down. "This is what May June's been after. Now, do I give it to her and get her off my back? Or keep holding the invisible threat like Joe Tom did? She's only guessing I might find out."

"How about Bry?"

"Let's settle May June first."

"Well, of course, I probably see this in a little different light than you. I'm not nearly as generous."

"You'd tell and threaten her."

"I'd make sure she deeded to Bry. Or be exposed and risk losing it all in a Cummings shoot out. Talk about messy. Nothing like money to bring out the worst in relatives."

"Tempting. Before her death even?"

"Hell, yes. Old broad'll live another ten years."

"What if I do nothing?"

"What if she advances her threats? She's bound to know you're in the attic. Missy Smith's just the worst gossip. If you think the volunteer head of the museum hasn't told that you're cleaning out again…"

"In that case, I'm surprised she hasn't attacked."

"Me, too."

They sat silently. "What about Bry?" Edna Earle ventured.

"Jeez. Talk about hard. Lied like a dog last night, Edna Earle. Told him I did nothing in the attic yesterday. Kept him away from everything."

"He is a legitimate McLeod."

"An illegitimate Cummings."

"He'll do better as May June's heir than Joe Tom's."

"He's already been Joe Tom's. Unless he challenged Ted."

"He wouldn't do that."

"To quote: Nothing like money to bring out the worst in relatives."

"If Joe Tom knew, then he divided it as he wished."

"So we're agreed to say nothing."

"Gave you my opinion. Worth what you paid for it." She pushed away from the table. "We'd better put on our happy faces. Bry'll be here any minute."

***

Happy faces. Guilty minds. Bethann and Edna Earle put everything but the silver service back in the trunk and dragged it into the Joe Tom room. They covered it with a quilt. They told no one.

Four weeks late, the definitive Atlanta Divines cookbook arrived. One case was shipped to Bethann, the rest to Kiki and their distributor. They popped champagne over the webcam that night, celebrated in separate kitchens. Even late, it was all they had hoped it would be. Bethann parceled her case out for favors, notably the phone and electrical work done in October. Sally took a dozen for the Grille to sell. They were gone by noon.

Ted came in from school when the semester ended. The smile on his face, the brisk hug, the peck on the cheek—Bethann knew something was up. "What you want, sweetie?"

"Well, I've been thinking." Bethann and Edna Earle exchanged quick glances. Now what? "It's really not fair to you for me to take four years to get through college when with summer school, I could do it in three. Get on to grad school quicker."

"Joe Tom's still paying for this, Ted. I don't see how it's not fair to me."

Edna Earle freshened the iced tea, pursed her lips, raised an eyebrow in Bethann's direction.

He finished the pie, pushed the plate to the middle of the table. "I thought I might stay closer to home. SMU, Dallas."

"Don't suppose Gina's taking any courses there this summer."

"She's thinking about it." He let out a long breath. "I mean, what am I going to do here this summer?"

"Well, I thought you might keep me company. What am I going to do?"

"What have you been doing?"

"Biding my time."

"Do I have to bide it, too?"

"Where is Mr. Loyal and True Blue who was going to be with me to the bitter end? Whose inheritance are we talking about?"

"I thought we both won on this."

"You'd better be a lawyer, son. I'd hate to think this argumentative attitude was wasted in some other profession."

He grinned broadly at her and got up. "I'm going to run into town. Shall I stop at Delmar's and get a check?"

They heard the tires squeal on the way out. Dust rose into the open windows. "Can't believe you gave him an argument about that."

"I really looked forward to one more piece of time with him."

"Bethann, he's nineteen. He's grown. Got to let him go."

"Well, that's pretty easily said if I was in Atlanta." She leaned back in the chair and closed her eyes. "Getting the cookbook made me homesick."

Edna Earle sat back down and patted her hand. "You got three and a half months left. Surely you can handle it. Maybe Bry can kiss it and make it better."

She opened her eyes. "The thought has actually crossed my mind that when I get to Atlanta, I'm still going to be homesick."

***

Four hours later, Bry brought Ted home, their tread heavy up the back steps, their typical light banter gone. Bethann looked up from the washing. "Where's your car?"

"Stolen."

"What?"

"We've put out a bulletin on it," Bry explained as he opened the refrigerator, helped himself to a beer. "He parked it in front of the jail and when he comes out, it's gone. Sort of an 'in your face' steal."

"Bolder than brass," Bethann murmured. "What would anyone want with a three-year-old car?"

"I'm sorry, Mom."

"Not your fault. Did you lock it?"

"It was in front of the jail."

"Who do you think hangs out there?"

Bry shook his head. "Enough. Nothing we can do till it turns up."

***

Bry showed up the next evening with knitted eyebrows and a closed expression. "You're not going to like this," he said as he moved to the sink and started washing his hands. They were covered with grease and soot. "Highway patrol found the car about a hundred miles from here over in the canyons. Burned."

"Burned? Bry, you don't think May—"

"I don't know what to think." He leaned on the sink

258

as he dried his arms with a kitchen towel. "They've hauled it in. It's down at the Wilson's Garage. Unredeemable. Insured?"

"Yeah." She puffed out her cheeks and blew slowly. "This is the last straw, you know that."

He nodded. "You want to bring charges?"

"Can we prove anything?"

He shook his head. "We had them in October and I let them go."

"What are you two talking about?" Ted asked as he came into the kitchen.

"Bunch of trouble that doesn't concern you."

"I think you need to tell him all of it, Bethann. He's a target just like you are. Somehow the stakes have been upped."

"Mom?"

"Basically, you get to go to both semesters of summer school."

His mother's trials the past nine months put before him, Ted wanted to stay the summer with her. He was furious. "What are they after?"

"Don't know," Bry answered.

Bethann remained silent. This was going to end and it was going to end tomorrow.

Chapter Twenty-Three

Bethann was admitted to May June's estate with little difficulty. The problem was keeping her eyes on the driveway and not darting from side to side, from flower beds bursting with geraniums and begonias to the tree-lined boulevard she inched the SUV down. The grounds were as lush as any golf course she had ever encountered. There were even sheep dotted around, giving the place a pastoral English air. Money, time, and taste—that was all it must take to live like a queen in the middle of nowhere.

She pulled into the area in front of the house. The door of the SUV was opened unceremoniously by a young man who introduced himself as Dan Kincaid.

"She's waiting in the house for you." His tone was formal, condescending, as he indicated the opened front door. "Millie'll show you in." The uniformed housekeeper, a fifty-ish woman with a no-nonsense scowl, waited in the doorway. Bethann pocketed her keys, grabbed a cardboard box from the front seat and went up the steps.

If the grounds were merely tasteful, then the interior was regal. The wooden floors shone where they weren't covered with Oriental or Navajo rugs. The furniture was straight from a manor house, the light fixtures brass and glass. There were stone fireplaces in each room they passed. At the back, a glassed-in garden room ran the width of the house. Here were wicker and bentwood, floral chintzes, a glass table, four sets of French doors opening to a stone patio. It was a room with the unmistakable stamp of a woman, a room where the weather would set the mood, a room where every footstep would echo, every laugh become a howl, every tear become a storm.

"Mrs. Fox," Millie announced.

It took Bethann a moment to find to whom she spoke, then a rocker moved slightly, and Bethann saw May June. She was turned toward a window, surveying the barns or perhaps watching the colts visible in the near pasture. She croaked, "Go on and bring the tea things," then lifted her left hand in dismissal.

Millie left Bethann standing in the doorway. She felt like the orphaned niece, the lowly ward, dumped on the spinster aunt's doorstep in a nineteenth century novel. Hell with this! She was the one that had requested the audience, not vice versa. She moved into the room.

The rocker tilted, turned, and ice blue eyes were leveled upon her. She raised her left hand and beckoned. "I believe you asked to see me. Come here, come here." Bethann went closer. "Sit, sit."

She obeyed, lowering herself into the adjoining rocker, putting the box she carried on the cold stone floor at her feet. "I don't see so well anymore, so my guests must be close. A red head. I'd heard as much." She settled back. "I do hope you like hot tea, although it would seem to be a bit warm for it. Millie will get you iced, if you wish."

"I like hot tea." May June couldn't have weighed a hundred pounds. It was hard to imagine a woman so small wielding so much power, demanding so much fear. There didn't seem to be anything of her in Bry, at least not physically, unless it was the stubborn set of the clenched jaw.

Millie set the silver tea service and bone china cups on the table between them and left. "Please serve, Mrs. Fox. My hands shake sometimes." May June looked to the outside again.

"Please call me Bethann. Would you like sugar, cream?"

"And my name is May June. The old formalities are all gone now, aren't they? Just tea, please."

It was like a visit with Lanelle's mother when Bethann was eight. Her grandmother had insisted that any well brought up daughter of the South should know how to serve tea. And so for one incredibly miserable, bright April Saturday afternoon, she had learned. All stiff backs and linen napkins, finger sandwiches and lumps of sugar.

Bethann handed her the cup and saucer. Her hands shook as she brought it to her lips, sipped. "Not quite hot enough. If you find it unpalatable, please ring for Millie.

The good help was gone thirty years ago."

"It's fine, May June." She sipped the tepid concoction.

"Very well, Bethann, what did you wish to see me about? You realize, I'm sure, that I've granted few audiences these last years. Yours is a special case. I'm seeing you only out of respect for Joe Tom. Undoubtedly that old harridan that keeps house for you told you that."

Bethann smiled to herself. Among other things, that would just about cover it. She held her tea cup in her lap, swirled the liquid, wished there were tea leaves she could read and divine how this would end. She hadn't liked Edna Earle's prediction of Bethann being tossed out on her ear. And if Bry knew she were here...

"In October, my barn was burned. I'm sure you know that." May June nodded, her attention still held by something outside. "I saw a Jeep leave the property, and it was determined to have come from here. New Year's, all my security lights were unscrewed. End of January, my house was broken into and ransacked, computer hard drive stolen, then returned. Bry came to see you. Two days ago, my son's car was stolen and found burned. Threats to me and to my property are one thing, May June. No one threatens harm to my son."

"Spoken like a McLeod. You're accusing me of all this mischief? Is there any concrete proof to this effect?"

"Not other than your Jeep on my property in October."

"Help isn't what it used to be, Bethann. You, of

263

course, are too young to realize that. Since the sixties, there's been no such thing as good help."

"Well, in my naiveté, I might have been inclined to believe that it was your help that wanted me off Joe Tom's place, didn't want me to inherit, had some mystic way of knowing what inheritors were in the mystery envelope should I fail to make Joe Tom's magic year. But no one, not even Edna Earle, could figure out why the hired help would do anything but the employer's wishes." She set the china back on the tray. "Then last month, I happened on just the right trunk in the attic." She pulled the folded papers from the box.

May June finally took her eyes from the outdoors and put them on her guest. Bethann held the papers up, just outside her reach. "Last month, I found the answer. Talk about a shock." She opened it and started to read. "That must have been some adventurous day, all the way to Oklahoma and back. 'Dated 20 April 193—'"

May June reached out her hand. For the first time, Bethann saw fear in her eyes. "Please don't read it aloud. The walls have ears."

"Do they now?" Bethann refolded the sheets, laid them in her lap, lowered her voice. "Let's see, how did it go? You and Joe Tom elope. Be a married couple in *every* sense of the word. Then he leaves for the army. You're bound to have known he was going. But you get pregnant. Can't admit you followed your lusts to couple with a McLeod. There was certainly no monetary advantage in that. Was it parental pressure that made you go after the Cummings heir? Didn't take much doing obviously. According to the county record books, you married him the end of June. Bouncing baby girl first part of January. How proud his family must have been of your combined fertility. How would they have felt about a bigamist as a daughter-in-law? Or were you praying Joe Tom would be killed overseas?"

She ignored the questions, her voice breaking from whisper to croak. "What are you going to do with this?"

"Well, I've been giving it some thought. Starting with the fear you must have felt when Joe Tom had the nerve to survive and come home." Bethann paused. "Did you really think you'd get away with it?"

"I've gotten away with it, as you say, for seventy years."

"But it's taken its toll, hasn't it? You rejected your daughter. Too much of Joe Tom in her? Afraid your husband would see a physical resemblance? And then, when God gives you a chance to make amends with Bry, what do you do? You treat him worse than your precious hired help!"

The old woman bristled. "You've only heard one side."

"I have all afternoon. I'm willing to hear yours."

***

"She's where?" Bry exploded, throwing his golf cap on the floor of Bethann's kitchen.

Edna Earle drew back, her eyes wide. "Where did that temper come from?"

"Edna Earle, I swear you'd better tell me the truth! What in hell is she doing at May June's?"

"I believe she went to tea." Edna Earle applied a little more elbow grease to the sugar bowl Bethann had uncovered in the attic. "Won't this look nice when it's polished?"

"Why would May June ask her to tea?"

"Why does that old woman do anything?"

"Edna Earle, you know a lot more than you're saying. Spit it out!"

She polished all the more diligently. "She'll be home soon, Bry. You can ask her yourself."

He switched tactics. "Did you approve of this?"

"Not particularly."

He finally sat down and she pushed a rag at him. "You can polish off some of that steam. Start with the teapot."

***

May June took a moment to compose herself. "When he ended up back here, Bry was the image of Joe Tom at that age. I can't believe the town couldn't see it, didn't run me out on a rail."

She flicked her eyes back to Bethann. "You have no idea the shame I felt when I found I was pregnant. I actually thought to tell my mother, to confess it all, but

Joe Tom had the certificate for safekeeping. There was no proving I was married unless we got hold of Joe Tom or went back to Oklahoma to the courthouse. So, instead of a scandal, I set my cap for Charles Cummings. And as you have pointed out, it didn't take long. It couldn't!"

She smiled to herself. "All in all, Charles wasn't bad, just not very interesting. He even insisted the doctor deliver our baby, not Edna Earle's mother, that gossipy midwife. Of course, this pleased me. I think I'd even convinced myself the baby was Charles'." She set her thin lips together. "Till the ice storm. The driver couldn't get out to the doctor. Only got as far as the midwife's. And she brought Edna Earle. Going to show her the way it was. Sniveling child. We've been a thorn in each other's sides all our lives. She saw my baby born. Saw the birthmark. So much for it being a Cummings. That baby was a McLeod."

Her eyes darted around the room. "I don't know how she knew, but Edna Earle did. I saw it in her eyes. Saw the awareness, heard the gasp. I felt doomed. God knows what windows she'd been looking through. "

Bethann wasn't going to tell. "She didn't give you away."

"Who would believe a child anyway? It was Joe Tom's return that had me worried. And I did so for five years."

"And he didn't give you away."

"No."

"Why?"

"We never spoke about it. We never spoke, period. I figure he was just always waiting to pounce. That that was his revenge for my betrayal. I never breathed an easy breath till he died."

"Then I moved in." May June nodded. "And it got complicated again. What if I found the certificate?"

"Precisely."

"What a dilemma. Let's see if you figure the way I do. I expose you as a bigamist. The neat little Cummings world of high finance and independence takes a major turn toward the blood-letting side. The only thing thicker than blood is money, and your empire would be cut up, down, and sideways. What a shame!" She shifted in the chair and leaned closer to May June.

"But the other side of that is not very pleasant for me. Bry is a very legitimate McLeod heir. In exposing you, I leave myself open for a court fight from him with my son. Not in my best interest."

Bethann tapped the papers on her lap. "You see, it really doesn't make sense for me to announce this." She held them out to May June. A shaky hand grabbed them, fisted them in her lap. "First, have a copy of the McLeod family tree from the family Bible, the object, no doubt, of your search. Notice Rae's name and Bry's. He knew, May June." She measured her words. "Joe Tom knew!

"And secondly, take that cursed certificate. But I am not so kind-hearted that I haven't made a copy. Let me assure you, old woman," there was menace in her voice, "if that mischief at my house doesn't stop, I'll publish it.

Cummings and McLeod estates be damned! I will protect my child." Bethann stood up.

May June turned watery eyes up to her. "As I protected mine." Her head and hands shook with age. "Bry inherits when I die. He'll be a very rich man. Now do you want to stay and marry him?"

Bethann shook with anger. "It's a real pity he couldn't be rich with a grandmother rather than rich without her."

"What does Edna Earle know about this?"

"As you said, God knows what windows she's looked through."

May June returned to her window gazing. "Millie will show you out."

"That's not necessary."

Halfway to the door, the voice called out from the depths of the chair, "You left your package."

"Two cookbooks. Compliments of Joe Tom's estate."

"Have a pleasant summer, Bethann. I hear Atlanta's beautiful in the fall."

***

Bethann held onto her emotions until she parked the car at the roadside overlook. By the time the keys were slipped into her pocket, she was sobbing. Relief? Release? It was over. Nine months of increasing terror had been reduced to three sheets of paper and a verbal acknowledgment of guilt by May June. She got out of the car and stumbled to the picnic table she and Kiki had sat on so carefreely. Had it only been nine months? God, it could have been a lifetime.

How ironic for Bry, for her. Unless May June changed her will, she would leave it all to him. Or did she lie about that, too? Bethann was trapped. If she revealed the marriage, she'd risk Bry's losing everything from the illegitimate Cummings side. Clever old woman. And to bring up the idea that Bethann could also be persuaded to marry for wealth—the venom that took!

She wiped her eyes, sought to steady her trembling chin. She hugged herself, although the May day was quite warm. She needed Bry. She needed to be held and stroked and told everything would be all right. But that wasn't going to be. She would and could never tell him.

***

Bry bolted up from the table and confronted Bethann on the back porch. "What the hell were you doing at May June's?" He blocked her way up the steps. "Oh, no. You're not going in there and exchange signals with Edna Earle. I want the truth!"

She looked up at him. He saw the tears run to the edges of her eyes, then she quickly looked away. "We had tea."

"Out of the blue, she calls and asks you to tea? You expect me to believe that?" He took her shoulders, gently turned her toward him. "You've been crying." His tone softened immediately. "What did she say?"

Bethann swallowed. "She wished me a pleasant summer and a good journey home to Atlanta. She's heard it's beautiful in the fall."

"Bethann." He drew her to him. "Please don't lie. I know her for what she is. Don't protect her."

"She's brought me nothing but fear and anger. I'd never protect her, Bry." She put her hands on his chest. "But we had tea. We came to an understanding. It's over. There'll be no more problems." She looked into his eyes. "You're right though, she's quite a presence. Could," she moved her hands up to the back of his neck, "could you just hold me, please?"

He took her into his arms, held her tightly. She trembled slightly. He'd only gotten a partial truth out of this. He looked over his shoulder through the kitchen porch window. Edna Earle stood just outside clear range. It would take awhile, but he would get the truth.

Chapter Twenty-Four

Ted left for summer school the day before Bethann flew back to Atlanta for a whirlwind three day, two night marathon. There were four book signings sandwiched in between three brunches and two wedding receptions. It was the same story as the New Year's visit: Kiki had joyfully overbooked.

The talk was of Bethann's return in time for the close of the season, for the Labor Day parties already booked. Jon had found an old restaurant site he thought appropriate for their tea room. Less than a mile from his dealership, less than two from their neighborhood, it was a block from the newest high-rise office building. A trendy coffee franchise had leased the other end of the building. It was more than adequate, but Bethann found she could do little more than smile and nod. The option to lease lapsed the end of June, but she couldn't make the decision. She couldn't reach for the checkbook.

"We'll keep looking, Bethann." Kiki said as they stood in the doorway of what could be their new business venture. "You do still want to do it, don't you?"

"You know I do." Bethann sipped coffee from the new franchise. "It's a dream come true and old Joe Tom gets to play fairy godfather."

"Well, some of your old, familiar rancor seems to have slipped. If I didn't know better, I'd say you'd rather be working on another dream come true." She pulled the door closed and turned the key the Realtor had given them. "How's the sheriff?"

"Just fine."

"Miss him?"

"That's neither here nor there. We've got other things to talk about. Like, how you can so continually overbook," Bethann commented as they got in Kiki's car.

"How about we talk about how you'd really rather stay in Cummings?"

"But I hadn't."

"Ted talks to me, you know." She watched Bethann out of the corner of her eye. "He thinks of me as an aunt."

"See, there's a perfect example of why I need to be in Atlanta. I'd be so much closer to him. Then he could talk to me like a mother."

"Sure. What Ted says is the sheriff is in love with you and you're sleeping together until you leave. You got some sort of deal. You kinda' left all that out of our conversations, Bethann."

"Ted talks too much. Way too much."

"Do you love him?" Kiki checked her lipstick in the rearview mirror while they waited at a light.

"I love Ted very much."

"Don't be obtuse. The sheriff. Do you love him?"

"No."

"Now look your lifelong friend in the eye and tell me that. Sell me, Bethann. Make me believe."

She twisted in the passenger seat and looked straight at Kiki. "No, I do not love the sheriff."

"Well, I didn't buy that. Good thing Marsh was the salesman in the family. You would have starved otherwise."

***

Bethann sat on the edge of her bed in Atlanta. Her bags were packed and by the door. Even without the personal things she'd taken to make Ranch McLeod home, she should have felt a pull to this room. She and Marsh had loved in it for most of their married years. But it felt so cold now. It was alien, no longer a part of her. She moved to the window, pulled the sheers apart, looked at the back yard. It showed signs of a year's neglect, Jon's benign care notwithstanding. Pressing her face to the cool window, she sighed. The joy of air conditioning. She'd better enjoy it while she could. No such luxury at home.

The word struck her. Had she just thought of that hundred acres with the creaking floors and appalling decor as home? The feelings that had stayed just beyond recognition in December came flooding back. Home. Wasn't she home now, in Atlanta?

She turned her back to the window, tried to picture

Bry in this room with its chintz draperies and cornice boards. There was no way. He was all leather and khaki and silver. She twisted the bracelet. Marsh had fit into this room only because she had closed her eyes to the decor of the study.

There it was. Bry didn't fit in her world nor she in his. After the cookbook, before and after the attic, she had to admit she had been bored. What was there for her in Cummings? She'd cooked, tinkered with some new dishes, read, gardened minimally, read some more, ridden. She had bided her time, played the old waiting game. The only part of her days that were full was when Bry was there. It was like when she and Marsh were newlyweds. She'd wait and wait for him to come home at night from his job. Hers had been neither interesting nor time-consuming enough. Even when Ted was born, she'd played the waiting game.

Then Atlanta Divines. No more waiting. She was happy and fulfilled and had her own goals. She'd become a more interesting person. Even Marsh had admitted it. To stay in Cummings was to take on the old life again and she didn't want that. Whether she loved Bry or not, she didn't want the old waiting game. Love hadn't been enough the first time, why would it be now? It was easier to stay in Atlanta than risk finding out. Surely, it was less painful. If she stayed in Cummings, she'd have to sort out all those jumbled feelings, have to admit to love again.

Have to submit to love again.

She pushed away from the window and pulled her checkbook from the bottom of her handbag. Time for a new life.

***

The airplane commuter hop seemed to take forever. In her newfound inspiration, Bethann was anxious to get the design programs loaded onto the computer and to begin the reconstruction plans for the tearoom. She gathered her bags, stuck her keys in her pocket and headed out into the terminal.

Bry met her just past security.

"What a pleasant surprise!" To her astonishment, her heart skipped at the sight of him leaning against the wall. Hadn't it just been three days? This wasn't going to be like the reunion they'd had in December. They were past that. Still, something wasn't right. He wasn't in uniform, and his golfer's tan showed up particularly well against the white open-necked golf shirt. She set her bags down at his feet and reached to kiss him. He hugged her with an unknown urgency. "Is something wrong? Is Ted hurt?"

"No, no," he rushed to disarm her fears while he gathered her bags. His difficulty in explaining himself further unnerved her.

She took his arm as they walked toward the exit and pulled so that his ear was even with her lips. "Couldn't wait to get me in bed? Really, Sheriff, it's only been two nights. Are we already booked into a motel or do I get to pick?"

That drew a smile out of him. "Insatiable." They were walking under the covered parking.

"My car was there." She stopped, wheeling him around. "It's been stolen, that's why you're here."

"No, Sam came up with me and took it back to Cummings."

"Keys?"

"Edna Earle found an extra set. We're over here." He started walking again and she trailed behind.

"Then why are you here, if it's not an accident or sex?"

He unlocked the doors and threw her bags into the back. She got into the front without waiting for him to open the door. They buckled their seatbelts.

As he started to turn the ignition, she reached over and stopped him. He took a deep breath and sagged back against the seat. "May June had a bad heart attack last night and she's in the hospital over here. I've always known the inevitable: that I would hear news of her imminent demise one day. I just hadn't thought it would bother me one little bit." He turned to look at her. "But it does." Bethann took his hands in hers and squeezed. "The last thoughtful thing she did for me was pay for Meg's headstone. Then it was anonymously. This morning, she asked to see me. I thought I hated her. Why do I feel bad about this? Why do I feel this great need to see her one last time?"

"The heart attack's really that bad? They do wonderful things in cardiology now."

"Delmar has his finger on the pulse, so to speak. Her heart was already in wretched condition. This is it."

Having seen the old woman less than a month before, Bethann wasn't surprised. She reached across the console for him, held him as best she could. "I thought your plane would never land."

"Oh, Bry," she breathed. She closed her eyes, saw only the check made out to the real estate company.

"Edna Earle is appalled that I want to see her."

"Hell with Edna Earle. You're the one's got to live with yourself."

"When she dies, Bethann, that's it. I never knew my father's people, never claimed or was claimed by the Cummings or Bright clans. When she dies, I have no one."

Bethann's heart broke. The sadness she had carried with her since she'd seen his birthmark and heard Edna Earle's story intensified a thousandfold. She wanted to tell him not to despair, that he had Ted. That he had her. But the words wouldn't go past the lump in her own throat.

"Will you go with me to see her?" He pulled back and looked into her tear-filled eyes. "You don't really have a choice since Sam took the SUV, but will you? You don't have to go in if you don't want to."

"I'll do whatever you want me to. I'll be there with you, or I'll wait."

He kissed her forehead. "Thank you, Bethann. Thank you for being here."

***

Bethann held onto Bry's hand as he threaded his way though the hospital, following the blue floor tiles from the information desk to the CICU. At the entrance to the waiting room, a sea of relatives parted. Whatever else they thought of him or he of them, he was May June's grandson, her next of kin. Bethann let her hand go lax, so he could drop it if he wished. Instead, he laced their fingers more tightly and pulled her with him through the double doors to the nurse's station.

"Yes, sir?" The nurse was young, pretty, considerate.

"May June Cummings. I'm her grandson."

She glanced at the wall clock. "She's been in and out of consciousness, but if you'll be quick and quiet..."

He nodded and she led them to the cubicle that held May June's frail body. Machines, tubes, wires, monitors, oxygen. For whatever pain the tragedy of Marsh's death had caused, it had spared Bethann seeing him as Bry saw May June.

Bry released Bethann's hand at the opened door. She stayed in the doorway, watching, not wishing to intrude. He stood at the foot of the bed, then moved to the side. The veins at May June's temples and in her neck and hands stretched like blue streams under translucent skin. Bry reached out a tentative hand to hers, took the curled fingers in his own.

She clutched his in return. Her eyes opened but she seemed to have trouble focusing on him. Finally, as if her sight cleared, she recognized him and gave a small croak. Her fingers weakly crawled up his wrist, and he bent down to hear what she strained to say.

A minute later he stood up and laid the old hand back on top of the covers. He just made it to Bethann's side when the warning beeps went off and the wave-lines on the monitors straightened. They stood silently together by the nurse's station while the doctor and nurses tried to perform their healing on a heart that had already given up.

***

Delmar was coming in the hospital doors as they left and Bry told him to take care of everything. They sat silently in the truck in the hospital parking lot, their fingers laced over the console that separated them. "You want to know what she told me?"

"If you want to tell me."

"I guess I could trade you for the truth about your visit with her."

"Perhaps a woman's dying words should be secret."

He looked directly at her for the first time since they'd gotten in the car. "She had the nerve to tell me she was sorry. That I was the last of a proud line and she was sorry." He measured the words, turned away and focused on the steering wheel. "Made up for all those lost years for me." His tone was sarcastic, but the meaning was wrenched from a soul saddened by years of being unwanted.

He started the truck, jerked it in gear. They rode to Cummings in silence. Bethann simply had nothing to say.

***

Speakers were set up in the church fellowship hall for the overflow crowd from May June's funeral. Bry took his place on the front pew before the preacher, with the family and yet apart from it. Bethann sat beside him. There were sniffles and tears all around, but he sat ramrod straight, a posture befitting an ex-MP, a sheriff, the only grandson. He looked at the choir, never turning his eyes to the casket, never responding to any word said.

May June Bright Cummings was interred in the Cummings quarter of the cemetery, next to her husband Charles, two rows over from Joe Tom. "Pity we couldn't have buried her between them," Edna Earle murmured as she and Bethann left the Cummings plot and headed towards Joe Tom to visit.

"Well, are you happy?" Bethann hissed at the headstone marking Joe Tom's resting place as she and Edna Earle stood side-by-side at the grave. "Caused enough trouble for one lifetime, did you?"

"Well, he had a helper."

"And they read the will when? I'm real curious about what she told me."

"Depends on which will."

"Now what?"

"Rumor has it she called Delmar out two weeks ago to draw a new one. Question is, did she sign it? They read tomorrow."

"How do you know these things?"

"Common knowledge."

"Are there no secrets?"

"None 'cept one."

"It gets to stay that way, too."

"You can leave with that knowledge?"

"Yes."

They both watched as Bry approached. "Delmar wants to see me tomorrow at one. I'm highly suspicious." He stood with his hands in his pockets and rocked back on his heels.

Edna Earle whispered. "I guess if you have the gall to leave a man like that, then you can just take that information with you to *your* grave."

Bethann shot her a dirty look before holding out an arm to Bry and encircling his waist. He kissed the top of her head. "Communing with Joe Tom?"

"Every once in a while I come give the old weasel the benefit of my opinion about the inheritance. Right now, I'm trying to figure out whether I'm going to burn that mystery envelope on his head or his feet."

Edna Earle eyed the length of the gravesite. "Why

not right below the belt?"

***

"I can't stand this much longer, Edna Earle." Bethann made another turn on the kitchen linoleum. "That will reading started over two hours ago. Where is he?"

Edna Earle snapped another bean pod and dropped it into the bowl on her lap. "You're wearing me out. Come put some of that energy to use and snap these things. We bought a bushel. Remember?"

"Yes, I remember." Bethann jerked the chair out and straightened the newspaper in front of her as she began systematically snapping the beans. "Where is he?"

"I assume he's in the front row at Delmar's. Hell, girl, half the county was supposed to show up. I don't know why he didn't just read it over the radio!"

"Suit me. At least I wouldn't have been waiting."

"Bry asked you to go. I heard him this morning."

"I couldn't. If she changed it so he didn't inherit, I could not have contained myself. I just couldn't've. Besides the fact I've got to see Delmar at five. Old goat enjoys making me squirm. It's probably over some stupid bill."

"Well, if she changed the will, it wouldn't be your fault. Old bitch's been doing precisely what she wanted all her life. Even died dramatically—the final words to the estranged grandson. Maybe we should write a book."

The sound of tires on the drive deprived Bethann of a

pithy answer. She started to rise. Edna Earle caught her hand and pressed her down.

Bry came through the door, his face expressionless. He pulled a chair between them and started right in.

"She rewrote two weeks ago. How's that for gallows humor? Or premonition. Basically, everyone on staff got cash. The longer they served, the more they got. Millie got twenty-five thousand." Edna Earle frowned. "Exception to the longevity rule would be Kincaid, the new chauffeur. Got fifteen." He picked up a bean from the sack, idly snapped it. "There were various personal bequests, the family jewelry got scattered real good, some of the rugs, keepsakes, a few prize bulls, stallions." His tone was conversational, almost as if he had practiced on the way out. "Cain came up a big winner."

Bethann's heart and stomach met.

"Got all the property over in the next county. She just sheared it away from the rest. Toward the canyons where Ted's car was found. All the land, all the cattle normally pastured on it, the little ranch house over there. For years of service. God knows, he earned it." He stopped to pick a bean string off his pants, casually add it to the pile of snapped bean heads and tails and strings. "I'm really glad he got that." He paused.

Bethann couldn't take her eyes off his face, although he wasn't looking at either of them.

"It saves me the messiness of firing him, since she left everything else to me." He said it casually.

Bethann wasn't sure she'd heard right. She let the

words sink in, then dropped her head to the table in relief. Edna Earle just sat with open mouth.

"No comment from you two?"

"I can't believe she really did it," Edna Earle said. "At last, she does something right."

Bethann raised her head. "I'm so happy for you." She moved to his lap and kissed him. He held her tightly then scooted her over to his right knee. He reached for Edna Earle and scooped her up to his left.

"I am not going to sit on your lap!" she fussed.

"Hell, you're not, old woman. You did Christmas."

"Well, you shouldn't have done that." But she let him give her a squeeze and she hugged his neck. "How does it feel to be the wealthiest man in four counties?"

"Don't know that I am. I've got to look at the books. Then see if Ted's wealthier. May June put hers in tangibles. Joe Tom played the market."

Edna Earle got up, brushed her dress down, straightened her apron. "Been over to survey your domain yet?"

"You two are my first stop." He turned his attention to Bethann. "Want to go with me?"

"I've got an appointment with Delmar in less than an hour. Some stupid bill thing. Meet you there?"

He nodded.

"You're taking this mighty calmly," Edna Earle observed. "What if she'd divvied it up differently? What if she'd ignored you?"

"I have never expected anything from May June. I

figure this is an old guilty conscience trying to clear itself with its Maker."

He stood, setting Bethann back in her chair and kissing her soundly. "First thing I'm going to do is open those damn wrought iron gates—and leave them open!"

***

Bethann came through her backdoor, a manila envelope in her hand. "I knew you'd still be here."

"Needed to finish the beans." Edna Earle looked up at her from the table. "Quick bill paying. That didn't take long."

"Walk in, walk out, and not a bill in sight. Just this little gift from May June. Delmar wasn't in any mood for conversation, although I did get one interesting little piece out of him. Bry inherited it all in the will she nullified. She cut Cain in after my visit."

"Probably to get him out of the picture peacefully."

"I think so."

"What's in the envelope?"

"I haven't dared look. Sure as hell wasn't going to open it in front of Delmar." She tapped it on the table. "Listen." It jingled. "What do you think?"

"Wedding rings."

"My guess, too." Bethann sat down and broke the seal. She tilted the envelope and familiar folded sheets of paper and three rings slid out.

Edna Earle picked them up. "Looks like what Annie

Lee described to me. Angus McLeod's wedding rings. A full wedding set. Joe Tom kept the certificate and May June, the rings. Even married, they didn't trust each other."

"But May June trusts me to not rock the empire boat. I guess the rings can turn up around here in the bottom of a box." She held the papers up. "Burn these?"

"You'd better."

"Yeah. If I ever need the information, I know where to look in Oklahoma."

Chapter Twenty-Five

"**S**o this is tradition." Bethann looked around the barn and corral, glanced over her shoulder to the flagstone patio. "May June held a whopper of a Fourth of July blowout every year?" Japanese lanterns hung between the trees and buildings, church tables were laden with side dishes and desserts. Funeral home chairs were stacked against the barn. Two large drum barbecue trailers were smoking as much now as eighteen hours ago when they'd started.

"Yeah. She invited all the Cummings relatives and families of people who worked here. Never invited me, though. So I thought we'd do it with a twist." The drive was lined with police and sheriff's cars while the rest of the populace of Cummings was parked in the pasture just back of the house. "The Cummings estate has provided the meat, the band, the place, the fireworks. The town's responsible for the accompaniments and their own good humor." He caught her around the waist. "What say I give you a personal moonlight tour later on?"

"Is this like the one I had last week? Where we ended up on a blanket by the master's favorite bass pool?"

He raised his eyebrows. "Never do the same thing

twice."

Sam sidled up. "I see you're trying to sneak away. No fair. Better come referee Edna Earle and Millie in the kitchen. Don't know why you kept her on anyway."

"Which one?"

Sam shook his head. "Either. Both. You know, Bry, handling women's not as easy as handling the department."

Bry said nothing but squeezed Bethann as they walked with the younger man to the house. She pinched him back.

"I've been giving personnel problems serious thought since I'm running for sheriff." Sam turned to look at Bry. "You sure you can't handle this and being sheriff?"

"Not no, but hell no." Bry laughed. "A few months on this place may have me wishing I was back with you. But come September first, Cummings County gets a new shot at law and order."

***

They sat on the corral railing. The party was over, the fireworks sparkle just a memory, the band's refrains no longer lingering in the air. The tables and chairs were stacked in the barn, ready to be hauled back in the morning. The populace of Cummings had shown up in full force, and if the amount of food and beer consumed was any indication, a good time had been had by all. Bry had stood on the patio and taken all the congratulations and thank-yous in stride. He shook hands, received the best wishes, heard the regrets that he'd no longer be sheriff. Bethann and Edna Earle had stood at the garden window and watched.

"Makes me want to cry," the old woman had said. "All these years he's had so little. That someone has to die before he finally gets the recognition and love he deserves. It's a real pity all this happiness has to leave him when you do."

"Let's not start on all this again, Edna Earle. The conversation is closed. I have seven weeks. I have a life in Atlanta."

"You have a life here. Plenty to do as mistress of this place."

"I am not mistress of this place."

"You could be. He'd move here in a second if you'd come with him."

"He'll move here anyway when I go. He can't properly handle this place without living on it. He knows that."

"What he needs to properly handle this place is you."

"Enough, Edna Earle! Aren't you going to come work here once I leave?"

"He hasn't asked."

"Since when has that stopped you? I don't think I asked either."

"I came with the property."

"Well, I guess now you can come with the man."

"He's looking for you. Better go on out. Millie and

I'll divide this territory up in the morning."

Now they sat on the corral railings, fingers laced together. He'd made a special point of bringing her here, lifting her up, joining her.

"Bethann, we've got to get something straight between us."

She looked at him, but he was staring ahead. "Okay."

"I love you." Now he turned to look at her. "Plain, simple, I love you. You've never said you love me. I understand that. We didn't go into this relationship with that in mind."

He released her hand, turned on the railing so he balanced with a leg on either side of it. "Compared to a year ago, I own the earth now. Just the acknowledgment from my grandmother that I existed as something other than an embarrassment—I only need one more thing."

He took her hand again, kissed it. "This is it, a one time offer, because, believe me, peach pit, I'll not repeat it or beg. Marry me when Joe Tom's year is over. Move in here with me. We'll mingle May June's and Joe Tom's households and make them spin in their graves." He kissed her fingers. "Please. You know it would work. You know we're right for this."

Bethann opened her mouth to speak, closed it on nothing but air. She wasn't surprised, but she was shaken. She had known this was coming. But she'd expected it in August as the moving truck was pulling away. She'd expected a final assault, not a frontal one.

"I guess you don't have to tell me now, although if

the answer were yes, you'd have already said so." There was sadness in his voice. He jumped down from the railings and stood in front of her. "I don't know what I expected. I guess things were going so well for me, I figured, why not try for it all?"

"Bry—" she held out her hand to touch his cheek, but he moved away. "I can't—"

"I don't believe that. You won't admit to yourself what—" his voice broke. Silently, he held his arms up to her, helped her down. "Can you get home by yourself, or do you need an escort?"

***

The bedroom ceiling fan spun in slow, lazy circles above Bethann. The curtains blew in the open windows. She kicked at the covers, sent them flying off the end of the bed.

Sitting up didn't help. She'd tried it. Nor pacing. Nor, obviously, lying down. Misery knows no proper position. She turned onto her stomach, flipped back immediately. Got up. Got dressed.

Damn four o'clock train whistled through as she sat on the front porch, a very straight bourbon being swirled idly in her hand. She tossed what was left of it onto the lantana her parents had planted in the spring. Almost threw the glass with it, but thought better of an uncontrolled red-headed temper.

It all boiled down to one simple question: did she

love Bry? She took a deep breath, concentrated on answering honestly. Oh, God, yes. In every way possible, yes. If she could have anything in the world at this moment, what would it be? Bry, pulling into the drive, running to her, holding her. She craved him. She wanted his touch, his presence. She had so easily adjusted her life to him.

The old Atlanta question reared its head. Admit to love—submit to love. Play the waiting game again. But would she here? Wouldn't she be more a part of his life and livelihood than she had Marsh's?

What about Kiki, Ted, the new tearoom? The plans were all sketched and emailed to Kiki and the contractor for approval. She had a real for-sure life in Atlanta. And love? Well, it would show up if it were meant to. Otherwise, she'd be happy again like she had before. Before Joe Tom. Before Edna Earle.

Before Bry.

Six months from now, this year would be a blur. Six months from now, she'd be so busy with the tearoom she'd not even miss Bry. It was a cinch she'd never miss this hot, dry miserable place. Six months from now, she'd know she'd made the right decision.

Now all she had to do was survive the heat and Edna Earle's displeasure for seven weeks. Then, as she'd said all along, she was out of here.

***

Bry sat at the depot and waited for the four o'clock to whistle through. He'd not been here in months. He'd not needed a place to think and brood. He'd pushed the Bethann question to the back of his mind. He'd enjoyed all he could, had relished having her, had found a contentment he'd never thought to have again. Even if there were things she'd not tell him. Like her visit with May June after Ted's car was stolen. Was that why she had been so anxious about the will? Had May June told her she'd cut him out—or put him in?

But he had something on Bethann. He'd not told her all of May June's last words, and if tonight was any indication, he'd not get the chance. Hell, he'd really like to know if the old woman was giving him anything other than her blessing. Maybe as Bethann took that red hair back to Georgia, she'd tell him what May June had meant by, "Bethann—she holds your future."

Chapter Twenty-Six

"Somebody has been conspicuously absent lately." Edna Earle put up the last of the breakfast dishes.

"You're a quick study, Edna Earle. It's the first of August, and you're just now realizing that Bry comes less and less because he's busy more and more."

"I'm sure that's it."

"He moved Range and Rover over to greener pastures three weeks ago."

"Um-hum." She untied the apron. "Your time's almost up. Getting any happier as the countdown accelerates?"

Bethann looked up from the legal pad where she'd been keeping track of lists for the past month: what went, what stayed, what was needed in the tearoom, what to include in the cookbook's inevitable second printing that wasn't in the first. "What do you want me to say? Yes, I'm happy because this ordeal is almost finished? No, I'm miserable because Bry's too busy to come over?"

"Girl, don't lie to me." She wagged a finger at her. "You are miserable because you two had a fight the Fourth."

Bethann grinned. "Dying to know what it was about, aren't you? Haven't you already asked Bry?"

She crossed her arms. "He told me to MYOB."

"Well, it's obvious you don't know what that means or you'd have been doing it all this time."

"He asked you to marry him."

"Is that a question or an educated guess?"

"Both."

"Yes, Edna Earle, he asked me to marry him. He asked me to move my Joe Tom belongings over to May June's and commingle with benefit of clergy. He'll make an honest woman of me if I'll make an honest man of him. Are you satisfied now?"

"No. You didn't say the right magic words for me to be satisfied."

"Give it up."

"I have one month to straighten you two out again."

"You have less than one month." Bethann gritted her teeth as she said it. "And the answer is no, no, *no*! I am going back to Atlanta and lead my life and forget this whole stupid year ever happened except when I open my bank statement. I am going to be four hours from my son instead of a time zone. I am going to go on doing what made me happy before all this mess began. I was a fulfilled woman then and I'm going to be again. I don't need another man!"

"The fact that he's a McLeod has nothing to do with this senseless decision?" Edna Earle's knuckles turned white as she squeezed them against her hip.

"He could be a Williams and the same decision would be made. This is not my home!"

Edna Earle paid no attention to the snap of the pencil that broke between Bethann's clenched fingers. "Hell, girl, if he was a Williams, he'd already have that ring on your finger! We don't take 'no' for an answer!"

"Leave me be about this, Edna Earle."

"Home's where your heart is. And yours is in on that damn McLeod couch!"

***

Bethann made the arrangements for the movers but they couldn't come until the day after Joe Tom's year was up. She would do the packing, not so much from a desire to save money, but to have something to do. It was getting harder and harder to occupy her time. She'd not realized how much of it Bry had taken until he was no longer there. He didn't call, but then neither did she. They'd seen each other only once, and then by accident, at Sally's. They'd eaten together but it was strained. It seemed that if she couldn't say yes to the proposal on the table, then there just wasn't anything to say.

Ted came back through Cummings in mid-August, stayed a few days. He'd definitely enjoyed his summer school, even professed to having learned something. She'd already shared the news of Bry's good fortune with him. He headed out immediately before she could warn him that the meeting might not be all he hoped for.

When he returned from the Cummings property two hours later, he merely stood in the kitchen and stared at her. "Tell me you didn't turn all that down? Tell me you didn't turn *him* down?"

"What exactly did he say, Ted?" Bethann stopped wrapping the espresso cups.

"That he proposed and you wouldn't say yes."

"That basically covers it. My life is in Atlanta."

"Hell it is!"

"Ted!"

"I mean it, Mom, he's a great guy! I love him, why can't you?"

"Well, I think we're talking two different kinds of love here—"

"You know what I mean. He's given up on you. Why did you let that happen?" He flailed his arms in frustration. "Well, I wouldn't beg you either. You deserve to be alone!"

The rest of his visit was strained.

***

Maybe she did deserve to be alone. And alone she was. Edna Earle showed up only perfunctorily, refused to help her pack. As the final days ticked down, Bethann realized she'd not felt so alone since Marsh died. Well, all that would change just as soon as she got back where she really belonged.

It was going to be a much larger move going back

that it had coming out. She was taking all the artifacts she considered valuable as well as everything of her own she'd brought out. She was leaving a bare bones hunting lodge for Ted and his friends. As for herself, she planned to never set foot on Ranch McLeod again.

Initially, they planned for Kiki to come and travel back with her, a kind of reverse first trip. But the tearoom wallpaper was being hung and the kitchen equipment installed, so she couldn't. Bethann spent her last night as a prisoner of Ranch McLeod packing Joe Tom's trunk. She cushioned the angel as it had been along with the silver. She'd taken to wearing the wedding rings on a chain around her neck. Their constant bump between her breasts reminded her of what she had to do before she left.

The morning after the last night she had to stay at Joe Tom's found her on Delmar's doorstep as he opened the office. "Come for all the papers, titles, deeds, have you? Prompt, Bethann, I'll say that. No grass grows under your feet."

"No grass grows here, period, Delmar. I want all you mentioned plus Joe Tom's mystery envelope. I have a right to know."

"I don't know that you do." He settled behind his desk. She stood in front of it and leaned over.

"The envelope, please, Delmar." She held her hand out. He grimaced and began unlocking the safe.

"Don't suppose you're going to tell me what you're going to do with this." He pulled it out, holding it just beyond her reach.

"Burn it. Stand on that old man's grave and burn it."

"Read it first, of course."

She slowly shook her head. "Not on your life. I don't want to know."

"Thought it might clear up who was doing all that mischief out your way." He handed it to her and she deftly slipped it into her purse.

"That stopped this spring. Or didn't you notice?"

"I'll have those papers ready in the morning."

"Fine. I'll pick them up on the way out of town. The movers come tomorrow morning. I leave when they do."

***

She'd informed Edna Earle at breakfast of her intentions. So she wasn't surprised, as she arrived at Joe Tom's gravesite, to see the familiar form sitting on his headstone.

"Just us? You didn't tell Bry?"

"Private party, Edna Earle. Just you, me, and the devil's own." She pulled the sealed envelope from her purse and set it on the ground. As she retrieved the matches from her pocket, her home-made necklace slipped from her shirt.

"Wearing those rings, are you? Just exactly what does that mean?"

"Haven't strung a necklace in years, thought I'd try it again."

"Um-hum." She watched Bethann strike the match. "At least let me see who's on that damn piece of paper. Let me die a happy woman."

"I thought the only thing that would put you in that circumstance would be me staying."

"That, too." She grabbed the envelope. "Please."

"What good is it going to do? Just as soon as you know, I'm going to know you know, and be dying to know myself. Then I might as well have opened it."

"Very well. You do it." She held out the envelope to her. Bethann took it and set it aflame.

"I told Delmar I wasn't going to look."

"I could cry. Like a baby, I could cry."

They watched as the envelope caught fire and began to char. Its bulk was considerably reduced when the outside corner disintegrated and the inside padding of tissue paper was revealed. It burned rapidly, leaving a core sheet of thick paper. Edna Earle craned her neck to see around the smoldering McLeod tartan and the melting wax.

"Don't see a thing. Maybe it's written on the other side." The flame died out and Bethann reached to strike another match. Edna Earle stayed her hand. "It's a sign, don't you see? He really wants us to know what he wrote."

"You are so full of it."

"Always have been. Come on, Bethann, one little peek."

Bethann wavered. "I brought the marriage certificate,

too, thought we might dispose of it at the same time. It'll make the next fire bigger."

"One little peek."

"Are you sure you're not the devil's advocate?"

"No. But I think Joe Tom wants us to know."

Bethann sighed. "Okay. I know when I'm beaten." She sat down cross-legged on the sparse grass. "Pick it up, read it. Aloud."

Edna Earle scrambled to do so. Gingerly, she slid the single piece of paper out. It was thick, like a large calling card. The side toward them was blank. She turned it over so they both could see at the same time.

"Damn," Bethann breathed. Her eyes were filled with the words and she shivered in the midday sun.

"Now will you go see him? Now will you tell him about—about everything?"

"I'm still leaving."

"Fine, Bethann, no one can stop you. I don't even know if anyone wants to right now. But at least leave honestly. Leave without any secrets, without any regrets of what you should have done or said."

***

It would be past sundown when Bry came in. First, she had tried the sheriff's department, only to be told he was out on county business. At the Cummings place, she was told he'd be in late because he was checking the south acreage on his way in from work. Did she care to go home and they'd see he called? Or would she rather wait? There was nothing left to do at home. She elected to wait.

Edna Earle's words notwithstanding, she'd already determined that she couldn't leave without telling him about May June and Joe Tom. She would give him the wedding rings. They were his, although if those two hadn't decided to misappropriate them, she'd probably have inherited them from Annie Lee. Maybe he'd let Ted have them when the time came. She sat clutching them throughout the better part of the afternoon, sipping iced tea served her by the new woman Millie was training as a housekeeper.

At dusk, she walked to the corral and found Range and Rover, rubbed their noses, turned down having one of them saddled by the new handler. Most of the ranch personnel were new. The majority had quit voluntarily in the wake of May June's death. The new owner had walked through once and those with the slightest bit of guilt had resigned.

She ate a light supper provided by the new woman and dismissed her after that. She roamed the rooms. She waited. Surely, this is what it would be like if she stayed. Dismissing the help, waiting, waiting, waiting.

At nine o'clock, Bry came in, found her on the patio, an empty wineglass on the table beside her. He was dusty, sweaty.

"Saw the truck. Anything wrong? Or is this a social good-bye?"

She bit back hurtful words. "Supper's in the fridge. Shall I get it for you?"

"I ate downtown on my way in." He tossed his hat onto the chaise lounge. "Do you mind if I change clothes before we start this?"

"No." She tried to catch his eye, but he wouldn't look at her.

Fifteen minutes later he reappeared, casually attired, a bourbon in his hand. "May June stocked a much better bar than Joe Tom."

"I noticed." She poured herself another glass.

They sat silently. "Bethann, you came to see me. You start."

She shifted her chair around to face him. The light from the garden room caught his features and softened them. He sat hunched forward, his elbows on his thighs, the drink cradled between his hands. She matched his pose. She'd had the better part of the day to compose this speech and had thought she had it at least twice. Now it slipped from her memory and she was on her own.

"Two things." Her voice was a whisper. "I got the envelope from Delmar this morning and went to burn it on Joe Tom as I said I would. Edna Earle came with me, so there's a witness. I wasn't going to read it, but it wouldn't burn right. Typical, huh? And Edna Earle talked me into seeing what he'd written there. Said it was a sign we were really supposed to know." He looked up at her and her eyes held his. "Want to guess?"

He shook his head.

"You and me." He took a big drink. "No lie. His scrawl, 'Bethann and Bry'. Just like that. Me, then you. Of course, Edna Earle takes it as a sign from the other world that my leaving is wrong. I want to know which other world we're talking about."

She took a gulp of her wine and it threatened to go down wrong. She coughed and turned from him. "So I guess it didn't matter if I made the year or not." She snorted a laugh. "By staying I cost myself six million. Go figure." She let her voice trail off.

He took a deep swallow. "There were two things."

"Yeah." She looked heavenward as if for inspiration. "Can we walk during this one?"

He hesitated before giving his head a quick nod. They rose, left their glasses on the table and started toward the front drive, walking slowly between the oak trees on the lighted path.

"We all knew May June was responsible for all my trouble. The question was why. In April, I found Joe Tom's treasure trunk. The one that gave us all those glories you've seen—the uniform, the Christmas angel, the silver teapot. What you didn't see was the family Bible and the marriage certificate."

He slowed his steps and rammed his hands into his pants pockets. She matched her pace to his.

"May June and Joe Tom were married. They eloped. Produced your mother who produced you. I had the certificate to prove what Joe Tom had held over her head all these years. May June was a bigamist. Just as soon as

I found that out, she figured I'd publish it, so she kept trying harder and harder to find it or scare me into leaving, so that if I already knew, I wouldn't tell. Last thing I was going to do was tell and risk your suing for Ted's inheritance. So when I gave her what she wanted, the certificate and my assurances, she quit the harassment."

He stopped halfway up the drive and turned to her. "Just because they eloped—what a ludicrous thought— doesn't mean my mother belonged to Joe Tom. She was born within the Cummings marriage."

Bethann looked at the pain and confusion on his face. Tentatively, she put out her hand and touched his left hip. "Your birthmark is a McLeod family congenital trait. Marsh had it. Ted does. According to Edna Earle, who was present when your mother was born, so did she." She let the information sink in. "You're a legitimate McLeod. As a Cummings, you're common law, at best."

"I'd never have wanted what Joe Tom gave to Ted."

"I know. But I couldn't expose May June and risk a Cummings bloodbath. Then you might lose all this. She told me the day I came over that she'd left it all to you. Then I heard she'd made a new will. I was so scared for you." She was whispering even though they stood in the middle of a deserted driveway.

"I figured Joe Tom gave you as much as he could and not risk a problem with me." Her hand still rested on his hip. He made no move to dislodge it. "In the family Bible, he penciled in your name and your mother's. He knew, in his heart, that you were his, Bry. He loved you. I know he did."

Bry drew his brows together. "Is that why you won't marry? I'm Marsh's cousin?"

"No." She shook her head. "My life's in Atlanta."

"No, Bethann," he breathed and held his arms out to her. She hesitated toward him then stopped just inches before touching. Her hands went around the rings.

"There's more." She looked at him steadily as she undid the catch and took the rings off. Refastening the chain, she finished. "The day May June's will was read, Delmar wanted to see me. I thought he was going to be carping about a bill. Instead, he handed me an envelope. In it was the marriage certificate I had given to her and these rings. The McLeod wedding set. They split the evidence of the marriage, trusting souls that they were." She handed them to him. "They're yours. Belonged to your grandparents." She put them in his palm and closed his fingers around them. "The marriage certificate was burned along with the envelope today. No more evidence. You're safe."

"Time for total honesty?" A touch of fear quivered through her, but she nodded. "May June had other words for me on her deathbed than what I told you. I mean, she said what I said she did, that she was sorry and that I was the last of a proud line." He stopped to reflect on that. "But she also said you held my future. I thought she was just giving us permission to marry. Like everyone else. Obviously, she was talking in more cryptic terms."

They stood in the driveway, no longer touching, the import of each other's words slowly sinking in. He'd made one more attempt at a marriage proposal. She'd given him a complex family history he couldn't share with anyone.

Wordlessly, they turned and went back up the drive. She didn't look back as she drove through the open wrought-iron gates.

Chapter Twenty-Seven

Bethann closed the door of Ranch McLeod for the last time. Turning around to face the front drive, she watched the departing moving van's dust trail as it swirled in the air. Her things would be in Atlanta in a week. One week—and a normal life again.

Carefully maneuvering the cat carrier into the passenger seat, she went around to her side and got in. Clicking the key in the ignition, Bethann stopped before she turned it. Looking up at the house, the wagon wheel bathroom window staring back, knowing the tartan couch once more ruled the living room, she felt her eyes grow moist. Damn it, she was not going to cry!

She switched the ignition and jerked the SUV into reverse. Pen and Tux complained all the louder. Disgusted with them, she flipped their carrier lock and released them, paying them no mind as they zoomed around the interior and settled on the quilt-covered computer in the back. All she heard was the echo of Edna Earle's censure that morning after breakfast. "Damn, girl, look at yourself! What do all those tears have to tell you?" Bethann remembered taking her face out of her hands and looking up at the old woman who stood beside her in the kitchen.

"That I'm going to miss you."

"Not me you're going to be missing. If you're crying like that, I'd say you've made a wrong decision. Your conscience is trying to tell you something."

"Edna Earle, don't start on that." Why had the old woman even shown up this morning? Obviously, one last parting shot was too good to pass.

Bethann forced her thoughts back to the present as she stopped on the far side of the ranch gates. She locked them, a final act, a defiant good-bye. That done, she started the journey home.

No way out of Cummings except through the very middle of town. She stopped at Delmar's, retrieved the titles and deeds and other assorted legal documents that held the keys to Ted's and her future. The lone stop light was red. There couldn't be tears going through here, not unless she wanted to fuel the gossip from now till Christmas. She dried her eyes and looked straight ahead.

Bry's truck was parked in front of Sally's Grille. One of the last few days he'd be in the truck. The posters for Sam's election were scattered around town, as were Evan's, his opponent.

Bry had not come out this morning. Had she really expected him to? Hadn't they said it all last night? But then, what was there to say that she hadn't been saying for a year? Since the first kiss. Since the first night. Since he'd said he loved her. Since he'd proposed. Damn!

damn! *damn!*

Finally, free of Cummings, up the hill, past the roadside park where she and Kiki had stopped to get their bearings a year ago. A lifetime ago.

She was keyed up enough to drive all night. Get home in the morning. Time for brunch. Enough coffee, she could do it. Run the dust of Cummings off her feet, off her tires. Forget Bry's kisses, his arms, his love.

This had to stop. Edna Earle could not be right. She had made the only decision there was to make. She had a son and a successful business. She needed to be closer to Ted. This land didn't need her, not like her son, her business, her friends, her house—no, her home—did!

Bry didn't need her like they did.

***

Bethann argued with herself all the way across Texas. Every two hours, she stopped at a drive-through, vying with the cats for the kiddie burger or the milk shake. Gas and the bathroom. Pen slept in her lap, Tux held on between the seatback and her shoulder. She filled the truck with Webber music and tried to empty her mind of everything but Atlanta and the good life that awaited her there. She'd be busy, fulfilled.

By nine o'clock, she was to Shreveport, Louisiana. Finding a fast food place for coffee, she went in to give herself a stretch. Coming out of the bathroom, she found herself in line behind what seemed like half the local sheriff's department.

She caught herself staring at the back of the man in front of her. The uniform was tan, like Bry's. Stetson, boots, just different accents. Still, she almost felt at home. She'd grown so accustomed to being around him, around his department, his uniform. This line of thinking had to stop. It was only natural she'd miss him. But hadn't she been missing him since the Fourth? She'd get over it.

She *was* over it.

The counter girl had to ask for her order twice and still Bethann answered distractedly. "Two cups coffee, large." She meant to take both to the truck, hum on into the night. Instead, she found herself sitting in a booth where she could keep an eye on the cats and watch the sheriff's department, too. She doctored the cup, made it too sweet, too creamy.

It took real effort not to stare at the deputies. She *had* to get past this. The door opened and another one came in. Taller, darker, older. Bry? He turned, and of course, it wasn't. Where was her mind?

In Cummings, Texas, with her heart. The realization came to her. Her love for Bry engulfed her, took her breath.

How could she be so stupid? So shallow? Her heart and mind weren't in Atlanta, hadn't really been since New Year's. Her heart, her mind—God, her soul—were probably sitting at the Cummings depot, being lonely, waiting for the four o'clock to whistle through. Such a long wait. Almost seven hours. In eight hours she could be halfway through Alabama. It was all interstate. Atlanta by breakfast time.

She stared at the pile of Stetsons on the hat rack. In seven hours she could be to the edge of West Texas. Home by breakfast time.

***

Dawn was attempting to push itself off on the world. Behind Bethann the sky had been lightening for an hour. Pen and Tux slept contentedly back in her lap and on her shoulder. The Louisiana coffee was long gone, replaced by stops at brightly lit interstate stores along the way.

Pulling over the hill, she sought the roadside park. Unexpectedly, joyously, Bry's truck was there. Was it a stroke of luck or the chance for a quick get away again if he rejected her?

That thought had surfaced about two in the morning. She had to contemplate the fact that he might actually tell her to take a hike, that her treatment of him had been shabby. She couldn't argue. She wouldn't argue. She'd certainly not belittle either of them or their love by begging. One confrontation, then she'd turn tail and go. She didn't really deserve the one chance she was here to ask for.

He was sitting on the picnic table and didn't turn when she parked on the other side of the truck. She slightly lowered the windows for air for the cats and switched off the ignition. He was bound to have heard her. Probably didn't figure anyone would be stupid enough to mess with the sheriff.

"Hey, mister, need some help?" She stretched her mind to remember what all he'd said when he'd come up on them a year ago. What if he was as sassy to her as she'd been then? Didn't she deserve it?

He turned slightly to face her, and she could tell he'd had as sleepless a night as she. "No," was all he said. But he continued looking at her.

"No car trouble?"

"No."

"Flat tire?"

"I could change it myself. Or don't you let your men do that?"

She fixed her lips in a straight line, afraid to show her pleasure at his humor, however sarcastic. "Are you sick?" she asked.

"Well, now, I might be sick." He turned back to the view of Cummings, making her come closer in order to continue the conversation.

"We've got medical help available," she offered.

"Specialists?"

She thought on that. "Mostly amateur psychiatrists. But they think they're as good as board-certified."

He didn't smile. "Well, I've got a heart problem." He continued on unflinchingly. "Mine's broken."

The game was over. Bethann's voice caught in her throat and she steadied herself by putting her hands in her back pockets. "Oh," was all she could manage. Blinking back the tears now, she screwed up her courage and went on. "We only have home remedies for that."

"I'm desperate. I'll try anything." He shifted his weight slightly on the table. "You know, I've got all the damn money I'll ever need and the right medicine just doesn't seem to be available, no matter the price."

The sun finally broke through the horizon and bathed them in light. They faced each other red-eyed and tired, in need of sleep and comfort.

Bethann took a deep breath and plunged on. "Home remedy is really just an incantation. But you'll know immediately if it works. You just say it once. You either get the desired result or you don't."

"Tell me." He balanced with a hand on either side of his thighs, his knuckles turning white from the pressure he put on the table edge.

He's as scared as I am, Bethann realized. "It's real simple." She inched toward him. He didn't move. Standing squarely in front of him, she looked him straight-on and said what she'd not been able to say for eight months. "It goes like this." She swallowed. "I love you."

He was silent. Unsuccessfully fighting back the tears, she continued. "Sometimes, you have to add more," a sob escaped, but still he didn't reach for her or touch her. "May I come home?"

"I see."

She swiped at the tears while he just sat there. How

long was this going to go on? There wasn't anything else for her to say and she was crying so hard she couldn't have said it anyway. Ten seconds more, then she'd go. Sneak back to the Ranch and then leave again in the morning. Sleep, God, she needed sleep!

She got as far as the mental count of three when Bry reached out a hand for her. Taking her by the wrist, he pulled her between his legs and began wiping the tears with his fingers. "Kinda' hard to do, isn't it?" She raised an eyebrow at him. "Come home, I mean." He kissed her eyelids. "It's hard to come home when you never really left."

"Oh, Bry!" Her arms curled around his neck and back. He embraced her tightly, rubbing her back, kissing her. She pulled back slightly and took his face in her hands. "I got halfway cross Louisiana and and I saw these sheriff's deputies—"

"Shhh," he whispered, placing a finger on her lips. A laugh caught in his throat. "You sure this is what you want? No business, no Hot-Lanta, just dust and horses and cattle and a working ranch with a working rancher. Oh—and McLeod tartan!"

"I'm having the damn thing recovered!"

"Oh, no, this McLeod wants it just like it is. I think we'll move it over to my place."

She lowered her voice. "You can't say you're a McLeod."

"I know," he whispered back.

"Anyway, May June will spin in her grave if you

move that old hand-me-down in."

"McLeod hand-me-down?" He smiled and laughed. "I think McLeod hand-me-downs will look just fine over there."

She shook her head at his sudden unexplained amusement. "I love you, Bry. You just don't know."

"I've got a good idea." He kissed her, warm and welcoming. "I couldn't sleep either last night. Knowing you were on the road. Really gone from me." He pulled her even tighter. "Let's sleep all day. Your place or mine?"

"Yours. It's air-conditioned." She pulled back as something under his shirt rubbed between her breasts. "What are you wearing?"

He pulled up the wedding rings from around his neck. "Got any ideas for a better location for them?"

She nodded.

"Reality check, Bethann. What about Atlanta Divines?"

"Kiki will just have to think of something. I'm sure she can find a buyer for my half." She set her forehead to his. "Can I run the ranch with you?"

"Sure. But why this sudden change of heart?"

"I waited too much for Marsh. I don't want to wait for you. I want to do with you."

He pecked a kiss on the tip of her nose. "Let's go across to a friendly state and get married today."

"And deprive Edna Earle of her last great victory?"

"You're right. Want to take her with us?"

"No." She kissed him lightly. "Ted has to be here. And Kiki will want to cater."

"I think I know why May June and Joe Tom eloped."

"Lust. They eloped for lust."

"Sounds good to me."

The radio in the truck crackled. "Hey, Bry," Sam's voice boomed over. "Edna Earle called. Wanted to make sure you go vote for me."

Bry jumped off the table and steered Bethann by the shoulders to the truck. He got in the passenger side and she curled onto his lap. He clicked the radio. "Tell Edna Earle to get her knickers out of a knot. I'll come get her and transport her to the polls."

"She'll like that."

"She at home?"

"Nah, they're all down at Sally's for breakfast. Fixing to hand the pool over to Evan. Better be the only thing he wins today." There was a touch of sadness in his voice. "Guess she's almost back to Georgia by now."

Bry handed her the radio receiver and showed where she was to press.

She clicked the button. "I don't think she's as close to Georgia as you think she is."

There was silence on the other end. "Bry," the voice was tentative. "You not alone?"

"No," he grinned as she leaned her head on his shoulder and unfastened the wedding ring necklace from around his neck, "and I'm not going to be alone again."

The End

—————————————

About The Author

Kay Layton Sisk

Native Texan Kay Layton Sisk began writing books in third grade featuring such wonderful creatures as The Rainbow Monster. That opus may be hidden deep in the closet with the *Star Trek* fanfic she didn't know she was writing throughout high school. Then life took over and didn't release her to write again until staring at a computer screen resulted in more words than numbers.

Today she makes her home with one husband and seven demanding cats. Although she is the author of 12 romance novels, After the Thunder Rolls Away is her first foray into women's fiction. As with all the others, it began with "what if?"

You may follow her at
www.kaysisk.com, **kaysisk.blogspot.com** (Sisker's Lair),
or **kaylaytonsiskauthor** on FaceBook.

After The Thunder Rolls Away

The lives of two families are forever changed when a car accident kills one spouse of each family. But which one? How do the remaining two rebuild their lives? And what if it had been two others?

Mark and Angel O'Shea, Eric and Paulina Eubanks-- best friends and business partners are driving home early one summer morning from a country club party when a deer darts out in front of Mark's new car. Paulina's sure driving saves them from the first deer, then the second, but the third is a surprise and they plunge off the narrow Texas highway down a ravine and into a slow-moving river.

There are four outcomes to this horrifying, community-changing event. Four ways the families may have to reconfigure their lives, hopes, and dreams.

But which outcome is it... after Fate steps in.